PIECES OF JUSTICE

PIECES OF JUSTICE

Margaret Yorke

WARNER BOOKS

A *Warner* Book

First published in Great Britain in 1994 by Warner Futura
This edition first published in Great Britain in 1994 by Warner Futura
Reprinted 1995, 1996

Copyright © Margaret Yorke 1994

The moral right of the author has been asserted.

A CIP catalogue record for this book
is available from the British Library.

ISBN 0 7515 1392 X

Typeset by Solidus (Bristol) Limited
Printed in England by Clays Ltd, St Ives plc

Warner
A Division of
Little, Brown and Company (UK)
Brettenham House
Lancaster Place
London WC2E 7EN

ACKNOWLEDGEMENTS

THE LIBERATOR, copyright © Margaret Yorke 1977. First published in WINTER'S CRIMES 9 edited by George Hardinge (Macmillan, 1977).

ALWAYS RATHER A PRIG, copyright © Margaret Yorke 1978. First published in JOHN CREASEY'S CRIME COLLECTION edited by Herbert Harris (Gollancz, 1978).

I DON'T BELIEVE IN SANTA CLAUS, copyright © Margaret Yorke 1979. First published in *Woman and Home* (December, 1979).

THE RECKONING, copyright © Margaret Yorke 1980. First published in *Woman* (August, 1980).

SUCH A GENTLEMAN, copyright © Margaret Yorke 1980. First published in MYSTERY GUILD ANTHOLOGY edited by John Waite (Book Club Associates, 1980).

A TIME FOR INDULGENCE, copyright © Margaret Yorke 1981. First published in WINTER'S CRIMES 13 edited by George Hardinge (Macmillan, 1981).

FAIR AND SQUARE, copyright © Margaret Yorke 1982. First published in *Ellery Queen's Mystery Magazine* (August, 1982).

THE FIG TREE, copyright © Margaret Yorke 1983. First published as BITTER HARVEST in *Woman* (June, 1983).

A WOMAN OF TASTE, copyright © Margaret Yorke 1983. First published as CRUISE A LA CARTE in *Good Housekeeping* (June, 1983).

THE WRATH OF ZEUS, copyright © Margaret Yorke 1984. First published in *Ellery Queen's Mystery Magazine* (May, 1984).

GIFTS FROM THE BRIDEGROOM, copyright © Margaret Yorke 1986. First published in WINTER'S CRIMES 18 edited by Hilary Hale (Macmillan, 1986).

Acknowledgements

ANNIVERSARY, copyright © Margaret Yorke 1986. First published in *Ellery Queen's Mystery Magazine* (November, 1986).

THE MOUSE WILL PLAY, copyright © Margaret Yorke 1987. First published in LADYKILLERS (J.M. Dent, 1987).

THE BREASTS OF APHRODITE, copyright © Margaret Yorke 1989. First published in NEW CRIMES edited by Maxim Jakubowski (Robinson Publishing, 1989).

THE LUCK OF THE DRAW, copyright © Margaret Yorke 1989. First published in WINTER'S CRIMES 21 edited by Hilary Hale (Macmillan, 1989).

MEANS TO MURDER, copyright © Margaret Yorke 1990. First published in A CLASSIC CRIME edited by Tim Heald (Pavilion, 1990).

A SMALL EXCITEMENT, copyright © Margaret Yorke 1991. First published in WINTER'S CRIMES 23 edited by Maria Rejt (Macmillan, 1991).

WIDOW'S MIGHT, copyright © Margaret Yorke 1991. First published in MIDWINTER MYSTERIES 1 edited by Hilary Hale (Scribners, 1991).

THE LAST RESORT, copyright © Margaret Yorke 1993. First published in 2ND CULPRIT edited by Liza Cody and Michael Z. Lewin (Chatto, 1993).

To Alexander, Shaun, Lucinda and Ben,
with love.

CONTENTS

PIECES OF JUSTICE

THE
LIBERATOR

My mercy mission began in Italy. I noticed him first on the plane: a coarse-featured, stout man with wide pores and purple thread veins on his face. He sat across the aisle from a still-pretty, faded middle-aged woman who seemed to be, as I was, travelling alone. When the stewardess with the drinks had passed, he leaned across with his glass in his hand and made some remark to the woman, who was reading. She looked surprised, but answered pleasantly. Thereafter, she was unable to return to her book for the rest of the journey, for he continued to talk, and when we boarded the bus at Genoa there he was, assiduous, by her side, helping with her hand luggage.

The hotel, in a small resort about forty miles north of Genoa, was across the road from the sea, a modern concrete block with balconied rooms at the front, and behind, single cells with the railway below. I had forgotten that: the railway line that runs along the coast, sometimes in front of the towns, sometimes to the rear, but always with express trains thundering through during the night, blowing their whistles piercingly at level-crossings.

With machine-like efficiency the hotel staff and the tour courier sorted the travellers, collected passports, and allocated rooms. The faded woman, the red-faced man and I all had rear-facing single cells. Off to the front, to their airy balconies, went the fortunate married, or anyway the twosomes.

Because of the trains I slept badly, and was angered at my own stupidity: I, usually so careful in my research, had slipped up over this booking which I had made in some haste after my sudden, premature retirement. I had felt the need for a change of scene and had quickly arranged a modestly priced package tour instead of the well-planned journey of some

3

cultural interest I usually took later in the year. Now I had a
bedroom which was no haven wherein to retreat in the heat
of the day, nor a place of repose at night.

I went down early to breakfast and saw the faded woman
at a corner table with her *prima colazione* of rolls and coffee.
She glanced up and murmured 'good morning' as I passed,
and her sigh of relief as I went on to sit some distance
away was almost audible. She sought company no more than
I did.

The pairs in their better rooms were sleeping late or having
breakfast upstairs; few people were in the restaurant so early,
but George was: I learned his name later. He came breezing
in, sparse grey hair on end and colour high. He had been for
a walk and already he glistened with sweat. He wore a bright
yellow towelling shirt, crumpled cotton slacks, orange socks
and leather sandals.

'Good morning,' he cried, walking up to the faded woman
and pulling out a chair at her table. 'I'll join you,' he
announced. 'Who wants to be alone?'

Plenty of people, I thought grimly, if the only company
available is uncongenial. I felt sorry for the woman, whom I
judged to be recently widowed, observing her ring and her
faint air of defeat. Most divorcées, I have noticed, soon develop
a certain toughness; the widows who do acquire it take
longer, softened as they are by sympathy.

He talked at her all through breakfast, and when various
couples who had been with us on the plane came into the
room he greeted them all jovially. Most responded with
reserved cordiality. He was all set to be the life and soul of the
fortnight and to wreck it for other people, particularly the
faded widow who would find escape difficult. I had seen this
sort of thing happen before but had done nothing about it
beyond protecting myself.

On the beach, later, I saw them among the rows of deck-
chairs. He had accompanied her to book them; thus they were
given neighbouring chairs and would remain together for the
fortnight. I saw dawning realisation of this on her face as they

trudged over the sand to their shared umbrella, and for a moment our eyes met.

She tried to get away. She was a good swimmer, and struck out boldly while he floundered in the shallows. I first spoke to her out there, in the water, clinging to a raft, and in the same way she made friends with a retired colonel and his wife and two more couples. These people, all aware of her predicament, would sometimes invite her to join them in the bar or to go out in the evening for coffee. I, keeping my own company rigidly, a book held before me, would see her with her other friends drinking *strega* with her *cappuccino*, briefly happy. Sooner or later, however, along would come George.

'Mind if I join you?' he'd blithely say, and would do it.

The couples were civil. They talked to him for a while but finished their drinks and then left, abandoning meek Emily, as I christened her, to her fate.

Meal-times were the worst. Because he had adopted her at breakfast, the head waiter had assumed them to be together and had allotted them a shared table for all meals. I had had to assert myself to be left alone. It was easier for the staff to seat people in groups and it took strength of will to stand against the system: as it always does. George spoke a bastard Italian, very loudly, expecting to be understood and becoming heated when he was not. The waiters, whose English vocabulary was limited to phrases connected with food, drink and cutlery, were at a loss to respond courteously to these aggressive attempts at dialogue. Emily would intervene when George paused for breath, speaking in a soft voice; her limited Italian was precise. George, however, soon shouted her down, like a dominant husband, so that her little attempts to improve understanding withered and died. He ate grossly, too, demanding extra portions and shovelling the food into his mouth, even belching. Afterwards, he complained of indigestion.

Emily tanned, under the sun; she even bloomed a little as a result of the food, which was very good; but she grew edgy, was restless, twitched her hands. And she was not sleeping. I could see her light on, late at night, when I leaned out of my own window to watch one of the trains rush past in the darkness.

She had paid a lot of money for this holiday and it was being ruined by an obtrusive boor.

I often walked round the town in the evening buying fruit and mineral water to consume in my room, and I enjoyed these expeditions. Once I met Emily, scurrying along, head down, arms full of packages. George was not in sight. I did not detain her by speaking, for he might be in pursuit – and he was: I saw him approaching, large belly bulging over his stained slacks, searching about for her.

'Have you seen Mary Jolly?' he asked. 'I've lost her.'

So that was, in fact, Emily's unlikely name.

'She's gone that way,' I said, pointing to a narrow alley between chrome-painted houses, where children played and cats skulked. 'You'll catch her if you hurry,' and I had the satisfaction of seeing him depart in the opposite direction from that taken by his quarry.

I caught her up myself. She was buying postcards, in a shifty, worried manner, peering over her shoulder as she made her choice in case he was on her trail.

'It's all right,' I told her. 'He's gone in the other direction. You can take your time.'

She looked startled for a moment; then she smiled, and I saw how pretty she must once have been.

'He means well,' she said.

Fatal words. I wondered how many other people's holidays George had wrecked over the years, and indeed, how his good intentions affected those he met in daily life at home.

'I never manage to miss him at breakfast, no matter what time I come down,' Mary-Emily confessed as we walked on together. 'Early or late, he's always there. And my room is too dark and dismal to stay in for breakfast. The trains in the night are so awful, too. Don't they wake you?'

I agreed that they did.

Mary-Emily had tried ear plugs, but could not sleep at all with them in her ears.

A morning glory trailed over the railing above a culvert alongside the pedestrian tunnel under the railway line. It was a dark, eerie passage, where sounds echoed in the vaulted concrete cavern, but above it the blue flowers were brilliant.

'It's so pretty here,' said Mary-Emily. 'The town, I mean, with the oleanders and the palm trees. And all the buildings. Look at that lovely wrought-iron balcony.'

I admired it, but I was thinking. An accident would be impossible to arrange, for George did not swim out far enough to drown, nor were there any cliffs, and there were people about most of the time. It would have to be done here, near the railway. Timed well, the sound of a train would mask any noise. No one would suspect an elderly spinster, a retired schoolmistress of modest demeanour. No one here would know that the elderly spinster had once worked with the French Resistance and was no stranger to violence. It was too late to save Mary-Emily's holiday this year, but no one else would have to suffer George in future.

I went on the organised coach trip to Monte Carlo, which I had not originally planned to do, but I bought the knife there: for my nephew, I said in my excellent French. The shopkeeper never suspected that I was English, just as no one had all those years ago, when after the German advance I was caught in Paris.

George and Mary-Emily had booked to go on the outing too, but when the coach was due to leave she had not turned up. George made the driver wait and went to find her, returning to say she had a headache and was not coming. He almost decided to stay behind in case she needed anything, but I persuaded him to come; she should have this one day off, I resolved, silently commending her resource, and I invited him to sit with me in the coach. He talked without pause throughout the journey, and I learned he was a widower who lived alone in Leeds and sold insurance; he had one son whom he almost never saw. Since his wife died, he told me, he had learned about loneliness and that was why he befriended the solitary. The effrontery of it! He supposed, by accompanying

me now, that he was benefiting me! No wonder his wife had
been unable to survive such insensitivity, I thought. When we
reached Monte Carlo I managed to elude him among the
crowds, to make my purchase unobserved.

At dinner that night Mary-Emily looked tranquil after her
undisturbed day. After the meal she went into the town with
the army couple, and when George followed them, I followed
him.

But there was no chance for action that night. I joined the
group at a café and we talked late, sheer numbers wearing
George down so that others might speak; because I was there
to dilute the mixture the couple lingered. Mary-Emily was
secretary-receptionist to a doctor in Putney, I learned. I
described my years of teaching in a girls' school but did not
mention the war. We walked back to the hotel together, and
Mary-Emily went up to bed ahead of everyone else.

In the end, I did it in daylight. At least, it was light above
ground. I found George, one afternoon, pacing up and down
the hotel garden wondering where Mary-Emily was. It was a
shame to waste a minute of such weather indoors, he said.

She was sure to be skulking in her room; when he had
given her up and gone down to the beach she would appear
in a shady corner of the hotel garden with a book, and
remain there, as I did, until she went down for a swim. This
was her latest tactic.

'She's gone to have her hair done,' I lied. 'And I'm just
going – I have an appointment after hers. Shall we go together? You could walk back with her.'

'She hasn't left her key,' he grumbled.

'I expect she didn't bother – I don't always leave mine – see,
I have it now,' I said, showing him the large, brass-tagged
hotel key.

He was so stupid that he did not know the hairdresser, like
all the shops, closed in the afternoons. If he did query it as we
proceeded, I would say the hairdresser was an exception. If
necessary, I would walk him round the town, always quiet at
this hour, until I found a deserted spot where I could do it, but

first we had to go through the tunnel. At that time of day the chance of its being deserted was good.

My luck was in. Not a soul was in sight as we entered the subway, and a goods train even rumbled obligingly over our heads as I plunged the knife in so that he died silently, and at once. There was just an instant when he gave me a startled, incredulous stare before his life gurgled away.

I withdrew the knife, slipped it into my pocket wrapped in a handkerchief, and walked unhurriedly back to the hotel. George would be found very soon. I must hope no one had seen us depart together, but it was a risk I had to take. If I had been noticed, I could say that I had felt unwell and had turned back, leaving him to continue his walk alone. Suspicion would never fall on me, an inoffensive, elderly woman.

Back in my room, I washed the knife and wiped it carefully, then rinsed the handkerchief in which it had been wrapped. That afternoon, when I bathed, I would have the knife strapped to my body with sticking plaster, and I would sink it out there, deep in the Mediterranean. I had not felt such satisfaction in a job well done for years. In those long-ago days I had swum rivers with a knife in my belt. People forget that the elderly have all been young once, and some have done remarkable things.

The murder was a nine days' wonder: various drop-out youngsters were questioned and grilled by the police, and known local ne'er-do-wells, but the tourists were never suspected. I said that I had walked with George to the mouth of the tunnel and had left him there; it is always wise to tell the truth.

Two days later we went home, as planned. Oddly, Mary-Emily wept at the news of George's death. She was tender-hearted: one of life's victims. That was why she had not been able to protect herself from him.

The next year, on Aegina, where I had gone after a week in Athens, I met a couple who, morning and afternoon, carried airbeds down to the beach, to roast. Or rather, the wife carried them, trudging behind her empty-handed mate. She bore also, slung round an arm, a carrier holding towels and suncream. Her skin grew scarlet; she panted; her eyes had the dulled look of a cowed beast. She was beyond protest – long past hope – but she should have her chance.

Disposing of him was easier than getting rid of George. Daily he paddled far out to sea on his mattress, then dozed, floating in the sun. People commented on his foolhardiness, lest the *meltemi* blow up suddenly. I never saw him swim, and guessed he could not; real swimmers show respect for the sea. I merely pierced his mattress with a penknife, swimming close to him on my back as if I had not seen him, ready to apologise when I gently thumped against him. Drowsing, he scarcely noticed me. I had entered the water from some rocks, away from the hotel beach, and I left it the same way before the air-bed began to sink, dropping the penknife in deep water. He had been floundering for some minutes before a water-skier's boatman noticed his predicament and turned. I had guessed that his blood pressure was high; he drank a lot, and looked a likely coronary candidate, so that if he did not drown, heart failure might account for him.

I was never sure, in fact, exactly what he died of; it was a tragic accident, everyone said, and the formalities were soon over. It was thought that the mattress must have been punctured on a rock. I hoped he was well insured.

Next year I pushed a woman from a cliff top near Nissaki. Daily I had watched her humiliate both husband and teenage daughter as she dictated their plans for the day in a hectoring voice which caused all heads to turn. She spoke to me with gracious condescension, and was at her most odious when ordering the Greek waiters about in her loud voice as if they were deaf. Once, father and daughter slipped off along the cliff path to the next cove without letting her know where they were going, and she was furious when they returned, sheepish but happy, after eating shrimps at the little taverna and swimming from the rocks. They did it again another day, and then I told her where they had gone, adding that I was going to walk that way myself. No one else was in sight. Her horrified face when I lunged against her and pushed her over the cliff top remained in my mind for some hours. She screamed as she fell. I walked back quickly the way I had come, and after her disappearance was reported, agreed we had started out together. She was worried, I said, because she did not know where her husband and daughter were, and had set off to look for them. I had left her after a time as I found it too hot for walking. Her body was washed up the next day on rocks beneath the cliff.

The daughter seemed very upset and the husband was stunned. I hoped they would not blame themselves for long and that they would make good use of their freedom.

Then Mr Bradbury, next door to me in Little Wicton, bought his scooter.

For years we had been neighbours, and Mr Bradbury left the village daily for his London office, getting a lift to the station with a friend. The friend retired, and Mr Bradbury bought the scooter. Thereafter, he tooted his horn in farewell to his wife every morning at a quarter to seven as he rode off. It did not disturb me, for I was always awake then, but it woke others. Besides, blowing one's horn at that hour in a built-up area was against the law. He tooted again each evening when he returned, an announcement to his wife, just as his morning signal was a farewell. When I mentioned to Mr Bradbury that he was disturbing people, he was quite rude and said that what he did was his own business.

Reporting him to the police would cause a lot of unpleasantness; and a man capable of such thoughtlessness for others would not stop at merely blowing his horn: who knew what went on in the privacy of his home?

His journey to the station took him along a quiet lane, and one morning I was there ahead of him, with a wire across the road. Several cars passed, running over my wire as it lay on the tarmac, and I let them go, watching from my vantage point behind the hedge. It was like old times; I had enjoyed planning this and felt quite youthful again as I waited for Mr Bradbury. My acquaintances in Little Wicton thought I was in London for the night, but I had driven back at dawn and hidden my car some way off; I would return again to London for two nights when the deed was done.

Mr Bradbury never saw the wire spring taut before him. I braced myself to take the strain; I had wound it round a tree as a support, finding a place in the road where two elms face each other on either side. He was travelling fast, the bike engine noisy in the morning air.

His ridiculous Martian helmet saved his skull from shattering, and he lived for a week before the rest of his injuries killed him. I remembered to remove the wire, not losing my head as he hurtled through the air, and I got away before the next car came along. Such a shock, I said to his wife later, when I came home to hear the news.

She grieved a lot.

'He loved that silly bike. Would blow the horn like that, saying goodbye, though I know he shouldn't have. I'd have got him to stop it, in a bit,' she said, looking bleak. She'd soon get over it, and find a way to use her life more profitably than spending it cooking and cleaning for one selfish man.

Mr Bradbury had an invalid mother, it seemed, whose fees in a private home used up much of his salary, and this was why they had never run a car. Mrs Bradbury seemed to think that she would now have to provide for the old lady though there was some sort of insurance.

It was a surprise, two months later, when the doorbell rang and I saw a woman whom at first I did not recognise on the step; her hair was quite grey and her face lined. It was Mary-Emily.

'Ah – you do remember me,' she said, as I struggled at first to place her among the generations of girls I had tried to ground in the rudiments of French grammar, and then realised who she was. 'I was passing and thought I'd see if you were at home.'

'Do come in,' I said, but I felt the first sense of unease. I was sure I had not told her where I lived. I don't give away detailed information about myself; old habits die hard. 'How are you?'

I asked. 'Still living at – Putney, wasn't it?' I pretended to be uncertain.

'Yes. I need not enquire about you. You don't look a day older,' said Mary-Emily.

It was true. I took care to keep physically active, and though I missed my work, now I was on the alert at all times, looking for opportunities to free others from bondage, so that my perceptions were acute.

I made tea for Mary-Emily and offered her a home-made scone. She told me she had remarried.

'You've met my husband and stepdaughter,' she said. 'You were in Corfu when his first wife died in a fall from a cliff.'

She could suspect nothing, but I knew sudden fear.

'It was such a coincidence that poor George should have been killed like that in Italy, and then Betty in Corfu, and that you should have been there both times,' said Mary-Emily, and took a bite of her scone.

'But Betty wasn't killed,' I objected. 'She fell – either accidentally, or it was suicide.'

'She could have been pushed,' said Mary-Emily. 'And wasn't there a fatal accident on Aegina, too, when you happened to be there?'

How could she have found that out? Anyway, it didn't matter. Nothing could be proved.

'Accidents do happen,' I said, pouring out more tea.

'Rather often, in your company,' she said, looking at me steadily. She had changed in character as well as in appearance, I realised; she was bolder. I decided to attack.

'Well – things have improved for you, haven't they?' I remarked. 'You've remarried, and that man and his daughter are no longer bullied or humiliated. I'm sure you're good to them both, and no one could miss that dreadful woman, just as no one could miss George.'

'George meant to be kind, though he failed,' said Mary-Emily. 'And Betty was domineering because both Hugh and Jane are so weak that someone has to take charge of them. You never saw them at home – only their holiday face. They still blame themselves for causing Betty's death by slipping off on their own.' She put sugar in her tea and stirred it. 'Hugh and his family were patients of the doctor I worked for. After Betty's death someone had to marry Hugh to save him – drive him on – and to fend for Jane. Better me than someone who wouldn't understand him. I try to remain kind, but I'm getting quite aggressive myself,' she said, and took a sip from her cup.

I waited for her to disclose the reason for her call. Was it to blackmail me? How had she found me?

'I believe your neighbour, Mr Bradbury, was recently killed in a road accident,' she said.

'Yes,' I replied. 'The roads are so dangerous.'

'You shouldn't have done it,' she said. 'I can see that you've set yourself up as some sort of judge, deciding that certain people should be exterminated, like the Nazis during the war. But I don't know why you picked Mr Bradbury. He seemed harmless, from what I can discover, and he grew beautiful begonias.'

My hand, holding my teacup, remained quite steady as I said, 'Picked him? What do you mean?'

'He must have annoyed you in some way,' she said. 'It was people who annoyed you whom you despatched.'

She was wrong. It was people who made life intolerable for others, not me, whom I removed. But I did not fall into the trap of replying. I tried instead to think of a way to silence her. For the first time since the war it seemed that I would have to act for my own protection.

'It will make a sensational case when it comes to court,' she was saying. 'Wartime heroine turned murderer. You see, I know all about you now. I traced you through the travel agent Hugh booked with that time. And in case you're thinking of a way to dispose of me, save yourself the trouble. Detective Superintendent Filkin from the local CID knows everything, and he'll be here soon. He allowed me some time with you first, for my own satisfaction, as I was the one to uncover your trail. It's taken me a year, and at last I've got proof of something you've done. There are marks on the trees where you stretched the wire across the road to bring Mr Bradbury off his scooter, and even after this lapse of time there were shreds of clothing found in the hedge where you hid. I'm sure they'll match something upstairs in your room. It was your speciality during the war, wasn't it? Dealing with German despatch riders. Commendable then, but criminal now.'

How could she have found out so much? I could not ask, for to ask was to admit. But she told me a little.

'You were the last person to see Betty alive. Her death didn't make sense – she'd never commit suicide, and she was much too capable to fall accidentally. I enquired at newspaper offices about other accidental holiday deaths, and I followed up some of them, asking if you were there at the time. It wasn't easy, but I discovered that you were on Aegina when there was an accident. The woman whose husband died told me you were there. Poor thing, she had a mental breakdown and has been in and out of hospital ever since.'

'I'm not surprised. That man had destroyed her,' I said.

'She could have protested,' said Mary-Emily. 'Or left him. But she was one of those helpless women who are good only at running a home. She married him for material security, which he gave her. She didn't deserve more.'

'Now who's making a moral judgement?' I demanded.

Mary-Emily ignored my comment.

'It can be proved that you were present on those three occasions,' she said calmly. 'It adds up to just too many coincidences. Maybe there were more, which I haven't discovered, but if so the police will ferret them out. They're very thorough. However, there will be enough proof from the Bradbury case to put you in prison for the rest of your life. You won't like that, will you, being confined – shut up? You're paranoiac, I suppose.' She set down her cup. 'I found out what happened at the school where you taught – how you started to bully girls who found their work difficult and eventually locked one up in a music-practice room for three hours. The headmistress wanted no scandal because of your war record, so she asked for your immediate resignation.'

My mind was batting about like a rat in a trap seeking a way of escape. There must be one; there always had been before, even from that cell I was once in, shut away from all light and freedom. I could never endure that again.

Mary-Emily got up.

'I'm going now,' she said. 'The superintendent will be here in a little while. There will be time for you to make some arrangements.'

I had the pills. I kept them just in case. You never knew. Not cyanide, like we had then, but strong barbiturates obtained from a gullible doctor who thought I needed sleeping pills. When she had gone, I swallowed them down with tea – I made a fresh pot – and laced the cup with brandy to help them along. I could see no other way. This would protect my reputation for posterity, for my deeds were on record for anyone to read, and save me from confinement.

Mary-Emily had surprised me. I would never have thought she could possess so much initiative. And then I realised that it was through me she had discovered her own power; she had married a weak-willed man and had been forced to develop strength of her own. She would not be a victim again. My own ill luck lay in the coincidence that two people whom I had liberated had known one another.

The pills are working. I feel drowsy already. That superintendent should be here soon. He'll arrive in a police car. I won't open the door, and it may take him some time to decide to break in. Will he realise what I've done and take me to hospital – yes – of course – and they'll use a stomach-pump. I hadn't thought of that. They may prevent my final escape. Why didn't I think of it? But Mary-Emily said there would be time to make arrangements. How long ago did she leave? I can't see the clock very well. Why, it's over an hour already – nearer two – the superintendent is late . . . very late. . . .

What's that noise? The doorbell? No – it's the telephone. . . .

Who can it be? Shall I answer it? I can't – my legs won't move – I can't reach it. . . .

Mary-Emily let the telephone ring for a full five minutes. She had been right. The old woman had taken something which by now had begun to work. She walked away from the telephone box from which she had been able to watch the house and see that no one had left it. Her car was parked near by and as she got in she glanced at her watch. It would take her about an hour and a half to get back to Putney, and by the time the old woman understood that there was no Detective Superintendent Filkin and that the police would not be calling, she would be beyond help. Mary-Emily hoped she would realise that, but she could not be certain if that part of her plan had worked. She had only one regret: that she had been too late to save Mr Bradbury. But his killer would despatch no one else, for whatever motive.

Mary-Emily, however, had learned that with some ingenuity, and a lot of daring, such things could, if necessary, be accomplished.

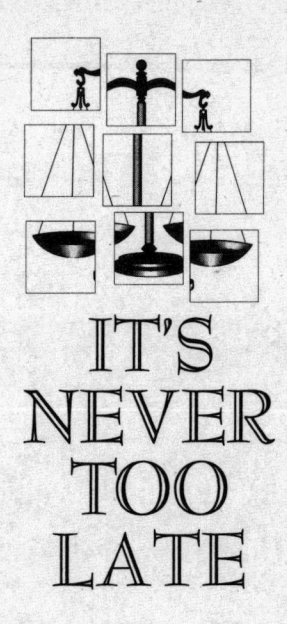

IT'S
NEVER
TOO
LATE

Stella suddenly appeared again yesterday.

She first rode into my life more than sixty years ago on a small pony when we were both twelve. I was on a pony too, that day when our mothers introduced us, but a shaggier, cosier one than Stella's, and we were both taking part in a gymkhana. Stella's mother was a widow who had recently married Mr Gregson, who owned the Manor House and most of the land around the village; my father was his estate manager. The gymkhana, an unambitious local affair, was held in one of Mr Gregson's fields, and when Stella and I met, I had just come second in a bending race.

Stella's pony was smart and speedy, but it knocked over some of the posts and was disqualified. This didn't please Stella, who rode off scowling. She was a pretty child with fair hair and a deceptively fragile look; in fact she was as tough as whipcord. I was square and sturdy, with dark hair cut in a straight fringe over my brown eyes. I looked rather like my pony, really, peering out at the world as I did from under my mane. My pony's name was Mr Chesterton, because of G.K.; he was a brave animal who did anything I asked of him and performed obediently in the games and competitions for which I entered him. He was not smart enough to appear at the county show, although I spent hours schooling him in the field behind our house as if he were. Everyone was very polite to me about Mr Chesterton because his nature was so kind and they knew I loved him dearly, but no one could commend his looks.

On this day at the gymkhana Mr Chesterton knocked down several jumps because he was too fat to be very springy, but he had a go at them all. He knew I wouldn't ask him to tackle anything that was really beyond his powers. Stella's pony

belted round when her turn came, and won. I must admit she
rode it bravely, and all the mothers said so too. I noticed that
my mother had rather a subservient manner when she spoke
to Stella's, and she agreed at once when Mrs Gregson
suggested we two girls should ride together in future; she
didn't like Stella going out alone all the time, and the district
was still strange to her. So after that every day we set out on
our contrasted mounts. Mr Chesterton often had trouble
keeping up with Stella's pony, whose name was Lochinvar.
We jumped fallen tree trunks, and some fences my father put
up in one of the fields. Stella jumped Lochinvar over the stone
walls that kept the sheep in, but I knew that Mr Chesterton
couldn't manage them, so we went round by the gates,
although Stella mocked and said that Mr Chesterton would
clear them if I made him, and that I must be scared. Before
Stella came I used to pretend to be a knight riding out to joust,
or a lone cowboy on the trail, but I knew it was no good
suggesting such ideas to her.

Towards the end of that first long summer holiday I
developed measles, no one knew where from. Stella had
already had them. She continued to ride every day while I lay
in a darkened room feeling dreadful, but then Lochinvar went
lame. He'd strained a tendon. Mrs Gregson told my mother
that Stella was bored without him to ride and without my
company. As Mr Chesterton was out in his field getting
steadily fatter with no exercise while my measles ran their
course, wouldn't it be a good idea if Stella rode him while
waiting for both Lochinvar and me to recover?

Of course my mother agreed, and when I protested, she
reproved me.

'Stella doesn't understand Mr Chesterton,' I said.

'She rides very well,' said my mother, and it was true. But
I had seen her force Lochinvar into a gallop along hard, rutted
tracks; no wonder he'd gone lame. She never considered his
welfare, just his performance.

'You mustn't be selfish,' said my mother.

From the window I watched Stella ride off on Mr Chesterton, who turned his shaggy head to cast a reproachful glance at our house before obediently carrying her away. He and I trusted each other; he would trust Stella too.

I didn't hear them return. Instead, my father came into my room. He sat on my bed looking grave, not speaking, and I knew something terrible had happened.

'It's Mr Chesterton,' he said at last.

Stella had put him at a stone wall she often jumped on Lochinvar. He'd refused.

'Quite right too,' I said. 'It's much too high for him.'

But Stella had insisted. She'd put him at it again, and at the third attempt, gallantly, he'd tried it. He couldn't manage it, of course. He'd hit it hard and fallen, breaking a leg. My father was there when the vet put him down.

Stella was thrown clear. She wasn't hurt at all.

The Gregsons were very sorry about it. They even bought me another pony, a bigger one, more suited to me now that I was growing, and better bred. I won prizes on him later.

Stella and I never discussed Mr Chesterton.

She was sent away to school, and then abroad. In the holidays there was always a whirl of gaiety at the Manor, with tennis parties and dances. I was often included, and Stella introduced me to everyone as Jane, her oldest friend, who'd never left the village in her life, imagine it. It wasn't true. Mother took me to London sometimes to stay with her sister, and we went to Cornwall for a fortnight every year.

After we left school our social lives overlapped less and less. Stella spent most of her time in London or abroad. She'd given up riding and had a sports car instead. I went to college, and then began to teach at the village school. I'd learnt the flute, and I joined an amateur orchestra in the nearby town. That was where I met Rob. He was gentle and shy, not very tall, and he played the French horn. He worked for the Forestry Commission. He walked me to the bus after our orchestral practices. Sometimes we went to the cinema, holding hands in the dark, and once he took me to a charity dance at the Town Hall, borrowing a friend's Austin Seven to fetch me. He took me home at 2 a.m., a daring hour for our village in those days, and kissed me in the moonlight.

One night he wasn't at orchestra practice, but two days later he came to our house and was waiting there when I got back from school.

Mother disappeared tactfully into the garden to dead-head the roses, and Rob told me he had been offered a job in British Columbia. It had great prospects, but a condition was that he must leave almost immediately. He sat looking at me, and both of us were tongue-tied. Then Rob drew a deep breath and was about to speak, when suddenly from outside there came the blast of an expensive car horn and the sound of tyres scrunching on gravel. A moment later Stella erupted into the room. She was tall, slim, and bursting with vitality. Rob's jaw dropped at the sight of her. Later I realised that my mother, hearing the car, had rushed up the garden in an effort to intercept her, but unsuccessfully. Stella bulldozed her way wherever she wanted to go and it would need a regiment to deflect her.

I introduced her and Rob to one another.

'That's your motor-bike outside, I suppose,' said Stella. 'I nearly knocked it over.'

Rob said nothing. I realised that his ownership of a mere motor-bike and not a car would disqualify him from inviting Stella's interest.

'Rob's going to Canada,' I said.

'What fun,' said Stella. 'When?'

'Almost at once,' Rob answered.

'Don't let me delay you, then,' said Stella. 'I expect you want to pack. And I've come to talk to Jane. I need her help.' She sat down firmly. 'Jane's my oldest friend,' she said to Rob. 'She rescues me when I'm in trouble.'

I sighed. It must be some man this time. When we were younger I'd been roped in to go with her on dates where she wouldn't have been allowed to go alone. I'd listened to her tales of hearts that she had broken, and I'd half-believed them. I'd lent her money when she'd used up her allowance.

'Wouldn't tomorrow do?' I began desperately, in anguish. Had Rob only come to say goodbye?

'No. It's urgent,' Stella said, and looked at Rob. 'Do you mind?' she asked him.

He got up to go. He shook my hand and went away and I never saw him again.

'Plenty more fish in the sea,' said Stella airily, when he'd gone. 'Remind me to find you someone.' She went on to tell me that she'd quarrelled with her latest admirer and was devastated, but what was worse, she'd borrowed her step-father's car without his permission while hers had a puncture mended, and she'd badly dented it. She wanted me to go back with her and spend the evening. My presence would calm the Gregsons down.

'They think you're good for me, you're so dependable,' she said.

It sounded as if I were already dressed in a mob cap and bombazine.

I went, of course. And the Gregsons forgave her.

Three days later she left the village again, this time for the south of France. But by then Rob had sailed.

Two months later Stella married a French count with a château and his own vineyards, while I stayed at home watching the postman for letters from Canada that never came.

All that was long ago. Since then, Stella's had three husbands. Her count didn't survive the war, and she had a terrible time, caught in Unoccupied France. Later she married an American, but that didn't last. When it crashed she sought me out again and spent hours recounting the history of her sufferings. And they were real. That was inescapable. Her time in France during the war had been shattering, and her American marriage was a disaster. But then Geoff came along and everything promised well.

Before her divorce from the American came through Mr Gregson died, and Stella's mother sold the estate and moved away. My father retired at this time, and my parents moved to a cottage on the fringe of the village. I took time off from helping with the move to go to court with Stella for the hearing of the divorce. Afterwards she remained in London to celebrate and I went home by train.

I didn't hear from her again until yesterday. I'd decided that at last things must be running smoothly for her; Geoff must have managed to tame her. The years went by, and sometimes I thought of Rob and wondered what would have happened if Stella hadn't interrupted us that day. Had he intended to say more than simply goodbye? I allowed myself sometimes to daydream and imagine a life in Canada, full of challenge, and a family of tough boys with crew-cut hair and checked shirts.

Then, yesterday afternoon, Stella arrived. Once again she drove up unheralded in a sleek sports car. Her hair was still blonde and her figure was slender. At first sight she hadn't changed at all. Then I saw the deep lines which no amount of make-up could obliterate, and the crêpey skin of her neck, and all at once the tight, hip-hugging pants and the skimpy sweater looked ridiculous.

'You do look well,' she said accusingly, when I'd greeted her with what I hoped sounded like pleasure and not the dismay I felt. 'You haven't changed at all.'

'I am well,' I replied. I am still sturdy – plump, some would say – and my hair is still mainly brown, though there is plenty of grey in it. But I had changed, as she would discover.

'I knew you'd be in. The same old Jane,' she said, and strode past me into the cottage. A small, squirmy dachshund followed her, its nails scrabbling on the floor.

'I'm afraid you've come at rather a bad moment, Stella,' I said firmly. 'I have to go out in five minutes.'

'Oh, you can put it off,' said Stella, flinging herself into a chair, still able to throw a long, slim leg over its arm, as she demonstrated. 'I've come for the night. I knew you'd put me up. After all, you're my oldest friend.'

We'd known each other nearly all our lives, but had there ever been any real friendship between us?

'I can't put you up, I'm afraid,' I said. 'My spare room's occupied already. If you'd telephoned, I'd have told you so. And I have to go out now, as I've said.'

'Who've you got staying? It's never a man, is it?' Stella asked, slyly. 'After all this time? And at your age?'

Our age, I thought grimly.

'It is, as a matter of fact,' I said. 'And he's very important.'

'Dear, dear. It's never too late, I see,' said Stella. 'Well, he won't give up, if he's keen.'

I'd told myself this about Rob, years ago. But some people are afraid to dare a second time.

'Why have you come, Stella?' I asked. 'Not just to see me, I'm sure. You must want something.'

'Oh, you are cynical. You've got hard, haven't you?' Stella said. 'Hard and bitter. I thought you would. But even so you won't let down your oldest friend when she needs you.'

'Why do you need me now?' I asked, with one eye on the clock. In three minutes I must go.

'It's Geoff. He's left me,' she said, and suddenly her face crumpled. It was dreadful to witness her distress; the make-up ran down her cheeks as she wept. 'He's gone off with some chit of a girl he met when we were in Bermuda. She's young enough to be his daughter,' she wailed. 'I'm all alone.'

That must be true. If she had other friends, why seek me out? We hadn't met for years.

'You've got plenty of money,' I said cruelly, for she had. Her mother had died and left her Mr Gregson's wealth. 'You'll soon find someone else. Have a wash, if you like, Stella, and make yourself some tea, but I must go. I don't know what time I'll be back.'

She should not do it to me again. My whole life might have been different if she had not come that other time, or if she'd gone away at once, finding me not alone. Or if I'd made her go. The years had taught me the importance of priorities: today was another landmark in my life and I'd promised Bill that no mortal thing should stop me from carrying out our plans.

I left the house without another word, got into my Mini and drove away. I did not go fast, and in the mirror I soon saw Stella's car behind me.

The village school had changed very little in the years since I had taught there. Now other cars were drawing up outside it, and parents were going in through the old iron gates. Bill was there, waiting. He opened the door of the car for me and kissed me in front of everyone.

'I knew you wouldn't be late,' he said.

I had married during the war, a kind, unexciting man I'd met while helping at a canteen for servicemen. He was killed in the D-Day landings, not long after our daughter was born. She'd married a local doctor and they were both away now for a few days' snatched holiday. Bill, their unexpected youngest child, was staying with me.

Stella, driving past, saw my ten-year-old grandson escort me into the school grounds for his annual sports.

ALWAYS
RATHER
A
PRIG

'**P**rimmy has come to live near Whipton,' said Daphne Blythe when she met Mildred Fisher in Fenwick's for lunch one day. Both were in town for a day's shopping, and they met like this two or three times a year. 'We ought to do something about it.'

'What?' enquired Mildred. 'She must be awfully old.'

'Eighty next year – that's all. I used to think she was eighty then,' said Daphne, and giggled.

Many years ago Mildred and Daphne had been pupils at St Wilhelmina's, where Miss Primrose ruled as headmistress. Most girls in those days left St Wilhelmina's equipped with the School Certificate, as it then was, a basic knowledge of the French language that included some ability to speak it, a sound grounding in the Christian religion, and well-mannered. Only a few went on to university, but some, in the brief years before marriage, were capable secretaries and others trained as nurses and therapists of various kinds. St Wilhelmina's had perished in the reign of Miss Primrose's third successor, worn down by rising costs and competition.

'We could have a party for her – give her a good lunch somewhere. We could round up twenty or so old girls, couldn't we? I can think of several who live fairly near. I'm sure the old thing would enjoy it. We can't just leave her there, unacknowledged. And what else can we do? I don't know that Robert—' Daphne's voice trailed away.

She had been going to say that Robert, her barrister husband, might not be enthusiastic if Miss Primrose were asked to dine, and Mildred understood this. Her own Gerald would feel exactly the same.

'A hotel would be better than a hen lunch in one of our houses anyway,' she said, imagining the scene in her own. If it were to happen, one might, perforce, get involved with other old St Wilheminians – those who lived near enough might take to dropping in, want to use the swimming-pool, and so on. It could lead to endless difficulties. Mildred's entertaining was mainly the kind that might lead to some sort of advantage.

'I don't suppose she gets taken out to lunch very often,' she added. 'It's a good idea, Daphne. Have you got the last school magazine? We could round up some names from that.'

So it was that in the next week twenty or so women, none of them young, who lived within forty miles of Whipton and who had been at St Wilhelmina's but had seldom or never met since, agreed to meet at a riverside hotel to feast their former headmistress.

'Who else is coming?' asked Naomi Kent.

Daphne read out the list of names.

'We'll all pay our own and I'll pay for Primmy,' she said. 'It should be quite fun. Have you kept up with anyone, Naomi?'

Naomi hadn't. She had been startled when Daphne announced herself on the telephone.

Daphne couldn't remember Naomi at all, apart from her name, but had discovered that she ran a bookshop in the area. A thin, dark girl, she thought, a few years younger than herself – Mildred had told her that.

'I could only come if it was a Wednesday,' Naomi said. 'I can't leave my shop very easily otherwise. But my assistant can manage for the last hour that morning.' By saying this she had expressed willingness to go to the luncheon. She must be quite mad, deliberately setting out to encounter that woman.

Daphne was saying that Wednesday was the best day for her too. Her Mrs Blossom came then.

Yes, and polishes the desk in Robert's study, Hoovers the room where he sleeps with Daphne, cleans out his bath, thought Naomi.

She had never met the adult Daphne. The mental picture she had of her lover's wife must be inaccurate, surely, after all these years.

None of this was her idea. She didn't want to stir things up. The fact that Daphne had included her in the scheme must prove that she had no suspicion.

The date was arranged, and on a July day Morris 1300s, Allegros, Minis, Ford Escorts, a Jaguar, and a Bentley all converged on the riverside hotel chosen by Daphne for the entertainment of Miss Primrose.

To everyone's surprise, for all her pupils remembered her as tall and of a commanding presence, Miss Primrose was a thin little woman compared with her hostesses. But her white hair was bound round her brow with a snood of black velvet, as all remembered, and her face was quite rosy, for she was healthy and worked daily in her garden despite the torrid heat of that amazing summer.

She gazed round at the assembled women, all well into middle age. Daphne had supplied a list of those attending, which was thoughtful, for some of them Miss Primrose had not found memorable. Daphne, though, she remembered: captain of hockey and captain of tennis, but never head girl. She had once reported a junior girl for smuggling forbidden sweets into school and another time she had led a movement to ostracise a member of the fifth form who had, in Daphne's opinion, let down the school by forgetting her lines in a performance of *The Tempest* before the assembled parents.

What a dull, worthy bunch they were, Miss Primrose mused, sipping gin and tonic. The most interesting and successful of her former pupils were not free to entertain her thus, for they were too busy. There was a hospital matron, a senior civil servant, two doctors. The women here today were, most of them, conscientious wives and mothers who now, with their own families grown up, provided meals on wheels for the elderly, were kindly grandmothers, and pillars of Women's Institutes throughout the land: worthy and good. How bored their husbands must be. Of course, some were widowed, like Ruth Gibbs – brisk and smiling, now a part-time teacher – and Felicity Downes, who looked mournful still, though her husband had died at least ten years ago and he had been rich and stupid, so that her condition now must surely be improved.

Had she wasted her life, Miss Primrose suddenly wondered, eating trout. Had she kindled no spark in a single soul? Was there no woman here today who was witty and wise? Thinking thus, she agreed aloud with Hermione Curtis that her daughter should certainly profit by reading modern languages at the university and thought that perhaps she might grow out of dressing in garments fit only for rummage sales.

It was the daughters of these women who were the active ones, able to progress along paths hewn by the generations preceding them. And these were good women. Miss Primrose looked at their plump faces, all smiling benignly. 'Do you remember?' they were asking one another, and talking of daring pranks like dormitory feasts and moonlight swims in the school pool. They were having a lovely time. Some might even meet again after today. It was impossible to imagine any of them in a gym slip and shirt.

One was different: Naomi Kent. For one thing, she had never married. But there had been some trouble. Miss Primrose fished the facts from her mind.

Yes – she'd had a baby, a daughter. In the war. So the girl must be well grown by now, probably married and a mother herself.

'Tell me, Naomi – what are you doing now, my dear?' Miss Primrose boomed in the voice which had announced the school hymn, 'Fight the Good Fight', at the start and end of each term.

'I run a bookshop, Miss Primrose,' Naomi replied. Though over fifty, she was still slim and dark-haired.

'It's dyed,' Mildred had whispered. 'It's not, you know,' Daphne had answered, scrutinising the smooth jet strands.

'How interesting,' Miss Primrose said. 'Are you holding up in these difficult days?'

'Oh yes,' Naomi said, though increasing costs and falling sales were a serious problem. She looked round at the well-nourished women. Had any of them suffered as she had, felt joy and pain like hers? They all looked so smug, with their prosperous husbands or, in the case of the widows, their adequate pensions. She had never had any security. Even now, though Robert and she were together again after so many years apart, what if he died? There would be no pension for her. 'Jemima – my daughter – is married now and she has a son,' she said. Robert had always helped to pay for Jemima, but the girl didn't know her father's name.

'How nice,' said Miss Primrose, and the other ladies rustled in their seats. Fancy admitting to it! They'd heard rumours, of course, but hadn't really believed—

Daphne wouldn't have invited Naomi if she had known.

'Jemima?' she asked, frowning.

'My daughter,' said Naomi, and longed to add, 'and your husband's.' Aloud, she went on, 'Oh, I'm not married. It was thought a scandal when it happened, but nowadays no one turns away from an unmarried mother. Most of us have probably at one time or another mentally prepared ourselves in case it should happen to a daughter.' And these women *would* try to be understanding and tolerant if their daughters became involved with married men, she thought wryly.

Suddenly Miss Primrose recalled something that had bothered her. She had recognised Naomi before any of the other women, but it was not because she had changed less than the others. She had changed a great deal – as a schoolgirl she had been quiet and shy, very unsure of herself, thin and plain. Now she had assurance, was slim but rounded, and she looked alive – she was the most alert-looking woman present. But more: Miss Primrose had seen her a few weeks before in a picture gallery with a grey-haired man who looked rather distinguished. They had not been paying much heed to the pictures, so rapt were they with each other, and this was what had struck Miss Primrose as unusual about them. It was rare to see a couple their age so mutually engrossed. She had assumed them to be husband and wife, but it seemed she was wrong.

Over coffee, the photographs came out, and Miss Primrose

admired families. Then her gaze was held fast. In one snapshot, smiling a little self-consciously, she recognised the man who had been with Naomi in the picture gallery.

'My husband Robert,' Daphne was saying with pride. 'He's a barrister – he gets some very big cases. He'll soon be a judge, I hope.'

After lunch they walked by the river bank. It was hot. Insects buzzed about, and the noise of the weir made background distraction. Miss Primrose attempted to talk to the women she had been seated away from during lunch. Each treated her with the old deference – habit died hard.

'Tell me about Naomi,' Miss Primrose instructed. 'About her daughter – so unfortunate—' Mildred might know the story.

'Oh, she was silly – got herself involved with a married man in some wartime escapade,' Mildred said. 'I heard about it from Betty Butts – she died, you remember. She was a friend of Naomi's.'

There was a small silence out of respect for the deceased Betty Butts. Miss Primrose felt sad that some of her girls should not have survived their headmistress.

'He'd married some addlepate during the war, Betty said – the man Naomi got mixed up with. Very pretty but no brains. And he had to stick to her or she'd collapse. He became quite well known later on, I believe, though I don't know who he was. Betty seemed to think his empty marriage drove him on to success – he worked hard because his wife was dull and his home life uninteresting.' Mildred paused in her recital. 'Some women are very stupid,' she declared.

'Had he legitimate children?' Miss Primrose enquired.

'Oh, yes, I believe so,' said Mildred. 'I'd forgotten about it until now – Daphne didn't mention that Naomi was coming. She can't have known anything about it – she seems a bit shocked. But then, she always was rather a prig.'

She may be, and you're complaisant, thought Miss Primrose, filled with dismay.

'I must talk to Naomi,' she said, and the ranks of her girls
eddied and flowed to allow this to happen.

'My dear Naomi, you look much younger than all your
contemporaries,' Miss Primrose informed her wayward pupil.

Naomi laughed.

'Perhaps I'm the only one of us who isn't playing a role,'
she said. 'The others all seem to be performing the roles they
think are expected of their husbands' wives.'

'That's all most of them are capable of,' said Miss Primrose.
'Though they are valuable citizens, I've no doubt. Good to
their neighbours and excellent cooks. Home-made jam and
full freezers. You've had a hard time, Naomi.'

'In some ways. But I've put that all behind me long ago.
Jemima is married – she's happy. I've had a lot of happiness
too. And I can retreat into my solitude now when I close up
the shop. As *you* can, Miss Primrose. You always could,
couldn't you? Being head must have been lonely – it is at the
top of any concern. But that's a compensation, isn't it –
enjoying solitude?'

'That's true, my dear.'

'And are you enjoying today? Seeing your girls, if you still
think of us like that? Do we disappoint you?'

'I wish I could have seen some of the others – those who
were too busy to come today. There were *some* with brains,'
Miss Primrose said wistfully. 'You have brains, Naomi. You
always had, though perhaps your school career was un-
distinguished.'

'It was,' said Naomi. 'And I don't know about the brains.
Perhaps. At least by using one's mind one can fight against
grief.'

'I hope we meet again after today, Naomi,' said Miss
Primrose. 'You are one of St Wilhelmina's better specimens.'

Naomi laughed. 'The others might not agree,' she said.
'They probably think I was a disgrace to you and the school.'

Dimly Miss Primrose remembered that first war. Dick had
been killed on the Somme. She thought of his serious young

face as he asked her to marry him on his next leave. They had told no one their plans, and there had been no next leave. She had gone up to Girton. After all this time she had almost forgotten, but not quite. Naomi, at least, had borne a child to her lover.

Miss Primrose thought about Robert Blythe. It was a good name for a judge. If he was so indiscreet as to meet Naomi where he might be recognised and fail to mask his emotions, he might never grace the bench.

'Daphne's children. Do you know what they're like?' Miss Primrose asked slyly. 'What do they do?'

'The boy's a solicitor. The daughter's a Cordon Bleu cook. They're both married,' she said, and turned her brown eyes upon the faded but very alert blue ones of Miss Primrose.

'Do *they* have children? Grandchildren for Daphne?' Miss Primrose pursued.

'Not yet. Expected, however,' said Naomi. And then, a little maliciously, she added, 'They live some way away. They fear interference.'

'I see.' Miss Primrose nodded. 'Thank you, my dear. Good luck with your shop.'

Naomi, dismissed, drifted away and found herself next to Mildred.

'Funny old thing, Primmy, isn't she?' Mildred said. 'I think she's enjoying her day. She's still spot on, though.'

'Yes, she is,' said Naomi. 'Remarkable. But so many old ladies like her are, don't you find? Riding bicycles and mowing their lawns. Tough.'

'I wonder if we'll be as tough if we live so long,' mused Mildred, rather surprisingly.

'Only the tough or the cosseted survive to a great age,' said Naomi.

Miss Primrose was ahead of them, walking with Daphne. The sun beat down on their heads as they drew near to the weir, the white one with the velvet snood and the grey one, old-fashioned lacquered set immovable, broad shoulders bent slightly to the small old lady beside her.

No one saw how it happened. One minute the two were walking along the bank above the weir, conversing; the next there was some sort of scuffle as Miss Primrose appeared to stumble. A cry rang out, then a real scream.

Daphne was gone, swept into the river and instantly over the weir. By the time the others had rushed forward to look for life-belts she had vanished.

It was Naomi who ran along the bank and found a boat which she paddled right up to the foot of the weir. But Daphne had disappeared.

Miss Primrose, apparently suffering from heat stroke, was taken to the hospital where she spent the night. She recovered swiftly, and at the inquest on Daphne, whose body was washed up further down the river, she said she had fainted. Daphne must have tried to prevent her from falling and in so doing had lost her own footing and slipped into the river, which was notoriously dangerous there, above the weir.

A verdict of accidental death was recorded.

Six months later, Miss Primrose read in *The Times* that His Honour Judge Robert Blythe had married Miss Naomi Kent, quietly at Caxton Hall.

'One of my more deserving pupils, Naomi,' Miss Primrose recalled. 'And never a prig.'

I
DON'T
BELIEVE
IN
SANTA
CLAUS

The bus would pick them up at the end of the lane. Timmy was to meet the others there. He wore his best gear; his hair was slicked down; there was a clean handkerchief in his pocket. He stepped along carefully, to avoid getting his shoes wet. It had snowed in the night, but now it was thawing and water dripped from every branch. Soon it would be dark; a few lights shone out from the houses he passed. Only five days to Christmas, and today's party was just the first of the season's festivities; it had been planned for months, and there would be games, competitions with prizes, and presents for everyone.

When he reached the meeting-place, Jean and Wendy were already there, waiting; no one else. Timmy sighed. As usual, the fellows would be outnumbered.

'I wonder what there'll be for tea,' said Jean. 'Chocolate cake, I hope.' Her eyes gleamed in anticipation.

'Greedy,' said Wendy. 'You are awful.' She smiled at Timmy. 'Sit by me in the bus, Tim?'

He recoiled. 'You two sit together,' he said. 'I'll be all right on my own.'

'I hope I won't feel sick in the bus,' Jean said. She did, sometimes.

Timmy wondered forlornly if there would be anyone at the party who might become his friend. He yearned for one, someone who would share his interest in wild flowers and birds; not difficult things at all, you'd imagine, and approved of at home, but no one seemed to cater for them.

Several times he'd tried to avoid these expeditions, especially the organised parties. He didn't like games such as Musical Chairs and Forfeits, he'd protested. They embarrassed him; he was too old for them. Everyone laughed at that. Dolly had tweaked his tie and told him it was time he found a girlfriend; there were plenty to choose from.

But they were so awful: giggly, like Wendy and Jean, with shrill laughs and loud voices. There didn't seem to be any quiet ones.

The bus arrived, stopping with a sigh of its air brakes and splattering Timmy's trousers with water as it went through a large puddle beside him. There'd be trouble about that when he got home.

He climbed up the steps after Wendy and Jean. Mrs Baxter, one of the organisers, stood at the top checking them off on a list. The bus was nearly full.

'All there? Wendy – Jean – there's a seat at the back for you. And Timmy, take that one, will you, next to Janet?'

Timmy knew when protest was useless. Besides, no single seats were left. He subsided into the place indicated with barely a glance at Janet, whom he did not know. Maybe, if he didn't speak, she'd stay quiet on the journey although she'd think him rude. He'd been told often enough that he mustn't be shy, must come out of his shell.

He had thought of playing truant today, hiding somewhere until the party was over and the bus had brought everyone home. But where could he go? And he'd be missed – there was always someone like Mrs Baxter checking up, someone who would fuss if anyone failed to appear.

Now she was making them all sing. Carols, because it was Christmas. Timmy resolutely shut his lips tight. He wouldn't sing.

After some time he realised that Janet wasn't singing either. Her hands, in knitted gloves, were folded on her lap and she was sitting quite still beside him. He stole another glance at her. She looked about his own age, he thought, though he wasn't very good at estimating things like that. She had curly hair and wore a blue woollen cap. He couldn't see her eyes.

He looked quickly away. She wouldn't do as a friend. That must be a fellow, one who would enjoy walking over the fields looking for rare species. Females didn't like such things; all they thought about was clothes, and getting you to carry things for them. But if only he could find someone, they might be allowed out together when the summer came.

'You've been very ill,' they reminded him. 'You can't go off alone.'

But he was as strong as the next one now. He clenched his fists as if to prove it. When the snow went, he'd show them. He'd walk through the fields, and the woods. Perhaps he could get hold of a bicycle.

'A bike – that's it,' he said, not realising he had spoken aloud.

'What?' Janet asked. 'What did you say?'

'Oh – I was thinking I'd like a bike, if I could get one,' Timmy said.

'Why can't you?' she said.

'I don't get much pocket money,' Timmy replied.

'You could save it up. Or earn it. Get a part-time job. Help in someone's garden or deliver papers.' To her, it seemed quite natural that he might do such things. And why not? Would they let him?

'I don't like parties,' Timmy said. 'Do you?'

'Not much,' said Janet. 'I haven't been to one for a long time. But if we all refused to go, what would happen to the tea? And then there's Santa Claus coming today. He'd be disappointed.'

'I don't believe in Santa Claus,' Timmy said grimly.

'Don't let Mrs Baxter hear you say that,' said Janet. 'If we don't pretend, they get very annoyed.'

'I don't care,' said Timmy, and waited to hear her answer, 'Don't care was made to care,' like Dolly would, but she didn't.

She didn't say any more at all.

The party was held in the community centre, which had been decorated with streamers and holly. Taped carols played loudly. Long tables were laden with sandwiches and jellies;

there were iced cakes and trifle. Balloons hung from the walls, and a tall Christmas tree covered in parcels stood in a corner.

'Presents,' said Janet, nodding.

She was greedy like all the others, Timmy decided.

'I got gloves last year. I got three pairs of gloves for Christmas,' said Janet. 'What I wanted was a book about birds.'

'You should ask Santa Claus for one,' said Timmy, looking straight at her for the first time. Her eyes were bright blue, matching her woolly cap. He looked away.

'What did you get last year?' she asked.

Timmy couldn't remember.

'I was ill,' he said. He'd been in hospital for a long time, and they'd rubbed his bottom with baby oil, to stop it from getting sore; that was what he remembered most. As if he were a little kid.

'Oh.' Janet asked no more questions.

Timmy decided he might as well sit next to her as anyone else at tea. She was certainly better than Wendy or Jean.

'How quiet you are, you two,' cooed Mrs Baxter, swooping at them with plates of jelly. 'Two shy ones, eh?'

Janet wriggled with embarrassment and Timmy thought briefly of throwing the jelly at Mrs Baxter. What would she do if he did? Stand him in the corner? But it was a Christmas party, and people weren't put in corners at parties.

In Musical Chairs, Janet carefully got out first by not trying at all to sit down. Timmy too had left it till very late but when he understood her intention, chivalrously took the last chair. He managed to be the second one out. They sat together and watched the others.

'There'll be Blind Man's Buff, and Statues,' Janet warned.

Timmy looked round for escape.

'We could hide in the cloakroom,' he said.

They'd be parted, since the cloakrooms were His and Hers, but that didn't matter. They slunk away.

Mrs Baxter routed Janet out herself and a man was sent for

Timmy. It was, in fact, Santa Claus, who banged on the door and asked if he was all right; then, when Timmy sheepishly emerged into the washroom, proceeded to put on boots, whiskers and scarlet robe.

'Reckon you know all about me,' he said, grinning. 'No need to pretend in front of such a big boy.'

He handed the presents off the tree. Janet got a piece of soap and Timmy a penknife.

'You said you wanted a book on birds,' he remarked.

'Yes. I can't tell them apart, except robins and sparrows,' said Janet.

'I've got several,' Timmy volunteered, then blushed. What had he let himself in for? He couldn't invite her home. Everyone would tease him.

'If I get the bike, I could bring them over,' he said.

'I might get one too,' said Janet. 'A bike, I mean. I could go baby-sitting for it. We could go for rides in the summer.'

'Now the draw,' cried Mrs Baxter, clapping her hands for silence.

On arriving at the party, each had been given a ticket for the mystery prize. A local paper was the beneficent donor, and a reporter had been sent to record the event.

Under cover of the excited murmurs, Janet asked. 'Are you going to the pantomime? *Mother Goose?*'

'I don't want to,' Timmy said.

'But your family will make you?'

'Mm, I'd rather see a film. Pantomimes are for kids.'

'But we are kids. They treat us as if we were. Tell us what to do, what to think.' Janet, aged seventy-one and a widow, looked sadly at Timmy, three years older, a widower who had lived with his daughter and son-in-law since his illness.

'The winning ticket,' Santa Claus called out. 'Number thirty-seven!'

'That's yours,' Timmy said, looking at the pale pink scrap of paper held in Janet's thin, wrinkled fingers.

Janet went up to fetch her prize. It was a large white envelope.

'Open it, dear,' Mrs Baxter urged.

Janet did, and Timmy, looking over her shoulder, saw with amazement what the prize was: a week in Majorca for two.

A great grin spread over Janet's face.

'Well,' she said. 'Will you come with me, Timmy?'

THE
RECKONING

On the morning of her husband's seventieth birthday, a Thursday in September, Ellen Parsons rose as usual at seven o'clock. She washed quietly in the bathroom, careful as she moved about not to disturb Maurice, who still slept, a straggle of grey hair falling across bald pate and spotless pillow. After she had cleaned her teeth and inserted her dentures, three stark molars on a pink plate new last year, Ellen, in her woollen dressing-gown, went down to the kitchen and put on the kettle. While it boiled she laid the table in the dining-room: blue and white striped Cornish crockery, honey and butter, knife and fork for the egg and bacon Maurice daily consumed after his porridge. Odd that he never grew fat, she often thought.

This was the last time she would sit across the table from him, and she hummed under her breath as she finished her early routine. The kettle boiled, she made the tea, and carried the tray upstairs, setting it on the table between their twin beds. When it had had time to draw, she poured out two cups, one for Maurice and one for her, with two lumps of sugar in his. But it didn't do much to sweeten him.

'Tea, Maurice,' she said, and took her own cup into the bathroom, where modestly she dressed out of his sight.

Maurice did not answer, but she knew that he would now sit up, yawn, showing his bare gums, belch, and drink his tea in gulps. She would return to the bedroom to do her hair in time to pour his second cup. By the time he was ready to rise, she would be downstairs cooking the breakfast.

She had decided to kill him in church one Sunday morning a year ago. The vicar's text has been from Ecclesiastes: *To everything there is a season and a time to every purpose under the heaven: a time to be born and a time to die . . .*

'I have not lived yet,' Ellen had thought. Her mind ranged over the forty years of her marriage and she saw herself as she was when she first met Maurice. Her father, a widower, had died after a long illness through which she had devotedly nursed him, never begrudging the toll of time and strength. Maurice, then junior partner in the firm of solicitors acting for her father, had called at the house to advise. Ellen, self-contained and composed as always, had offered Madeira and home-made sponge cake. Maurice had called again. He said she should decide nothing in haste, and recommended that she should keep the house for the present. Ellen, weary from the strain of her father's illness, was glad to accept this counsel. Never one for idleness, she busied herself in the neglected garden and set about washing curtains and paint-work indoors. Maurice watched both her and the house revive under this treatment. One day he brought her some violets; another time, a book of poetry. She looked forward to his visits; he had such a sweet smile.

Soon she exchanged one form of bondage for another. She and Maurice, after their marriage, continued to live in the large Victorian house on the edge of the village, and here they were still, with the house as isolated as it had always been since the village had expanded internally, without enlarging its boundaries. Here their daughters, Jane and Priscilla, were born. Jane now lived in Australia; she had run away and married a young farmer of whom Maurice disapproved and they had immediately emigrated. Jane wrote happy letters and sent snapshots of their four children; she urged Ellen to come out for a visit and see her grandchildren, but Maurice would not go himself nor allow Ellen to go without him. Priscilla read sociology at university; now she worked in public relations in London. She seldom visited her parents, and when she did it was just for an afternoon when she would be accompanied always by a different young woman, usually frail and fair in contrast to her own dark vigour. Ellen did not like Priscilla very much these days, and she often thought wistfully of the solemn, precociously bright child she had been. Now she frightened her mother, but Ellen was used to fear.

Maurice insisted that his life should run smoothly. The smile that had once charmed Ellen was seen more and more rarely. Meals must be punctual to the second; children should be seen and not heard; arguments were not allowed; and only Maurice's opinions might be expressed. During their short engagement Ellen had anticipated long talks with him such as she had enjoyed with her father; reading the same books, Dickens and Trollope, for example, as her father had liked; and walking in the hills. But Maurice read only legal tomes and the biographies of politicians, and he did not like walking. In fact, it soon became clear that he liked nothing but himself. He worked hard and in time became senior partner of his firm; most nights he brought papers home to study. He was respected in the town.

When the girls grew older, Maurice gave permission for Ellen to join the Women's Institute; it was a seemly activity for her, he said. She enjoyed the meetings for they brought her into contact with other women, the only company she had when Jane married and Priscilla went to London. No wonder the two girls left home as soon as they could, for their father allowed no parties and never encouraged their friends to visit the house. If any dared to come they were subjected to such an interrogation about their lives and views that few ventured there a second time. The only guests invited by Maurice were business acquaintances whom he took to his study for brandy. The Parsons did not entertain.

Ellen's fragile links with other people dwindled after Maurice retired, for if they came to tea he would sit scowling and looking at his watch, finally leaving with some remark like, 'See that dinner is on time, Ellen,' in front of them, humiliating her.

But now all this would end. The resentment that had simmered for so long had boiled at last. She meant to go to Australia before she grew too old. The house was hers, and all the money that Maurice had made would be hers too.

The days of our age are threescore years and ten.

Ellen had read the words many times. Maurice had now ended his seventieth year and she was resolved. Despite constant complaint and a genuine bronchitic tendency, he was fit for his age; he had always been carefully tended. Ellen, though nine years younger, was not wearing so well. But she had made her plans with care and at last the time had come to carry them out.

The post brought nothing from either Jane or Priscilla. Jane would not have forgotten; she was meticulous over such things, but she must have missed the mail. What a pity Maurice would not now receive her card, Ellen thought, buttering her toast.

She gave him her present when he had finished *The Times* leader – a thick woollen dressing-gown. She had bought it with Ben, their jobbing gardener, in mind, for it would be unworn. Maurice thanked her without enthusiasm, saying he would have preferred camel colour to maroon. Ellen had known that Ben would like maroon better.

Breakfast over, Maurice went to his study and Ellen set about her chores. After she had made the beds and tidied round, she went into the garden and cut three marrows that were ripe; they would get old and woody if left on the plants. She carried them into the house and down the flight of stone steps leading to the cellar. The door was locked and bolted. Ellen took the key from a hook above the lintel and undid the door. She laid the marrows on a shelf inside. Strings of onions already hung on the walls but otherwise the cellar was quite bare; it was dark, lit only by a tiny window high on one wall and covered with a strong iron grid.

The marrows deposited, Ellen went upstairs again; she shut the cellar door but did not lock it.

Now it was time for her weekly shopping trip to town. Every Thursday Ellen made this expedition, her one outing in the car. Maurice decreed that once a week was quite sufficient if she planned ahead; there was a butcher in the village, and the post office sold sugar, tea, and a few items in tins.

She got the car out of the garage, backing it up against the house so that the exhaust pipe was exactly opposite the cellar grid; a black, smoky mark on the surrounding brickwork showed that this was customary. But today she backed too far and broke the glass. She smiled as she switched off the engine and uttered a shriek.

Maurice had heard the crash. He came storming out of the house to inspect the damage to the car, which was nil; the exhaust pipe had missed the iron bars and gone straight through the glass. Ellen had practised this manoeuvre till she could have done it blindfold. She stood wringing her hands and apologising meekly while he castigated her for her incompetence; then, as Ellen knew he would, he went to discover what had happened in the cellar, for most of the glass had fallen inwards. She followed him.

Automatically he reached for the key and found it missing from its hook.

'You've been down here this morning, Ellen,' he accused.

'Yes, Maurice. I brought those three marrows in. You told me yesterday to cut them.'

'You didn't lock the door. How many times must I tell you everything?' he exclaimed, opening the door and striding angrily inside.

In an instant she had slammed the door behind him, turned the key and thrust the bolt across. For a moment she leaned against it, panting, her heart pounding. It had worked! She had spent so long devising her scheme, thinking of first one plan, and then discarding it for another: it must seem to be an accident. Now she could truthfully say when she was questioned that she had forgotten to lock the cellar after taking in the marrows and had returned to do it. How could she have known that Maurice was inside?

She hurried up the stairs before he had time to realise what had happened and begin to beat upon the door. In a few minutes she had started the engine of the car and left it to run, leaving the choke well out as it was cold. The rich mixture filling the cellar with fumes through the new aperture would make Maurice unconscious very rapidly; a mere five minutes in a closed garage with a high-powered car could prove fatal, she had discovered during her researches in the public library. Maurice was due for a much longer diet of fumes from their medium-sized saloon.

She left the car and walked away, for she could not have listened to his cries; soon they would cease. There was nothing he could stand on so that he could reach the grating; he would go to the door, and without a weapon he would not be able to break it open.

She went to the garage and took out the bottle of distilled water kept there. Very slowly she returned to the car, opened the bonnet and topped up the battery, her eyes away from the cellar. There was no sound apart from the car's engine, which by now was warming up and beginning to run unevenly. She pushed in the choke. Maurice always insisted she warm the car up thoroughly before driving off; it helped preserve the engine, he said, though Priscilla mocked this theory and said with modern cars it made no difference. The battery topped up to her satisfaction, Ellen put away the distilled water and closed the garage doors; Maurice would never allow them to be left open while the car was out, although the garage was at the back of the house and could not be seen from the road. Then she went into the house. She could scarcely hear the car purring, its engine ran so sweetly. She went to her sewing-box and took from it the wad of leaflets about travel to Australia which had lain hidden there for weeks, under her embroidery. How should she go? By boat, she thought: a large and luxurious liner calling in at other places on the way. No one came to the door while she turned the pages of the brochures; no one ever did on Thursdays. In fact, visits from tradesmen were discouraged by Maurice, who cared for no form of caller.

Ellen had made a cake for the church bazaar and promised to deliver it before she went to town today. When she had finished dreaming over the booklets she put them away, fetched the cake, and took it up the road, two hundred yards, to the vicarage, where she stayed for a cup of coffee. It was pleasant, sitting in the vicarage garden in the September sunshine, and Ellen lingered there praising the late roses. When she reached home again the car was still ticking over, though it had got rather hot and the water temperature showed high on the gauge. Ellen moved the car forward so that the exhaust pipe no longer protruded through the cellar window. She laid a sheet of slate that normally covered the kitchen drain against the opening to keep the fumes inside. She heard no sound from the cellar.

Then she drove to town and did her shopping.

When she returned more than an hour later she removed the slate and replaced it over the drain, leaving the engine of the car running. She unloaded her parcels and put them away. Finally she opened the garage doors and put the car inside, having allowed another good supply of carbon monoxide to enter the cellar.

It was now time to prepare lunch, and for once it would not matter if the meal was late. How wasteful, she reflected, peeling Maurice's usual two medium-sized potatoes and slicing runner beans fresh from the garden. She had made his favourite pudding, crème caramel, the day before: a birthday treat. She put the grill on for the chops. Soon she would have to start looking for Maurice. She could spend some time searching the house and garden, and then go up the village to enquire if anyone had seen him. She needn't think about the cellar until later, much later; perhaps she need not think of it at all, until she told the police that he was missing. That was the part she dreaded: finding him. But he would be dead; most certainly by now he had been dead for hours. His age and his bronchitic chest would have sped him on his way, and he would not have suffered long. Only his hands might be torn and bruised if he had clawed at the cellar door. He would be lying on the threshold, she was sure; in fact she might not be able to open the door against the weight of him the other side.

She dished up the meal and put it in the low oven. Then she

went upstairs to wash and do her hair before calling him, as she always did. Her hair-brush was placed bristles downwards on the dressing-table, and she never saw the sleepy wasp among them as she lifted it. She felt only the sharp, searing stab of the sting above her temple as she began to use the brush on her limp, grey hair.

She became giddy almost at once and stumbled to her bed. Three years ago she had been stung on her arm, fainted, and recovered only because Maurice had been there, seen her cyanosed face and called the doctor instantly.

This time, he could not save her.

SUCH
A
GENTLEMAN

It was the dahlias that reminded me. This morning I went into the garden to cut some for the house; just now they are at the height of their blowsy glory, standing bright in the beds, bending against their supporting stakes in the late summer bluster that has sprung up in these past days after a long, still, hot spell, and smelling tangy. They have a defiant air, brazenly glowing, looking too vigorous to fall victim to the first blackening autumn frost.

It was on a day like this, ten years ago, that it happened. I had been in the garden then, too, ferreting out strands of bindweed, aware only of the sun on my back, the sigh of the wind, and the strong scents of the blooms around me, all thought suspended. Through the open window I heard the telephone ring, and went to answer it, muttering crossly at the interruption, kicking my muddy boots off by the kitchen door before entering the house.

It was Edmund, my godson. He asked me to come over, at once. It was urgent. His voice sounded calm, but it was ten-thirty on a Wednesday morning, and Edmund should have been at the office.

'Is something wrong?' I asked.

'I want to talk to you Phyllis. It's important,' he said.

Then why won't you come to see me, I wondered irritably.

But one had a duty to one's godson and I had promised his mother. So I went.

Helen Rossiter and I had been childhood friends; we went to school together, were married within weeks of each other and were parted only when the war came. Helen's husband was in the RNVR. She went to live in Scotland, in a remote cottage within reach of where he was based; she remained there for

61

two years, alone for most of the time except during her husband's brief leaves, and until Edmund was born. Then his ship was torpedoed, and there were no survivors.

Helen and the baby came back to Speyton, where they lived with her parents for the rest of Helen's life. She worked in a local munitions factory until the war ended; after that she did part-time work in a welfare clinic until her illness forced her to retire.

I was away from Speyton for much longer, at first with my husband, and then, after Dick's plane was shot down and he became a prisoner-of-war, with the WAAF. Once, I came back to Speyton on leave and saw Helen for the first time since she was widowed. Her face was pale and lined, and her hands were cracked and stained, partly, I suppose, by her work in the factory, but also by the hours she spent in her parents' garden, digging for victory. She grew quantities of vegetables and kept hens and a goat, in order that Edmund might be healthily nourished despite food rationing.

He was an amiable child, with large brown eyes and sandy hair. I was not accustomed to small children, but he appeared to enjoy my company. I wheeled him out in his pram to watch the trains pass at the level crossing by Speyton junction, and he waved joyfully at the engine drivers who always waved back. We used to meet Helen at the bus stop as she returned from the factory, and Edmund did his best to spring out of his confining harness in his eagerness to greet her.

I found Helen much changed. She had always been quiet; now she was withdrawn and remote, except when she played with the chuckling baby.

After his release at the end of the war Dick remained in the RAF. He was posted to the Far East and I joined him there. We had some good years, until one day I came home early from a wives' committee meeting and found him in bed with Valerie Fenton.

'You might at least have gone somewhere else,' I hurled at them both before rushing from the house again.

It turned out that Valerie wasn't Dick's first. Perhaps it was my fault: I'd become tough and independent during my time alone, while he'd had all those wasted years in the prison camp. Maybe if I'd been willing to forgive him we could have put it behind us and started again, but I was too hurt to try. As it was, Dick resigned from the service, we divorced, and within a year he married a girl of twenty-three. As far as I know they're still living happily ever after.

If we'd had children, it might have been different.

After the divorce I went back to Speyton. Where else should I have gone? I opened a fashion boutique geared to the needs of women of my own age, thus far not catered for in the town, and I'm doing very well. Since Wednesday is early closing day in Speyton and I don't open the shop at all that day, that's why I was at home when Edmund telephoned.

While I was abroad Helen's father had died. She and her mother and Edmund continued to live in the old house. Helen still gardened in most of her spare time, but she grew flowers now, and from her I learned about dahlias and delphiniums. Slowly, over the months we picked up and re-wove the threads of our friendship, and I got to know Edmund.

He had grown into a quiet boy, well-mannered, solemn, and tall for his age; he had knobbly knees, and wrists that were always sticking out of his too-short sleeves. He was interested in butterflies and moths and had a collection to which he constantly added, but I didn't like his habit of keeping specimens alive for hours in a preserving jar, often until suffocation point was reached, before mercifully gassing them. Only if their wings were threatened with damage as they beat against the glass did this budding lepidopterist hurry their despatch. Then he stretched them out and mounted them on pins in a glass case, for display.

Just before Edmund took his GCE exams Helen fell ill. She made light of it, but after the first operation she gave up her work at the clinic and spent more time than ever in the garden. I saw her every weekend and often on Wednesdays too. She was much happier in these last years and talked about the past, breaking the silence of more than a decade. To her, her dead husband was still a young, vigorous man; I sometimes wondered whether, if he had lived, he might have found her dull after so long. How much had she changed because of his death? How much of her quietness was inherent?

Anyway, when Edmund was twenty-one, she died.

He had done well at school, and could have gone on to university, but he had insisted on staying at home to help his grandmother, Mrs Rossiter, look after Helen. Meanwhile, he started work in a solicitor's office in Speyton as an articled clerk.

The fiction that Helen would recover was staunchly maintained, but only Mrs Rossiter really believed it, and perhaps that was because she was too frightened to admit the truth to herself.

'Look after Edmund for me, Phyllis, please,' Helen implored, on a good day just before the end. And of course I agreed.

After her death I suggested to Edmund that he might now take up his university career, but he told me that it was too late: he could not face the thought of student life after nearly three years in the tranquil office of Tresswell and Geddes. Besides, in two years he would qualify. I pointed out that he had done none of the things most young men of his age considered part of the normal pattern: for instance, he had never crossed the Channel. Why didn't he take a year off from Tresswell and Geddes and hitch his way round the world? His mother had left him her little estate and he could afford it.

Humouring me, he did consent at least to take a holiday.

He came back with Louisa.

It seems that they'd met in Penzance, where he'd gone instead of to Greece, as I'd suggested.

Like Edmund, Louisa was an orphan; she lived with an aunt who ran the small private hotel where he stayed. He found her weeping one evening because she saw no escape from the round of waiting at table and housework that was her lot. She loathed the summer visitors, with their noisy, mannerless children, and she hated the winter commercials, who tried to flirt with her.

Of course, I did not learn all this at once, but by degrees after Louisa arrived. Since Helen's death I'd formed the habit of going to see Mrs Rossiter once a week or so; this kept me in touch with Edmund indirectly, in accordance with my promise, and I liked the old lady, who had astonished me by her fortitude. On the first occasion after Edmund's return from his holiday she led me to the window and showed me Louisa reclining in a swing seat. In fact, all I saw was a large, shady hat, some long ash-blonde hair, and a pair of slender legs; the face was hidden behind a fashion magazine.

Mrs Rossiter hastened to tell me as much as she knew.

'The child was deeply unhappy. It seems she was a sort of Cinderella, helping her aunt run the hotel and getting no time to herself. Edmund was the first young man to show her any respect,' she said. Mrs Rossiter sighed. 'He was always such a gentleman, even as a little chap.'

We were both silent, remembering Edmund's unfailing courtesies, so much a part of him that perhaps we took them too much for granted.

'They're married,' Mrs Rossiter went on. 'They got a special licence, down there. It was the only way the aunt would let her go.'

It seemed a drastic method of escape. Couldn't the girl have got some other job? I said so, aloud.

'Yes, dear. I thought that too. It seems so hasty,' Mrs Rossiter said. 'But she hasn't any qualifications. You know what Edmund is, Phyllis. She must have appealed to the chivalrous side of his nature.'

'Maybe,' I said dubiously.

'She's very pretty, too,' said Mrs Rossiter.

Edmund had never shown much interest in girls. He'd spent most of his free time with his mother.

'She hasn't much to say for herself,' Mrs Rossiter continued. 'But I expect she's shy. Well,' she heaved a sigh. 'I'd better introduce you.'

The young couple remained in the old house with Mrs Rossiter for some time, during which local surprise over their whirlwind romance died down. Edmund continued in the usual way in the office, and Louisa was often to be seen in Speyton wearing trendy new clothes and pushing Mrs Rossiter's laden shopping trolley. She spent a good deal of time in the hairdresser's and was sometimes difficult to recognise in her newest style or colour; indeed, it was hard to decide what was her natural hue, since it was certainly not the ash-grey blonde she had been at first. She had a lot of leisure, for Mrs Rossiter continued to run the house with the help of a daily woman as before, and Edmund looked after the garden.

I found it impossible to get to know Louisa. She was always polite but made small conversational effort herself and I was forced to communicate by the question-and-answer method I find works with children.

Six months after the wedding Edmund and Louisa moved to a new bungalow on the other side of Speyton and I saw much less of them. It was clearly sensible of them to move to a place of their own, and Louisa would now have plenty to do. Mrs Rossiter perked up after they left, and began to play bridge again.

The years passed. In time Mrs Rossiter died and the old house was sold.

Edmund always remembered my birthday and would come round in the evening with a bottle of sherry. We'd open it, drink a glass together, and then he'd hurry away, back to his Louisa. Once or twice a year they both came to dinner with me, occasions I regarded as rather a chore but which were essential if I was to remain in contact with my godson, as I had promised. Punctiliously, they would invite me back, Edmund telephoning from his office to say that Louisa had asked him to fix a mutually convenient date. The bungalow was always spotless and the dinner perfect. While Edmund served the meal from an expensive hotplate, Louisa talked to me about my shop. She was interested in fashion, but she never came in; our style was not hers.

One evening, the last time I had dinner there, Louisa was

more talkative than usual and told me that they were going to Rome the following week. I had never seen her so animated. She took me into the bedroom and showed me several new dresses she had bought, and a glamorous nightdress with a matching negligée. I expressed due admiration, pleased to find her, after all, capable of some enthusiasm, and looked with interest at their bedroom, which I had never seen before. It was painted all in white, the fashion then, with an off-white carpet and mushroom-pink curtains. The large bed was covered with a white spread. On a shelf below the window was arranged a collection of small china animals, and there was a bowl of roses on the dressing-table beside Louisa's silver-backed brushes. With a shock, I realised that they had been Helen's: but why not, after all?

No one could criticise Louisa's housekeeping; all was immaculate, perhaps too perfect. It was sad that there were no children; Edmund's grandmother, Mrs Rossiter, and I had often speculated about it, but of course only to each other.

We went into the sitting-room. Edmund was seated on the sofa with the coffee tray on a table in front of him. He was holding one hand over his eyes, as if he were exhausted; he had not heard us enter. As soon as he saw us he rose quickly to his feet, smiling his gentle smile: suddenly I saw him as he would appear to a stranger, tired, harassed, nearly middle-aged. But Edmund was not yet thirty. I took my coffee and looked at him again; he had grown a moustache in the last year and it drooped over his upper lip, adding more lines of sadness to his face. He was sad, I realised, appalled: sad, and defeated. How long had this been so?

We talked about Rome and all they would see there. Last year they had been to Paris, the year before to Amsterdam, but Louisa had not cared for either place; not warm enough, she said, though there was plenty to see in both. It was difficult to imagine Louisa happy in a museum or art gallery, though Edmund would be. They both talked a lot, but I suddenly noticed that they rarely addressed each other directly, only me.

Well, they'd been married some time. At the start the dice had not seemed to be loaded in their favour, but they hadn't broken up after six months as people had expected. Doubtless they were just in a doldrum patch now.

They went to Rome ten years ago, and it was on the Wednesday after their return that Edmund telephoned asking me to come.

I reached the bungalow about twenty minutes after his call. The gate was closed so I parked in the road and walked up the path. Bright dahlias, like my own, flanked the side of it; they had grown a lot in the recent wet weather and the dead blooms needed cutting. The lawn was overgrown, too, and I was surprised, for Edmund was meticulous about its weekly trim. Of course, they'd been away and he hadn't caught up yet with the arrears. But I'd have expected him to get the mower out immediately he came home.

He had seen me coming, for the front door opened before I could ring the bell. A bottle of milk still stood on the step and automatically I picked it up before entering.

'Well, Edmund?' I said briskly, giving him the customary peck on the cheek.

'It's good of you to come, Phyllis,' he said. We'd dropped the 'Aunt' as soon as he grew taller than me.

'Did you enjoy your holiday?' I asked. 'How's Louisa?'

'She's gone away,' he said.

So that was it. She'd left him. After a moment I rallied, thinking that worse things than this could happen, and that Edmund was, by the calendar, still a young man, even if he did look fifty.

As he did.

'You look awful. What happened?' I asked. 'Didn't you go to Rome?'

'Oh yes. We went.' Edmund said.

'You look as if you could do with a brandy. Have you got any?' I said abruptly.

'I've had too much already,' Edmund said, with a faint smile. 'It's in the kitchen.'

Without waiting to hear more, I went out to the kitchen. The brandy bottle, half empty, stood on the table with a dirty glass beside it. There was another glass, broken, on the floor; my shoes crunched as I stepped on a fragment. On the draining board were heaped some plates with the remains of half-eaten meals stuck to them: scrambled egg, a piece of cheese, and half a tomato. Clearly, Louisa was not at home.

I poured out a stiff drink for Edmund, found a clean glass, and poured another for myself; I was going to need it. Then I went back to Edmund.

'I loved her, you know,' he said, and took the glass.

'Of course, Edmund. I know that,' I said, in a hospital-nurse voice. 'Now, are you going to tell me about it?'

'Yes, please,' he said. 'There isn't much time.' He began to pluck at the cover of the sofa and I longed to tell him not to fidget. 'I want you to understand, even though no one else will.'

'I'll do my best, Edmund,' I said.

'She was so pretty,' he said. 'When I met her, that first summer, she was like a butterfly in a cage. I had to set her free.'

He lapsed into silence, meditating, for some seconds. Then he spoke again.

'I thought it would be all right in the end. She was so very young, you see. I could wait. In time it would come right. She thought so too. She kept telling me so. "Just wait, Eddie, till I've known you longer," she said at first.' He paused again and I waited, still baffled.

'Later she said other things,' he continued. '"Don't frighten me." Or "How can you be so cruel? I thought you loved me." And I did love her. So I waited. I kept on waiting.'

Bit by painful bit the story was disclosed. For eight long years she kept him waiting, an untouched bride, feeding him on hope alone. I could not believe my ears, but as he went on talking it slotted into place: her little-girl clothes; her remote manner; Edmund's drawn features; the way they spoke to each other, as if they were strangers.

She'd been attacked and almost raped by a lodger in her aunt's hotel, it seemed: enough to terrify any young girl, though she had escaped the final outrage. Of course Edmund must rescue her from a place where such a thing could happen, and of course he must wait chivalrously for her to recover. Meanwhile, he cherished her in every way, giving her everything she asked for and waiting on her hand and foot. For it was Edmund who had kept the bungalow so speckless: housework was anathema to Louisa. He got up early and did the cleaning before he went to work; in the evening, when he came home, he cooked the dinner.

'But I used to meet her at the butcher's,' I said, stupidly. 'She did the shopping.'

'Oh yes, she was good at that,' he said with pride.

He'd failed his final exams, he told me now. He'd studied at night, and done housework with the dawn; in the intervals he'd kept the garden bright and tidy, but that he had enjoyed. Not surprisingly something had suffered, and it was his work. In the end though, he'd managed to devise a better routine and finally he'd qualified; he had to, for keeping Louisa contented was expensive. Often he thought the moment had come when at last he might claim some reward, but though she sometimes let him kiss her, she remained like a marble block, or so I understood.

'But you could have got a divorce,' I said, almost too horrified to speak. 'An annulment, I mean.' Of all people, he, a lawyer, must have known that.

'Oh yes, I know. But what would have happened to her then? She couldn't possibly look after herself. Besides, I loved her,' he said.

'Oh Edmund!' I exclaimed. I wanted to shake him, and I wanted to weep. 'Well, couldn't you have found a girlfriend, then?' It seemed the only other thing to do.

'I tried it,' he said, bleakly. 'But it was cheating, you see. Besides, I couldn't really spare the time.'

But in Rome all was to have been different. Louisa was sure

that the warm climate and the romantic aura would affect her favourably.

'And did it?' But I'd no need to ask, looking at him now.

I thought of the new nightdress I'd been shown. She'd put it on, he said, and twirled about in front of him, wearing it. Then she had blown him a kiss and said, 'I'm nearly ready, Eddie. Just a little longer.'

He sat there with his head held in his hands, his elbows on his knees.

'She needed a doctor, Edmund,' I said.

He'd thought of that, and consulted several. All had told him that nothing could be done without Louisa's co-operation. The advice columnist of a woman's magazine, to whom in desperation he'd written, had supplied some useful addresses and several booklets, but whenever he suggested any positive steps to Louisa she wept and said, 'But Eddie, I thought you loved me, and if you do you'll wait until I'm ready.'

'She'd had that awful experience, when she was so young, you see,' he said. 'And I did love her.'

'Edmund, where is she now?' I asked at last.

He looked at me, and nodded his head; then he smiled, and I was suddenly terrified.

'She's free,' he said. 'She always wanted to be free.'

'Edmund, where is she? Tell me!' I said, laying my hand on his knee.

'She's waiting in the car,' he said. 'I was going to take her out to some peaceful spot and free her there, but in the end I did it differently. The car's in the garage,' he added helpfully.

I got up at once and left the room. A door from the hall led into the garage, and I opened it.

Louisa lay on the back seat of the car, covered with the white eiderdown from her own bed. Her head was placed carefully on a pillow in a clean white case. She had been strangled.

I waited with Edmund until the police arrived. He had sent them a letter asking them to call at mid-day, and they did.

'But why, Edmund?' I kept asking him. 'Why?'

On Sunday evening, when they'd got home from the holiday, she'd been tired and wanted her supper in bed. He'd brought it, she'd eaten it, and he'd come to take the tray away.

'Something came over me,' he said. 'I don't remember properly what happened. I think I felt that if I was a little bolder, she'd give in. Women often say no at first, don't they, when really they mean yes. All they want is a little persuading.'

He'd tried to make love to her, and when she resisted he caught her by the throat, held her till she ceased to struggle, and then realised she had beaten him for ever.

'You didn't mean to kill her, Edmund,' I whispered.

'No,' he said, and then, 'I suppose I didn't.'

Suddenly, oddly, I remembered the butterflies he had kept imprisoned in his jars when he was a child.

'Oh, Edmund dear,' I said.

I visit him in prison, regularly. He's working in the library and studying in his leisure time. His moustache has gone and he looks much younger. With remission for good conduct he'll be out soon.

At the trial it emerged that Louisa was pregnant. She'd had several lovers, the police discovered, two before ever she had met Edmund. The prosecution asserted that Edmund had found out and that jealousy was the motive for the murder.

He never told the police, nor his lawyers, what he had told me.

A
TIME
FOR
INDULGENCE

Looking in the mirror, I see a white, fat face – pale eyes, sparse brows, which now I pencil over darkly. My lips are a bright bow of painted pink. My hand shakes as I apply mascara to my scanty lashes. I add rouge over my cheekbones and powder the whole. My mask is on for the day.

In the bathroom adjoining our hotel room, my husband is taking his morning bath. The water slurps and splashes. He will be some time yet; the ritual toilet lasts for over an hour as first he shaves his jowly chin, then soaps his scrawny body with its grizzled hair.

Last night, in the four-poster bed in this hotel bedroom, my husband used me. He plunged and groaned, trying to make of me a mustang to meet his bucking. Above us, the canopy stretched, silent witness of intimate encounter. Later, in sleep, he pushed me away, taking for himself the centre of the dipping bed, snoring heavily. When I tried to win for myself enough space to find some rest, he lashed out at me with a flailing arm. At last I took my pillow to the armchair and dozed a little. This morning my feet and ankles are sadly swollen.

Why not twin beds, you ask.

My husband frequently, even now, demands his rights, and insists they remain within reach. A holiday, he has said, is a time for indulgence.

I am wearing my white linen sundress, which exposes my flabby white arms and much of my heavy shoulders, though wide straps conceal my underwear. My husband has always liked me to be dressed in white, so to please him I seldom wear colours. I will go down to the terrace and sit there in the sunshine, waiting until he comes downstairs, for I must not

go into breakfast without him. You would expect me to have
no appetite after such a night, but I am constantly hungry. At
the thought of coffee, hot toast, bacon and egg, saliva runs in
my mouth.

While I wait, others enter the hotel dining-room: the
slender, pale girl with the fine dark hair that falls to her
shoulders, and her tall young husband with the full soft lower
lip. His hand guides her ahead of him, possessively touching
her back, and she turns to smile intimately at him.

I think of a day in Venice: of a pale slender girl in a full-
skirted muslin dress sprigged with small flowers and with a
wide-brimmed hat on her dark hair, her husband's hand firm
on her elbow as they cross the Piazza San Marco: myself.

He always took thought for me. In those first years before
the war a daily maid helped with the heavier work in our
small house in Wimbledon. I saw that all ran smoothly to
please my husband, as was my duty. The silver shone with
polishing; the furniture gleamed with beeswax; tasty, nourishing meals were punctually served. For a time I went to a
cookery school, to learn basic methods, and embellished these
by advice from books whose complicated recipes I followed
with increasing success. We gave little dinners for some of my
husband's friends. He would give me a bouquet of flowers on
the day of such a dinner; the guests, when he brought it to
their notice, thought it a charming thing to do.

Our intimate moments were troubling to me. I had none of
the knowledge girls seem to acquire so easily these days, and
I was too timid to ask advice from other young women; such
matters could not be mentioned to a mere acquaintance and
I had no close female friend, nor a sister; my mother was dead.
A husband to provide for her was what every girl hoped for
then; a job was a stop-gap until marriage was safely arranged,
and to remain unmarried was to be labelled a social failure.
Careers were for the few, who were thought eccentric and
unwomanly. How different things are today! I envy modern
girls their independence. Now no woman need pay for her
keep in a manner that degrades her.

For years I imagined that all women felt as I did about these things. Then came the war.

My husband, who worked in a bank (I had met him there, paying in money for the draper in whose shop I was employed as cashier), had earlier joined the Territorial Army; he enjoyed their manoeuvres and meetings, and looked well in his uniform. I was pleased that he had this interest and never minded that it took him away from home for hours, sometimes for days; for me, these intervals brought blessed rest. He was called up even before war was declared, and was soon in France, a commissioned officer. I felt proud.

In the collapse of 1940 he was taken prisoner, and he spent the rest of the war in various camps in Germany.

Left alone, childless, I let the house for the duration of the war and joined the ATS. At first I worked as a cook, for this was my only skill, but when I found that army food, cooked in bulk, could never resemble the tempting dishes I had been used to concocting for my husband's pleasure, I applied to become a driver and was accepted for training. I reasoned that this work, carried on outdoors and often alone in a car or lorry, would offer relief from the pressures of noise and constant company which I found trying. I was not good at mixing, and was older than many of the other girls.

I was a conscientious pupil and was soon proficient at the wheel, taught by a brisk middle-aged sergeant with a red face and a surprising amount of patience. I learned some mechanics, and took pride in maintaining my vehicle in efficient order. For the next five years I drove lorries round Britain to gun sites and supply depots.

I wrote regularly to my husband and arranged for parcels to be sent to him. He replied at intervals, terse notes with requests for things he wanted, but I knew his letters would be read and censored and expected nothing more. He studied for a law degree while he was in the camp, but he failed his examinations. He did not try to escape. Escapers, he said when at last he came home, were a nuisance to those who had settled down to a course of study in an effort to profit from their captivity. He blamed his examination failure on the fact that he was obliged to give background help to would-be escapers, acting as look-out and so on, which disturbed his studies.

Because I was married, I did not go out on 'dates' like the other girls. In my spare time I knitted warm garments for my husband and for other servicemen. I became a good knitter and found it peaceful employment, though I don't knit now. I went to the cinema often; there were plenty of good films to see then. Sometimes I went to concerts; I still listen to them on the radio if my husband is not in the house; he does not like music.

I was content. It was as though my life in Wimbledon with my husband had never been. I did not look ahead.

I was given a stripe, and then a second; as a responsible married woman I was an obvious candidate for an eventual sergeant's stripe, even a commission, but I never rose higher. I was not flighty, likely to get into trouble, like so many girls. Their conversation, as they talked about their amorous adventures, often shocked me; it surprised me, too, describing pleasure they obtained from experiences that would have been only distasteful to me.

Then, one fine warm night, walking back to the billets with one of the men who helped maintain our vehicles, everything changed. He suddenly slid his arm round me in the darkness, turned me to face him, and kissed my lips. Holding me close to him, he remarked that I was a fine girl, always cheerful, though my husband had been so long in the prison camp and wasn't I missing him?

I was so astonished by his action that I did not push him away at once. Nor did I connect what had happened with the encounters I had had with my husband. The soldier's lips were soft and warm. He kissed me again, his battledress rough against my hands which, to my amazement, were holding him. He led me away to a far corner of a field and undid my jacket, then my shirt. What followed was unimaginable bliss. I no more thought of protesting than I would have of refusing to take my vehicle out when ordered. We spent a long time together in that field, but it never happened between us again; he was posted away soon afterwards and I did not hear from him at all. But I remembered.

I did not become pregnant, but now I understood the other girls better and was kinder to them.

The war ended and my husband came home. We returned to Wimbledon. I hoped that things would be different between us, more as they had been with the soldier, but nothing was altered: if anything, matters were worse than before, for now I knew the difference. One night I wept, and in the end, when he berated me, told him the reason.

He beat me with his army belt, then used me again, violently and viciously.

'I will never forgive you,' he said. 'Behaving loosely, while I was behind the wire suffering for my country and half starved.'

'I know, I know,' I wept. 'I'm sorry.'

His thoughtfulness for me increased after that. Every day he telephoned me at half-past ten, using the office phone. He had not returned to the bank, but was now, after all those years of study, a solicitor's clerk. If I went out shopping, I had to hurry home to receive his call. He rang at odd times during the day, too, and if by chance I was out I had to account for where I was when he came home. Every evening he wanted to know exactly how my day had been spent.

I worked harder than before to ensure that the house was perfectly kept and the meals as good as ever, to afford no further cause for complaint.

I was always tired. The nights were dreadful and I slept little, but each afternoon I dozed off with a comforting box of chocolates beside me. My husband did not know about the chocolates, and I told him I had spent the time reading. He selected books he considered appropriate for me, improving volumes of biography or history, never fiction, bringing them home from the library, but I read few of them for I could not concentrate on their sober contents. I bought magazines, secretly, and paperback romances, which I read with my feet up on the sofa. I had no close friends. I seldom went out to coffee mornings for my husband's morning call made it difficult unless the hostess lived close by. Soon I gave up trying and my few acquaintances dropped away.

Our dinner parties resumed, with my husband's business connections as guests, and again he brought me flowers on the evenings of those days.

'What a good husband,' the guests would purr.

When we were invited back, he no longer took me with him but would telephone to say I had a migraine, and must be excused. He would lock up all my shoes in a cupboard then, leaving me only my slippers.

'I'm not letting you go out to behave like a trollop,' he would say.

He would return very late on such nights, elated, and his elation might last for several days. I would lie motionless in bed, feigning sleep, expectant and afraid, but I would be unmolested. It frightens me now to think of the possible reason for his exalted mood. I shall never know if I am right.

Food was my solace, and soon I grew fat, eating cream cakes at four-thirty with my cup of tea.

Why did I stay?

At times I thought of leaving him, but where could I go and what could I do? I had no money of my own, and no training apart from my ability to cook and to drive most sorts of vehicle. I could not divorce my husband, obliging him to pay me alimony, for it was not he, but I who had committed a matrimonial offence, as he pointed out to me when once I went so far as to pack a small bag and rush to the front door in the middle of the night. He would hunt me down, he said, wherever I went, disgrace me publicly but never let me go. I believed him.

'You are my wife,' he told me sternly. 'You are mine.'

Gradually the desire to escape withered away; I grew resigned, like one in gaol, to my endless sentence. Sometimes I would think of that long-ago interlude with the young soldier, whose face had faded by now from my memory; I would murmur his name under my breath, and try to remember the tenderness he had shown me.

Then my husband retired, and the few hours' respite I had had each day were gone. He took up growing orchids, making a success of them, in a large greenhouse which he built in our garden. Each July a neighbour tended it while we went on our annual holiday, always to a different cliff-top hotel at some seaside resort. In the mornings we would walk over the headland, often along hilly, difficult paths, and in the afternoons my husband would swim in the hotel pool while I, in my white sundress, would sit watching him pant splashingly up and down, and rise to hold his towel for him when he emerged.

My husband is old now, but he is still vigorous. I do not enjoy our holidays as I trail after him on our long walks, or pour his tea in hotel lounges. Sometimes I play clock golf with him, or croquet, though I do not care for games.

Last year there was a tragic accident at the place where we were staying. A young girl fell to her death from the cliff top near the hotel. A path led there from the hotel garden, and the girl, a guest in the hotel, had walked that way with her husband after dinner. Her husband – they were on their honeymoon – had returned to the hotel to fetch a coat for her as the night was getting chilly. He left her, he said later, sitting on a rock watching a ship, brilliantly lit, passing on the horizon. They intended to stroll further before going to bed, perhaps down to the shore to seek for shells in the light of the moon. Steps cut from the cliff descended near to where he left his slender, pale wife in her white dress. When he returned, she had vanished. He thought she might have gone down to the beach, and searched there for her, but could find no trace of her.

The girl was dead, dying before the stars went from her eyes.

Were there stars in my eyes after that brief war-time interlude? No one remarked on them at the time.

My husband had kindled nothing in me. His touch was death.

Last year, as that young couple went out into the moonlit night together, my husband set forth on the walk he took after dinner each evening. He no longer insisted that I accompany him, tittupping over the grass in the high heels he decrees I must wear. I stayed in the hotel lounge, glancing at a magazine. He was not gone long, but said it was time for bed when he returned. His walk had done him good; he was alert, elated, as on his return from dinner-party visits without me; and as on those nights, he did not trouble me. We missed the commotion when the distraught young husband returned to the hotel and the search for his missing wife began.

When I washed my husband's shirt the next day, I found a long dark hair clinging to it. I looked at his jacket and saw another there. I brushed the jacket well, not comprehending at the time.

It was only much later that I remembered other accidents at places we had visited. Four years ago a young girl who lived in the neighbouring town – not a guest in the cliff-top hotel – was killed in a fall, and there was another similar case the next year at the place where we stayed. The verdict on those two deaths was misadventure, for too little of the bodies was left, after some weeks' immersion in the sea, to prove anything else. Crabs, I have read, devour human flesh in the ocean. I have never cared for the strong flavour of crab.

I know what he did to each girl before she fell. Perhaps he prevented her screaming by strangling her first. It must always have been so quick.

It is going to happen again.

He has noticed this slender young girl in white with the fine dark hair. I have seen him watching her. It is myself as I was when young, and in his mind he kills me each time he does it, after the violation.

Last year he miscalculated, for the tide did not come up in time to prevent the girl's body being found. The moonlight helped too, and the searchers saw her white dress caught on a rock.

Her young husband was suspected of her murder, but on some detail of evidence not made clear in the papers it was later decided that he was not her attacker. That was when I remembered the hairs on my husband's clothes. We had long since returned to Wimbledon.

That girl last year was the daughter of my lost young soldier lover of a single night. He came to the hotel the next day, a sad man, well into middle age now, a widower, we learned. He was bewildered by what had happened. I would not have recognised him after all those years if I had not heard his name.

I saw him sitting sadly in the garden, and went up to him to express my sorrow over the accident. The girl and her husband had looked so happy, I told him, and he seemed pleased, but, understandably, his manner was abstracted. I asked him if he had been in Lincolnshire during the war, and he looked surprised but said he had. A friend of mine was stationed there, in the ATS, I said, and named myself.

He did not remember.

I will follow my husband tonight when he goes for his evening stroll. I will follow him every night until my chance comes. This year I have a bright, sharp knife in my bag. I brought it with me from my kitchen at home, for my plan was made long ago. I will plunge it into him. But now I must do it before he can attack his next victim, seizing my opportunity to save not only her life but also her young body from his abuse. Somehow I must find enough strength in my poor weak legs to creep up behind him undiscovered, and in my hand for the deed.

Perhaps I will do it tonight.

What happens to me when I have killed my husband does not matter, for I am dead already.

FAIR
AND
SQUARE

Mrs Ford stepped aboard the SS *Sphinx*, treading carefully along the ridged gangplank, her stick before her. It would be unfortunate if she were to stumble and injure herself before her holiday had properly begun.

Her holiday.

Mrs Ford had developed the custom of avoiding some bleak winter weeks by going abroad. While ostensibly seeking the sun, she sought to give her family some relief from having to be concerned for her. She tried hard not to be a burden to her middle-aged sons and daughters and their spouses.

She had been cruising before. She had also stayed in large impersonal hotels in the Algarve and Majorca, where it was possible to spend long winter weeks at low cost, enduring a sense of isolation among uncongenial fellow weather refugees. On her cruise, Mrs Ford knew she could expect near insolence from certain stewards because she was a woman travelling alone. With luck, this would be counterbalanced by extra thoughtfulness from others because of her age.

Her cabin steward would be an important person in her life, and she had learned to tip in advance as a guarantee of service and her morning tea on time. There would be patient tolerance from couples who were her children's contemporaries; they would wait while she negotiated stairways and would help her in and out of buses on sightseeing excursions ashore. Older passengers in pairs would be too near her in age and too fragile themselves to spare her time or energy, and the wives would see her as an alarming portent of their own future.

There would be plenty of older spinster ladies in cheerful groups or intimately paired. Eleanor Ford would not want to join any such coterie.

87

The best times would be if the sun shone while the ship was at sea. Then, in a sheltered corner, she would read or do her tapestry while others played bridge or bingo or went to keep-fit classes. She would have her hair done once a week or so, which would help to pass the time. She hoped she had brought enough minor medications to last the voyage. The ship's shop would certainly sell travel souvenirs and duty-free scents and watches but might be short on tissues, indigestion remedies, and such.

Each night Mrs Ford would wash her underthings and stockings and hang them near the air-conditioning to dry by morning. For bigger garments she would be obliged to use the laundry service. She would go on most of the shore excursions, though they tired her and she had been to all the ports before, because to stay on board would mean she had abandoned all initiative. She would send postcards to her smaller grandchildren and write letters to her sons and daughters.

She would long for home and her warm flat with all her possessions round her and her dull routine – yet this morning she had been pleased, leaving it in driving sleet, at the prospect of escaping to the sun. Most people would envy her, she told herself, wondering which of her fellow-passengers, who had looked so drab waiting at the airport, would, by the whim of the head steward, be her table companions throughout the cruise. She had requested the second sitting and been assured by the shipping office that this wish would be granted – otherwise what did you do in the evening after an early meal? As it was, Mrs Ford would be able to go to bed almost at once when dinner was over with a book from the ship's library, which was likely to be one of the best features of the vessel.

Her cabin was amidships, the steadiest place in bad weather, and not below the dance-floor, where she might hear the band, nor the swimming-pool, where the water might splosh to and fro noisily if the ship rolled. She had been able to control these points when booking. What she could do nothing about was her neighbours. They might be rowdy, reeling in at all hours from the discothèque, or waking early and chattering audibly about their operations or their love lives – Mrs Ford had overheard some amazing stories on other voyages.

As she unpacked, she thought briefly about Roger, her husband, who had died six years ago. He had been gentle and kind, and she had been lucky in her long life with him. He had left her well provided for, so that even now, with inflation what it was, she could live in modest comfort and put aside enough funds for such an annual trip. She had so nearly not married Roger, for it was Michael whom she had really loved, so long ago. Setting Roger's photograph on her dressing-table, she tried to picture Michael, but it was difficult. She seldom thought of him after all this time.

That night, climbing into her high narrow bunk, she had a little weep. It was like the first night away at school, she thought, when you didn't yet know the other pupils or your way around. It would all be better in a day or two.

In the morning she had breakfast in her cabin. The ship had sailed at midnight, and beyond the window the sun shone on a gently rolling sea. Mrs Ford had taken a sleeping pill the night before, and so she felt rather heavy-headed, but her spirits lifted. She would find a place on deck in the sun.

On the way, she stopped at the library and selected several thrillers and a life of Lord Wavell, which should be interesting. She found a vacant chair on a wide part of the promenade deck and settled down, wrapped in her warm coat. After a while, in the sunlight, she slept.

The voice woke her.

'You're not playing properly,' it charged. 'Those aren't the right rules.'

Mrs Ford's heart thumped and she sat upright in her chair, carried back by the sound to when she was twelve years old. She was playing hopscotch with Mary Hopkins, and Phyllis Burton had come to loom over them threateningly – large, confident, and two years older, disturbing their game.

'This is how *we* play,' came the present-day response, in a male voice, from the deck-quoit player now being challenged on the wide deck near Mrs Ford's chair.

'They're not the right rules,' the voice that was so like Phyllis's insisted. 'Look, this is how you should throw.'

Long years ago Mrs Ford's tennis racket had been seized from her grasp and a scorching service delivered by Phyllis Burton. 'You played a foot-fault,' she had accused – and later, umpiring a junior match, she had given several foot-faults against Eleanor Luton, as Mrs Ford was then, in a manner that seemed unjust at the time and did so still. All through Mrs Ford's schooldays, Phyllis Burton's large presence had loomed and intervened, interfered and patronised, mocked and derided.

She was good at everything, but though she was older she was in the same form as Mrs Ford. She wasn't a dunce, however – it was Eleanor who was a swot, younger than everyone else in her form. In the library she was unmolested; her head in a book, she could escape the pressures of community life she found hard to endure. Eleanor was no joiner, and neither was she a leader – it was Phyllis who became, in time, head girl.

There came the sound of a quoit, thudding.

Mrs Ford opened her eyes and saw large buttocks before her, shrouded in navy linen, as their owner stooped to throw.

'We enjoy how we play,' said a female voice, but uncertainly.

'Things should always be done the right way,' said the owner of the navy-blue buttocks, straightening up.

In memory, young Eleanor in her new VAD uniform stooped over a hospital bed to pull at a wrinkled sheet and make her patient feel easier. Phyllis, with two years' experience, told her to strip the bed and make it up over again, although this meant moving the wounded man and causing him pain.

'But the patient—'

'He'll be much more comfortable in the end, it's for his own good,' Phyllis had said. And stood there while it was done, not helping, although two could make a bed much more easily than one.

Phyllis had contrived that Eleanor was kept busy with bedpans and scrubbing floors after that, until more junior nurses arrived and she had to be permitted to undertake other tasks.

Michael had been a patient in the hospital. He'd had a flesh wound in the thigh and was young and shocked by what he had seen and suffered in the trenches. He and Eleanor had gone for walks together as he grew stronger. When he cast away his crutches, he took her arm for support – and still held it when he could walk alone. They strolled in the nearby woods, and had tea in the local town. Phyllis saw them once and told Eleanor so, and soon after that Eleanor was switched to night duty so that she scarcely saw Michael again before he went back to the front. She didn't receive a single letter from him, and after months of waiting, although she never saw his name on the casualty lists, she decided he had been killed.

Later she met Roger, who was large and kind and protected her from the harshest aspects of life for so many years, leaving her all the more ill-prepared to battle alone, as now she must.

'Games are no fun unless you play fair and square,' said the sturdy woman with Phyllis's voice.

Mrs Ford looked away from her and saw a thin girl in white pants and a red sweater and a young man in an Aran pullover and clean new jeans – the deck-quoit players. The older woman was leaving, walking away, but the damage was done.

'Come on, Iris, your turn,' said the man.

'No, I don't want to play any more,' the girl said.

That had happened long ago, too. Eleanor had not wanted to play games after Phyllis Burton's derisive interventions.

There was some murmuring between the two. The man put his arm round Iris's shoulders but she flung it off and, head down, mooched away along the deck, disappearing eventually round the corner. The man watched her go, then moved to the rail and leaned over it, gazing at the water.

Mrs Ford was trembling. The woman was so like Phyllis, whom she hadn't heard of since 'their' war, so long ago. Strange that someone else should waken her memory. Phyllis, if she were still alive, must be well over eighty now – eighty-four, in fact – and this woman was what? Getting on for sixty? It was hard to tell these days.

Mrs Ford found it difficult to settle down after that, and spent a restless day.

Proper table allocations, not prepared the night before when seating had been informal as passengers arrived, had now been made, and Mrs Ford was pleasantly surprised to find that she was at the doctor's table, with two couples past retirement age and a younger pair. The doctor was also young, reminding Mrs Ford of her eldest grandson, who was thirty-five. She didn't know that her elder son, that grandson's father, now chairman of a group of companies, had personally visited the shipping office to request special attention for his mother, particularly a congenial place for meals. He and his wife had been on a cruise the year before – their first – and had seen for themselves what Mrs Ford's fate could be. Her children all loved their timid mother and respected her desire to maintain her independence – and, far from relaxing about her when she went away, they worried. On a ship, however, there was constant attention at hand, a doctor immediately available, and swift communication in an emergency.

Mrs Ford felt happy sitting next to the doctor, waiting for her soup. She would eat three courses merely, waiting while others ate their way through the menu like schoolboys on a binge. The doctor told her he was having a year at sea before moving, in a few months' time, into general practice. It was a chance to see the world, he said.

He was a tall blond young man with an easy manner, and he liked old ladies, who were often valiant, building walls of reserve around themselves as a defence against pity. Mrs

Ford, he saw, was one like that. There were others who
thought great age allowed them licence to be rude, and took
it, and the doctor liked them too for he admired their spirit. He
ordered wine for the whole table and Mrs Ford saw the other
three men nod in agreement; they would all take their turn
to buy it and so must she. This had happened to her before
and it was always difficult to insist, as she must if she intended
to accept their hospitality. She liked a glass of wine.

Phyllis Burton, if she were a widow, would have no
difficulty in dealing with such a problem. She would, early on,
establish ascendancy over the whole table.

After all these years, here was Phyllis Burton in her mind,
and just because of the dogmatic woman on the deck this
morning.

Conversation flowed. The doctor asked about Mrs Ford's
family and listened with apparent interest to her account of
her grandchildren's prowess in various activities. It was
acceptable to brag of their accomplishments, but not of one's
children's successes, Mrs Ford had learned. Everyone disclosed where they lived and if they had cruised before – or,
failing that, what other countries they had visited. Both
retired couples had been to the Far East, the younger pair to
Florida. The doctor revealed that he was unmarried, but his
face briefly clouded; then he went on to describe the ship
making black smoke off Mykonos (such a white island) due to
some engine maintenance requirement. He laughed. It had
looked bad from the boats taking the passengers ashore.

Mrs Ford had enjoyed her meal. The passenger list was in her
cabin when she returned after dinner but she didn't look at it.
She read about Lord Wavell, falling asleep over him and
waking later with her spectacles still on. Then, with the light
out and herself neatly tucked under the bedclothes, she
dreamed about Michael. They were walking in the woods
near the hospital, holding hands, and he kissed her sweetly,
as he had so long ago, her first kiss from an adult male, right-
seeming, making it easy when afterwards Roger came along.

She woke in the morning a little disturbed by the dream, but rested.

The next night the Captain held his welcoming party, and at it Mrs Ford, hovering on the animated fringe of guests, saw the doctor talking to a pretty girl in a flame-coloured dress. She saw them together again in Athens, setting off to climb the Acropolis.

Mrs Ford decided not to attempt the ascent – she had been up there with Roger on a night of the full moon and preferred to hold that memory rather than one of a heated scramble that would exhaust her. She waited in a tourist pavilion by the bus park, drinking coffee, till the groups from the ship returned. This time the doctor was alone. With her far-sighted eyes, Mrs Ford peered about for the girl but did not see her.

Then she heard the voice again.

'What a clumsy girl you are. I don't know why you can't look where you're going,' it said, in Phyllis's tones. 'Look at your trousers – they're ruined. Scrambling about like a child up there!'

'I'm sorry, Mummy.' Mrs Ford heard the tight high-pitched reply of someone in a state of tension. 'I slipped. It will wash out.'

Mrs Ford, on her way to coach number four, glanced round. The tourists wouldn't pause for coffee – meals were paid for on the tour and they were returning to the ship for lunch before taking other excursions before the *Sphinx* sailed that night. Behind her she saw a tall, well-built woman with carefully coiffed iron-grey hair, in a tweed skirt, sensible shoes, and an expensive pigskin jacket. Beside her was the girl Mrs Ford had witnessed talking to the doctor, her blonde hair caught back in a slide at the nape of her neck. On her pale trousers there was a long, dirty smear.

It was to the mother, however, that Mrs Ford's eyes were drawn. Just so might Phyllis Burton have looked in middle age.

That evening Mrs Ford consulted the passenger list with a pencil, reading it with care to winnow out the mothers and daughters travelling together. The father might be present too, unobserved so far by Mrs Ford. She marked several family groups with a question mark. There were no Burtons. Of course not. But the resemblance was so uncanny, she would have to find out who the woman was.

In the end it was easy.

The next day the sun shone brightly and the sea was calm. Mrs Ford decided to climb higher in the ship than she had been hitherto, and explore the sports deck in search of a quiet corner where she could sit in the sun. Stick hooked over her arm, a hand on the rail, she slowly ascended the companion-way and walked along the deck to a spot where it widened out and some chairs were placed. In one sat the blonde girl. Beside her was an empty chair.

'Is this anyone's place?' Mrs Ford enquired, and the girl, who had been gazing out to sea, turned with a slight start. A smile of great sweetness spread over her face and, confused, Mrs Ford was again in a wood, long ago, with Michael.

'No – oh, please, let me help you,' the girl said, and, springing up, she put a hand under Mrs Ford's elbow to help her into the low chair. 'They're difficult, aren't they? These chairs, I mean. Such a long way down.'

'Yes,' agreed Mrs Ford, gasping slightly. 'But getting up is harder.'

'I know. We found it with my grandfather,' the girl said. 'But now he's got his own chair for the garden – it's higher, and he can manage.'

'Your grandfather?' Mrs Ford wanted the girl to talk while she caught her breath.

'He's lived with us since my grandmother died – before I was born,' said the girl. 'He's still quite spry, but a bit forgetful. He's a lamb.'

'And are you like him?' She was, Mrs Ford knew.

The girl laughed.

'Forgetful, you mean?' she said. 'Maybe I am – Mummy always says I'm so clumsy and careless. But then, she's so terribly well organised herself. Granny was the same, Grandpa says. She always knew what to do and made instant decisions.'

Roger had always known what to do and made quick, if not instant, decisions, Mrs Ford reflected. 'I dither a bit myself,' she declared. 'I miss my husband a great deal. He cared for me so.'

'That must have been wonderful,' said the girl, seeming quite unembarrassed by this confidence.

They sat there in the sunshine, gently chatting. The girl's mother was having her hair done, she said. They were cruising together – her mother had had severe bronchitis during the winter and it had seemed a good idea to seek the sun. Her father couldn't get away and so she had come instead. What girl would refuse a chance like this? Her mother had a great desire to see the Pyramids and that would be the high point of the trip for them.

'But you've travelled before?' Mrs Ford asked. Her elder grandchildren, this child's generation, were always whizzing about the globe.

Mummy hadn't liked her going off just with friends, the girl said, but she *had* been to France to learn the language. There had been family holidays in Corsica, which she loved. They rented a villa. She had two brothers, both older than herself.

'What are their names?' asked Mrs Ford, still feeling her way. She didn't know the girl's yet.

'Michael's the eldest – he's called after my grandfather,' said the girl. 'The other one's William, after Daddy.'

Mrs Ford's gently beating old heart began to thump unevenly. Should she say she had known a Michael, long ago? But the girl was going on, needing no prompting.

'Aren't names funny?' she said. 'I'm glad I wasn't called after Mummy – her name's Phyllis, after her mother. It would be confusing to have two Phyllis Carters, wouldn't it?'

'I suppose it would,' Mrs Ford agreed, and now bells seemed to be ringing in her head, for her Michael's surname had been Carter.

'I'm called after someone else Grandfather knew,' said the girl. 'It's quite romantic, really. There was this nurse he met in the war – the First War, you remember.'

'Yes, my dear, I do,' said Mrs Ford.

'She was very young and shy and kept being ticked off by this older, bossier nurse, Grandfather said. When he went back to France he wrote her lots of letters, but she never answered. Wasn't that sad? I'm named after her. Her name was Eleanor.'

'Oh,' said Mrs Ford faintly, and her head spun. Letters?

'She must have married someone else or something,' said the girl. 'Or even died. All the letters were sent back to Grandfather. Mummy found them when she helped him clear up after Granny died, in her desk, locked up. She burned them without telling Grandfather. It would only have upset him.'

'Yes, I suppose it would,' said Mrs Ford. There was just one fact that must be confirmed. 'Your grandmother?' she asked.

'Grandfather married another nurse,' said the girl. 'Mummy's exactly like her, he says.'

Mrs Ford took it in. All those years ago Phyllis Burton had intercepted letters meant for her. Why? Because she wanted Michael for herself, or because she sought, as always, to despoil?

'And have you uncles and aunts?' she asked at last.

'No, there was only Mummy,' the girl replied.

So Phyllis had managed just one child, and had died before this grandchild had been born, while Mrs Ford, with two sons and two daughters, had survived into great age. And Michael had never forgotten, for this girl bore her name.

She could cope with no more today.

'What a nice little chat we've had,' she said. 'We'll be meeting again.' She began to struggle up from her chair and the girl rose again to help her.

In the days that followed they talked more. Seeing them together, the mother would walk past, but if Eleanor was talking to any man among the passengers, or a ship's officer, the mother would break in upon them at once.

In Mrs Ford's mind the generations grew confused and there were moments when she imagined it was this confident, domineering woman who had been so perfidious all those years ago, stealing letters meant for another, not this woman's long-dead mother. At night Mrs Ford shed tears for the young girl who had been herself, waiting for letters that never came and in the end giving up.

But she'd had a long, full, and happy life afterwards. And Michael hadn't persevered – hadn't tried to find her after the war. Perhaps Phyllis had already made sure of him; she'd borne him just one child.

On deck, Mrs Ford heard Eleanor being admonished.

'A ship's doctor won't do,' came the dominant tone. 'I've plans for you, and they don't include this sort of thing at all. It stops the instant you leave the ship, do you hear?'

Eleanor told Mrs Ford about it later.

'He's a widower. His wife died in a car crash when she was pregnant,' she said. 'But it isn't just that. Mummy wants me to marry an earl, if she can find one, or at least some sort of tycoon, like Daddy.'

'It's early days. You don't really know each other,' said Mrs Ford.

'I know, but he's only doing a short spell in the ship, then he's going into general practice. We could get better acquainted then, couldn't we?'

'Yes,' agreed Mrs Ford.

'And as for earls and tycoons—' Eleanor put scorn in her voice.

She'd learned typing and done a Cordon Bleu cooking course, Eleanor said. She'd wanted to be a nurse, but Mummy hadn't approved. The girl seemed docile and subdued – too much so, Mrs Ford thought.

Michael Carter, she remembered, had seemed to have plenty of money, though neither had thought about things like that, when during that long-ago war they took their quiet walks and had tea in a café. Phyllis Burton might have destroyed the innocent budding romance simply because that was her way, but she wouldn't have married Michael unless he had been what was called, in those days, 'a catch'. She'd have made sure of the same for her daughter – and the daughter was repeating the pattern now.

'You're of age,' Mrs Ford said. 'Make your own decisions.'

Later the mother spoke to her. It was eerie, hearing that voice from the past urging her, since she had become friendly with Eleanor, to warn her against the doctor.

'But why?' Mrs Ford asked. 'He seems such a nice young man.'

'Think of her future,' the girl's mother said. 'She can do better than that.'

'He'd look after her,' Mrs Ford said, and she knew that he would. The girl was timid and lacking in confidence; the doctor, experienced and quite a lot older, would make her feel safe, as she had felt with Roger. 'It depends on what you think is important,' she said, rather bravely for her, and Eleanor's mother soon left, quite annoyed.

Mrs Ford smiled to herself and stitched on at her *gros point*. She'd help the young pair if she could. Nowadays, as she knew from her own family, people tried things out before making a proper commitment, and though such a system had, in her view, disadvantages, there were also points in its favour.

Mrs Ford did not go to Cairo. The drive was a long one from Alexandria, and she'd been before – stayed with Roger at Mena House, in fact, years ago. She spent the day quietly in Alexandria. The doctor, she knew, had gone on the trip in case a passenger fell ill, as might easily happen. That evening he said that someone had fainted, but nothing more serious had occurred.

The next day was spent at sea, giving people a chance to recover from the most tiring expedition of the voyage. Among those sleeping on chairs on deck, Mrs Ford saw Eleanor's mother. Her mouth was a little agape and her spectacles were still on her nose. In her hand she held an open book. Perhaps she was not as robust as she seemed, Mrs Ford mused – her

own mother, after all, the Phyllis of Mrs Ford's youth, had not
survived late middle age.

On the upper deck, Eleanor and the doctor were playing
deck tennis. Mrs Ford, seeing them, smiled to herself as she
walked away. Youth was resilient.

Several days later the *Sphinx* anchored off Nauplia. The
weather was fine, though a haze hung over the distant
mountains and there was snow on the highest peak, rare for
this area. Mrs Ford stood in line to disembark by the ship's
launches with the other passengers going ashore. Stalwart
ship's officers would easily help her aboard and she liked
feeling a firm grasp on her arm as she stepped over the
gunwale into the boat.

A row of coaches waited on the quay. Mrs Ford allowed
herself to be directed into one. She would enjoy today, for
while Mycenae, their first stop, was a dramatic, brooding
place, holding an atmosphere redolent of tragedy, Epidaurus,
in its perfect setting, was a total contrast. They drove past
groves of orange trees laden with fruit. The almond trees were
in bloom and the grass, which later in the year would be
bleached by the heat of the sun, was a brilliant green.

The haze had lifted when the coach stopped at Epidaurus.
Mrs Ford debated whether to go straight to the stadium,
which so few tours allowed time to visit and where it would
be peaceful and cool; in the end, walking among the pines and
inhaling their scent, she decided to visit it again.

She walked past the group from her coach as, like docile
children, they clustered around their guide and, sauntering
on, using her stick, she turned up the track to the left of the
theatre where the ascent was easier than up the steep steps.

At the top she turned to the right and entered the vast semi-
circle of stone. She moved inwards a little and sat down,
gazing about her, sighing with pleasure. Below stood her
group; she had plenty of time to rest and enjoy her sur-
roundings.

The sun was quite strong now and she sat thinking of very

little except her present contentment. A guide below began
the acoustic demonstration, scrabbling his feet in the dust,
jingling keys, lighting a match. Mrs Ford had seen it all before.
Then her eye caught a flash of bright blue lower down –
young Eleanor's sweater. She was almost at the bottom of the
auditorium and with her was a tall young man easily
discerned by Mrs Ford's far-sighted eyes to be the ship's
doctor. They were absorbed as much with each other as with
the scenery, Mrs Ford thought as she watched them together.

Then a voice behind her called loudly.

'Eleanor!' she heard. 'Eleanor! Come here at once!'

Mrs Ford reacted instinctively to the sound of her name and
she turned. Her pulse was beating fast and she felt her nerves
tighten with fear. Since her youth no one had talked to her in
such a tone.

Down the steep steps of the aisle between the seats, Phyllis's
daughter, whose name was also Phyllis, came boldly towards
her, striding with purpose, Phyllis the malevolent, Phyllis the
destroyer. Mrs Ford's grip on her stick, which was resting
across her knees, tightened as the lumbering figure in its
sensible skirt and expensive jacket approached. Her pace did
not slacken as she drew near. Mrs Ford knew with a part of
her mind that it was not she but her young namesake below
who was the target of the imperious summons.

She acted spontaneously. She slid her walking stick out
across the aisle, handle foremost, as Phyllis drew level, and by
chance, not deliberate design, the hooked end caught round
the woman's leg. Mrs Ford tightened her grasp with both
hands and hung on, but the stick was pulled from her grip as
the hurrying woman stumbled and fell.

She didn't fall far – she was too bulky and the stairway too
narrow – but she came to rest some little way below Mrs Ford
and lay quite still. No one noticed at first, for there were
shouts and cries filling the air from tourists testing the
amplification of the theatre and attention was focused below.

Mrs Ford's pulse had begun to steady by the time people
began to gather around the body. Her stick lay at the side of

the aisle. She retrieved it quite easily. She returned to her coach by the same way she had come, away from all the commotion, and was driven back to Nauplia where the ship waited at anchor.

There was talk in the coach.

'Some woman tripped and fell.'

'It's dangerous. You'd think there'd be a rope.'

'People should look where they're going.'

'She must have been wearing unsuitable shoes.'

The doctor was not at the table for dinner that night, and over the loudspeaker the Captain announced that though sailing had been delayed this would not interfere with the rest of the timetable – the next port would be reached as planned.

Mrs Ford's table companions related various versions of what had happened ashore to cause the delay. The woman, Eleanor's mother, had stumbled in the theatre at Epidaurus and in falling had hit her head against a projecting stone, dying at once. Someone else thought she'd had a stroke or a heart attack and that this had caused her to fall, for she was a big woman and florid of face. The Greeks had taken over, since the accident had happened ashore, and the formalities were therefore their concern.

'Terrible for the daughter,' someone remarked. 'Such a shock.'

'The father's flying out,' someone else said.

Mrs Ford ate her sole meunière. She had only wanted to stop Phyllis from interfering. Hadn't she?

Her son, meeting her at the airport some days later, found his mother looking well and rested. He knew about the accident – it had been reported in the newspapers.

'What a terrible thing to happen,' he said. 'It must have been most distressing. Poor woman.'

'Well, she saw the Pyramids,' Mrs Ford replied.

What a heartless response, thought her son in surprise, and looked at his gentle mother, astonished.

THE
FIG
TREE

The fig trees were bare when, fugitives from the winter, we arrived two weeks ago, but now the first leaves are showing glossy green against the silvery branches. In the woods, the spring air is fragrant from the pines, and the ground is dotted with flowers – cistus, wild lupin, lavender – tall, purple spikes unlike our native blue – even asphodels, and here and there the brilliant blue of tiny gentians.

I know the names of most of them, for Bernard brings back samples from his walks, enthusing over them, putting them in pots on window-sills. I prefer cultivated flowers, myself, planted in orderly fashion, not rampant, wild, undisciplined. Here, everything grows too large, too fast, for the sun is warm. Against the blue sky, in the clear light, the cliffs are sharply etched in burnt sienna in the highest parts, silvergrey elsewhere, above the pale, deserted beach.

The season has not yet begun, and there are few people about, so that those one sees are noticed and remembered. I recognised Teresa the moment I saw her come out of a villa at the edge of the tourist complex along the road. She got into a shabby rented Mini, and drove off.

This area is not what it was. We came here first some years ago, lent the same villa, Casa Bianca, by our friends who own it. Then, there were only a few other private villas in the quiet road, but now this tourist estate has been built and is to be extended: there are builders working, concrete mixers churning, bulldozers to be heard.

It is more than twenty years since I last saw Teresa – nearer thirty. She has put on weight. Long ago, we worked together in the typing-pool, but I rose through the layers of the organisation, becoming a permanent member of the staff in the publicity department, while Teresa soldiered on among ledgers and invoices.

Bernard was in the accounts department then. He became acquainted with Teresa, and joined us when, on fine days, we ate our sandwiches in the park. At that time, he was a tall, good-looking young man, with thick sandy hair and a broad frame. He's balding now, and I keep him on a strict diet because of his blood pressure.

He played tennis well, and so did Teresa. I, because I had no natural ability for the game and have always hated to perform badly, did not play. After a set or two in the evenings at the club, Teresa would be red-faced and perspiring when I sauntered along, cool in a linen dress, in time for a drink.

I had no trouble taking Bernard away from Teresa, though events played into my hands. He had drifted towards her, I knew, through circumstances rather than inclination, for he was always weak, but I saw his potential. He was quick and astute, with flair; all he needed was impetus, which, in time, I supplied.

When a post in the publicity department fell vacant, I casually suggested he might be the man for it; my judgement was already of value to the firm, as it is still, and he was appointed.

In those days he wanted to give up commerce and become a botanist, but I ask you, what future is there in flowers? Their use is for adornment. Teresa encouraged this folly, suggesting he might, at least, pursue horticulture.

After our marriage I permitted him to indulge his interest as a hobby; it was a healthy one, involving scrambling about into inaccessible spots after rare blooms, although I think golf might have done as well and led to useful contacts.

Our home near Dorking has a lovely garden. I see that the gardener plants, in rotation, wallflowers, tulips, salvias, dahlias; and at intervals the rosebeds are renewed with the latest varieties. Bernard has his corner where the gardener does not go; he cultivates wild sweet peas, untidy briars, sprawling shrubs, and some flower seeds higgledy-piggledy, anywhere. Near the house, however, all is tidy; the hedges are well-trimmed, the lawns closely pared.

In his own interests, I had to save Bernard from Teresa, all those years ago. He had begun taking her to the cinema, to dances, and their names were linked, but when he moved to my department it became easy to distract him during our lunch breaks by talking shop, which Teresa, still buried in her invoices, did not always understand and which I would never let Bernard explain.

In the end, fate intervened. Bernard was to take Teresa to the works dance, and I had invited a contemporary of my father's to be my partner, a bachelor who was almost my uncle, and who was always willing to oblige me. I certainly wouldn't go without an escort, but I planned to detach Bernard from Teresa during the evening, and effect an exchange.

However, on the day of the dance, Teresa slipped and fell as she got off the bus going home from work. She banged her head and broke her arm. It was a nasty tumble. I went with her, of course, to the hospital, where, as she was concussed, she had to remain for observation.

I promised to tell Bernard that she wouldn't be able to come to the dance, and to explain. Instead, I telephoned her parents, who came the next day and took her home to convalesce. It turned out that Bernard did not know where her digs were; they always met at the cinema or some other place for their evenings out. He didn't know her home address, either, and I pretended ignorance too.

By then, I'd replaced her at the dance, putting off my father's friend by saying I had a headache and wouldn't be going. Bernard had expected to meet her at the hall where the dance was held; instead, he found me, apparently 'stood-up', as he seemed to be himself.

She wrote to him. The letter came to the office, for their acquaintance was so slight and new that she had no other address for him. I had anticipated this, and was watching out for her round, childish handwriting. She'd printed PERSONAL in the corner of the envelope.

I read the letter, of course, before tearing it to pieces and flushing it away for ever in the ladies' lavatory. It told him her address and extended an invitation from her parents – her father was a farmer – to spend a weekend with them in the country. She'd be off work some time, she said.

In the end, she never came back. She had decided that city life was not for her and had found a job with the local vet – imagine! She sent me a note to this effect, but as far as Bernard was concerned, she had broken their date and disappeared without an explanation.

Bernard and I were married the following spring. Without me, he'd have got nowhere, but now he's the chairman of the company, a semi-retired post because of his poor health, but carrying a substantial salary and with many 'perks', as they're called. We've travelled all over the world, sometimes on business – sometimes not.

Unlike Bernard, I've worn well. I'm still a size 12; my hair – tinted of course, to a rich, glossy chestnut – is thick and lustrous, and my skin is clear. Bernard, unfortunately, has had a number of illnesses through the years – an ulcer, a minor heart attack, and now he is very deaf as the result of an infection he caught in Brazil. He has an efficient, inconspicuous aid, but is careless about using it and one may speak to him for several minutes before discovering that he has not heard a word.

When we returned from Bermuda in January, Bernard developed bronchitis. The hard winter at home was prolonged, so when he recovered we accepted the offer of Casa Bianca for March. Bernard was anxious to see the spring flowers; they were over when we came here before.

Our routine is established. I see to the house in the morning, and supervise the maid – an unskilled but willing woman from the village. She speaks a little English. To get him out of the way and to occupy him, I send Bernard off to do the shopping.

We have lunch in the villa but go out to dinner in the

evening, otherwise it's no holiday for me. He buys bread and lettuces, tomatoes, whatever we need to drink, at the *supermercado* up the road. It serves the holiday complex and stocks most ordinary groceries. Bernard takes the car, as it's bad for him to carry weights.

After he's brought the shopping home, and I've checked that he's forgotten nothing, he goes for his walk, looking for flowers among the pines and the mimosa on the headland. He has a siesta after lunch – it's surprising how hot it can get at midday, when the breeze drops.

I have a rest, too – apart from Bernard of course: the villa is large and cool and we each have our own spacious room. There's a pool, where Bernard swims in the afternoons. I can't swim, myself.

Teresa hadn't entered my thoughts for years. Perhaps the reason I knew her at once was because she looked flushed and hot as she got into the car, just as she used to after playing tennis. I saw her full-face as I walked towards her on my way back after buying some postcards. There was a girl with her, and a small child – a boy, I thought, though it's not always easy to tell these days, with their unisex clothes. They all drove off in the car.

I was curious enough to walk past their villa later, and saw the girl on the patch of lawn outside playing with the child. A young man was there, too, but I didn't see Teresa again, and tried to convince myself that I'd made a mistake and it wasn't her, after all.

But two days later Bernard drove straight past the Casa Bianca when he came back from the shops. I always listen for him – I want to get on with unpacking the shopping he's bought and making the day's arrangements – and I saw the car go by. I went out to the patio and looked up the road.

Bernard had stopped outside the villa where I'd seen that woman. He got out of the car and came round to open the passenger door. Teresa – or her double – got out; Bernard leaned into the back of the car for her packages and carried them for her into the villa. Their heads were turned to each other.

I knew fear, but I stilled it: it was all a long, long time ago. What could be said, now, that could threaten me, or my comfortable life which I'd worked so hard to secure?

He did not return for half an hour, and then he was in an over-excited state. I told him to calm himself, on account of his blood pressure.

'Who do you think I met in the shop?' he exclaimed, and before I could attempt a guess, he told me. 'I knew her immediately,' he said. 'I suppose she must have changed – everyone does, after all – but to me she looks just the same – a little plumper perhaps, but it suits her.' He smiled.

I ran my hands over my lean hips in their elegant white linen trousers. Teresa would look ridiculous in trousers; at least she seemed to have enough sense not to wear them.

'She's staying just down the road in that complex,' he babbled on. 'With her daughter and son-in-law, and their little boy – Simon, he's called – and a baby. The young family have all gone off for the day in the car and she's on her own there.

'She's got four children, imagine,' he continued, obsessed with the subject. 'But only these two grandchildren so far. Perhaps that's why she still looks so young. She's not dried up, barren, as we are.'

Dried up? Me? And I chose not to have children.

Before I could argue, he went on, 'I've asked them all round to drinks this evening, when the young ones get back and before the children have to go to bed.'

'You've invited the children?'

'Why ever not? They've no one to leave them with, anyway,' said Bernard.

'Her husband?' I grated. 'Teresa's?'

'He's dead.' At this, Bernard looked sad. 'She went to work for a vet, it seems, and married him. He was quite a bit older than Teresa, and he died a year ago. She seems to have had a happy life.'

'You found all that out in half an hour?' I asked.

He stared at me for a moment, then said, 'How did you know how long I was there?'

'You're always back by ten-thirty,' I said. 'It's after eleven, now.' A quick recovery.

'All those years ago, when she never turned up for that dance, she'd broken her arm,' he said. 'You went with her to the hospital and promised to tell me what happened, but you said nothing.'

'I didn't know what had happened to her,' I lied. 'I wasn't there.'

'She said you were on the same bus. You always went back together.'

'I got off at an earlier stop,' I said. 'She was concussed – she must have been hallucinating.'

'How do you know she was concussed?' he pounced. 'You told me you knew nothing at the time.'

'Some time later the girls in the office heard she'd had an accident and gone home to her parents,' I invented.

'You never told me,' said Bernard.

'Why should I?' I asked. 'It wasn't important.'

'She wrote,' he went on. 'She wrote me a letter. I never received it.'

'Oh well – posts are unreliable.'

'Perhaps,' he replied, and took off his hearing-aid.

They came, in the evening: the young man and the girl, the small boy, the baby, wheeled in a pram and mercifully asleep, and Teresa in an unfortunate pink dress.

The boy kept running about with his arms outstretched pretending to be an aeroplane – they'd flown out, of course, from Gatwick – and then he started to push a toy car up and down the patio, making engine sounds till I wanted to scream.

Luckily, with such weather, we had drinks outside; though it isn't my house, I couldn't have endured the child racing around the rooms.

Bernard offered them all the use of our pool. They had said that the one among the villas was often crowded.

'Come any time,' he said, without reference to me. 'But take care – it's deep. It's not safe for Simon unless someone goes in with him.'

They had accepted instantly.

'I love swimming,' said Teresa.

What a sight she must look, in her costume, flesh obscenely bulging.

She didn't talk much, sitting on the patio with a gin and tonic beside her, but she looked at me now and then with an odd expression. If I hadn't known it was impossible, I'd have thought her glance expressed pity, but if there was any pity about, it had to be mine, for her.

This morning Bernard was back promptly from the shop, alone, and soon he set off for his walk along the cliff. I had a hair appointment. I have to have it attended to regularly, particularly here, where the sun can affect my rinse. When I returned, Bernard was still out. Sometimes he forgets the time, and I go to meet him. I don't like lunch to be late.

I went to meet him today.

They were sitting together on the flower-studded sandy ground under a pine tree, holding hands. Bernard and Teresa, for all the world to see: a fat, red-faced woman in a blue skirt and cream-coloured shirt, and a thin old man with a sun-tanned, balding head.

An old man: yes, he looked it.

To reach them, I must walk over a narrow path at the side of a quarried hollow in the hillside. I'd been there before, and refused to go along this track which, at one side, fell away sheer to the beach, and on the other bordered a deep pit, scored with ravines, an occasional shrub clinging to patches of loose soil here and there. Bernard had wanted to show me some rare flowers that grew on the further side.

He'd been showing those flowers to Teresa, I supposed. Couldn't they see me? They weren't very far away.

I called out sharply.

'Bernard! It's lunch-time.'

They did not stir, and she did not release his hand.

I called again.

'Come over,' Teresa said then. 'Come and look at this fig tree. We think we can see its leaves coming out as we watch.'

At the rim of the ravine, near them, I could see a fig tree, boughs outspread, but what nonsense to think they could watch it unfold. I could not let Teresa know, however, that I was afraid of the narrow path with the drop on each side, and I could not let her go on sitting there, holding my husband's hand.

There was a longer way round, through the pines, and perhaps they had taken that path themselves, but it would take some minutes to find it and I knew the matter, now, was urgent.

I started along the narrow path. I was still wearing the high-heeled sandals I'd had on to go to the hairdresser's, and my foot slipped. I fell down into the ravine, bumping and bruising my thin body as I tumbled, clutching at the soft, sandy sides as I tried to halt my fall, but my hands could find no hold.

I must have lost consciousness, for it's almost dark now. Haven't they gone for help? I've called and called, but at this time of year few people come this way; that was its charm, for Bernard. My voice doesn't sound very loud, even to myself, and my arm's all twisted behind me. I can't move. I can never climb out alone.

Above, outlined against the darkening sky, a fig tree stands at the edge of this pit. I seem to remember seeing two people standing beside it, peering at me, and I see one of them, Bernard, removing his hearing-aid.

He'll have to tell someone I'm missing, won't he? Someone will come and save me. Won't they?

A
WOMAN
OF
TASTE

There was trout on the menu. Mrs Finch's mouth watered and she licked her lips, around which the creases of age had filled with runs of vermilion lipstick. She'd begin with the soup, and follow the trout with veal, which was done in a rich wine sauce. She enquired of the steward what else was in the sauce: it was important, at the start of the cruise, to establish herself as a woman of taste.

After forty years of married life, she knew that Harold would choose the soup and the trout, but he might prefer beef to follow the fish. There were several types of vegetables to accompany the main dish, with French fries and creamed potatoes. Mrs Finch would have chocolate gâteau to follow, then biscuits and cheese and fruit – a peach, perhaps – at the end. She waited calmly, her mind composed, her taste buds agreeably anticipating the treats in store, while Harold pored over his half-moon spectacles at the menu, one plump, pigmented hand tapping the table.

The Finches were at the First Officer's table, which conferred on them a certain status; but in any case, by their demeanour, they would have established themselves as persons of consequence. There were several tables for two in the dining-room, but Harold never asked for one of these when they cruised; he needed an audience for his *savoir faire*. Mrs Finch was always relieved by his wish for company, for thus she was spared from having to make conversation with him and could concentrate on her meal without distraction. They were experienced cruisers now, and Mrs Finch had her new outfits ready: well-tailored slacks to enclose her heavy thighs; pretty silk shirts and waistcoat tops; uncrushable dresses for the afternoons; and her evening attire – four different long ensembles and two short ones. Harold had his white dinner jacket and several frilled shirts, to be worn with a variety of ties. They had brought a lot of luggage.

Some years ago, Harold Finch had retired from the Civil Service, where he held a good position. He had his index-linked pension, the income from shares he had prudently bought, and the rents of two houses he owned. Mr Finch had always had an acute business sense, sharpened by his experience at the Ministry. He sold the house in Orpington where the Finches' family had grown up, and had bought a flat in Eastbourne. This was easy to close when they went away.

Before Harold retired, and after the children left home, Mrs Finch had enjoyed some pleasant years. She went to coffee mornings and even held some of her own in aid of causes approved by Harold, and she met her friends at cafés in town. She had attended a course of flower-arranging lectures in the afternoons, and another on dressmaking, but that had been a failure since Harold always went with her to buy her clothes and would not pay for things he had not selected. She couldn't scrimp enough from the housekeeping to buy fabrics or enjoy even a minor splurge, for Harold always inspected her housekeeping accounts and demanded an exact explanation for any expense, with bills for proof of outlay.

'Harold's very good,' she often told her friends, when she met them wearing, for instance, her new sheepskin coat – she hadn't wanted one, it was so heavy to wear, but he'd insisted. 'He likes me to have nice things.' But he'd never allowed her to learn to drive, though he could have afforded a second car with ease.

Now, in Eastbourne, there were no friends; they'd all been left behind in Orpington and the only companion Mrs Finch had was Harold. He went shopping with her these days, and would insist on brands of goods other than those she had found satisfactory for years. He complained in the butcher's about meat he declared was tough, though Mrs Finch had found it perfectly tender.

'It must have been in the cooking,' she anxiously declared

on one occasion, to be smartly rebuked by her husband.

'Nonsense, Amy. You've been cooking pork for forty years. You certainly know how to do it now,' he informed everyone in the shop.

Mrs Finch's fat, sagging cheeks had flamed as she paid for her liver and shoulder of lamb.

There were no coffee mornings now, and no friendly classes in this hobby or that. Mrs Finch had suggested that Harold might like to follow some such pursuit of his own, but in a hurt voice he had said that he had looked forward to spending time with her, now that he was at leisure, and had expected her to share this sentiment.

'Oh, of course, dear, I do,' Mrs Finch had hastily said. 'I just thought you might find it dull.'

He was under her feet, as it were, all day. When she wanted to vacuum their lounge, with its new, pale carpeting patterned in darker brown, he was reading the paper there, and making notes to do with his investments. When she went to prepare the lunch in the kitchen, he would come to watch how she scraped the potatoes and rubbed fat into flour to make pastry, and though he defended her cooking in front of the queue at the butcher's, he criticised it at home. His sudden appearance behind her when she was standing at the sink, or perched on a stool at the table, for her legs often ached and she rested them when she could, would always startle her, lost in some dream as she constantly was. He came to the library, too, and would not let her take out books of a type she enjoyed – romances set in days gone by, for instance – but would suggest biographies instead, about long-dead politicians or generals.

She could no longer watch television in the afternoon; Harold thought the programmes showing then entirely frivolous, unless she could assert that they contained genuine expert advice on improving one's own home management. They walked on the front every day, even in terrible weather, well wrapped up in their sheepskin coats and each with a fur hat on their heads.

But they went away a lot. Mrs Finch, in her mind, lived from holiday to holiday, as soon as the one was ended beginning to long for the next, like a child unhappy at school counting the days to the end of term, or a prisoner awaiting the end of his sentence. On their cruises, they'd 'done' the Canaries, Madeira, and most of the Mediterranean. At other times of the year, they'd packaged themselves and flown to Hong Kong, Bangkok and Delhi. Sometimes Harold talked about going to China, but was uncertain about the food: too much rice made one flatulent, he embarrassingly said to their travel agent, the new one in Eastbourne who was getting to know them so well. Bundled in coaches, they'd seen a great deal of the world, led in pedestrian files by foreign guides around Jerusalem, Valetta, Athens and Rome.

At the Captain's welcoming party on this first night of the cruise, Mrs Finch would wear her new cornflower-blue chiffon; blue had always brought out the colour of her eyes. Garbed in this expensive dress, the Captain of the SS *Sphinx* would recognise that she was not just one of your run-of-the-mill passengers but a person of some status, Harold had said as they chose it. She'd enter the ladies' deck-quoits contest, and play bingo. Harold would calculate how far the ship sailed each day and take part in the tote – a small expense, and justified, for he worked it all out in so studied a manner, keeping records from previous trips and using a calculator, that he often won. Mrs Finch would go to paper-flower-making classes and millinery lessons, and even keep-fit sessions, for these were part of cruise life and so Harold approved of her joining in. He played deck quoits himself and would take part in quizzes, for he prided himself on his well-stocked mind.

One thing Mr Finch missed very much, while away, was the *Financial Times*.

They wouldn't join in the dancing, after dinner. They never did that, though when they were young, and courting, Harold had often taken her to dinner dances. He'd stopped, once they were engaged. She sighed. In those days she'd been so romantic. In no time at all, it had seemed, after they were married, the children had arrived. The boys were civil servants like their father, well on up their ladders now that they were middle-aged; the girl had been a teacher and was now a headmaster's wife. At Christmas, the parent Finches stayed in rotation in one or other's household, dispensing appropriate presents to their grandchildren whom they saw rarely and scarcely knew as individuals, though Mrs Finch kept a tally of their birthdays and hoarded photographs. Harold didn't care for children and had wanted to see as little as possible of his own when they were young.

Their cruising routine evolved – morning tea in the cabin while they studied the ship's bulletins about the day's events at sea or ashore; then breakfast, with fruit juice, cereal, bacon and egg for both, followed by toast and marmalade. On the first morning Harold sent away the dark chunky marmalade at their table, demanding Golden Shred, and complained about the tea, which he said was too weak. He made the steward brew more.

'It doesn't do to let them get away with it,' he told the rest of the table, the younger couple and the woman with the glasses. 'You're paying, after all.'

The other husband, whose name was Paul, nodded. The woman with glasses demanded the chunky marmalade back again. Mrs Finch had the oddest feeling that in fact she didn't really mind what sort she ate but was doing it just to be awkward.

At boat drill, on the first day, Harold demonstrated his expertise at their muster station by helping first-time cruisers don their life-jackets and showing them where their whistles were kept. Mrs Finch looked away while this went on. She knew Harold liked to touch the women, even the plain ones.

He never touched her now, but she didn't really mind; in fact it was quite a relief. It had all been rather a disappointment after the expectations she had had in her ardent, eager youth – just a series of shoving grunts and groans followed by instant, heavy sleep while she lay wakeful.

Thick cream, whipped to a perfect texture, melted around Mrs Finch's teeth – few of them now, alas, her own – while she thought of the past and then dwelt, in her mind, more hopefully on the next weeks which would be spent afloat. She'd hardly be left alone with Harold at all. And in June they were going to Rhodes.

Amy Finch's legs, though short, had once been slender. Her ankles were still neat, and she had small feet. In Naples her husband bought her a pair of shoes, expensive ones, choosing the style and making her try on countless pairs, testing the salesgirl's patience as well as her linguistic powers. The Finches, despite their travels, spoke only their native tongue. The shoes Harold had selected pinched Amy's toes, but she hoped they'd be more comfortable after a while. Harold insisted that she put them on that evening for dinner, and under the table she slid them off, losing the left one when it was time to leave the dining-room after the long meal; theirs was the last table to finish, by the time Harold had sampled almost every course and persuaded Paul, the other husband, to do the same.

'You're paying for it,' he declared, and Paul's pointed nose nodded in agreement.

The Finches and the younger couple, Paul and Eileen, joined up for coffee each evening, afterwards taking part in or observing, according to what was arranged and Harold's opinion of it, the entertainment provided. Paul and Eileen had allowed themselves to be taken over by Harold without a struggle, to Mrs Finch's immense relief. Harold needed an audience besides herself and each holiday began anxiously for her until one was secured, usually some inexperienced couple glad of the protection offered by Harold's expertise. Now, Paul and Eileen stood little chance of making other friends, for Harold required total subservience from his satellites. On coach excursions the two couples sat in neighbouring seats and walked together round the sites. At sea, they occupied adjacent chairs on deck.

Paul and Eileen were camera-happy, and at Pompeii they snapped one another in front of crumbling walls. In Athens, Paul posed Eileen, in her green trouser suit, in front of the Parthenon, but by the time they got to Crete Harold was directing the shots, himself behind the lens aiming at the other three, and sometimes requiring a simple exposure of merely himself beside a plumbago in bloom. He used a lot of film and Paul had to buy more from the ship's shop. Harold had already asked to be sent prints of the best results. Amy knew he would not pay for them.

While the Finches and their new friends were taking photographs, the lone young woman, Julia Fane, who sat at their table, would be perched on some boulder, sketching. Wherever they stopped she made swift drawings, and Paul, looking over her shoulder once, saw strong straight lines, some squiggles, and notes about colours written at the side.

To the other four, Julia was an enigma. When the ship was at sea she would be tucked in some corner out of the wind absorbedly sketching. If anyone came to sit near her, she would rise and move without a word. She resisted attempts by Paul and Eileen, before the Finches took them over, to include her in their forays ashore and refused invitations to join them for coffee. She didn't want to seem rude, she said, to the first suggestion, but she preferred to be on her own; to the second she remarked that she never drank coffee after meals.

She was seldom seen in the evenings. Paul and Eileen were puzzled and wondered where she could be. Harold thought her not worth bothering about. She must be up to no good, travelling alone at her age, he told Amy. Amy couldn't understand what he meant.

One evening at dinner the talk turned to baggage and the problems of coping with it at stations and airports.

'You should never have more than you can carry yourself,' Harold declared, fixing Julia with an icy stare from his pale blue eyes. She'd stand helpless at the carousel, for sure. He knew her type, waiting for some man to help her.

'I can carry my own case,' Julia replied in even tones.

'Amy certainly can't,' Harold said, and seemed to be boasting.

Paul and Eileen were listening in some bewilderment to this dialogue; there were undercurrents they could not interpret, as if Harold were on the defensive.

'Then how do you manage?' Julia asked. 'You must have a lot of luggage, with so many beautiful clothes, Mrs Finch.' She turned to Harold. 'Do you always secure a porter?'

'Porters cost money,' Harold answered. 'Amy fetches a trolley.'

Julia merely smiled in response to this. There was something about her smile Amy didn't quite like.

In Heraklion, the Finches, with Paul and Eileen, were walking back to the ship for lunch when they met Julia. She was sauntering along, her sketchbook under her arm, in no hurry at all.

'Hullo,' Eileen said. She was by nature a kindly soul and had said to Paul that she thought Julia, who couldn't be much more than thirty, must be shy.

'Hullo,' Julia answered, pausing.

'Been drawing again, have you?' Amy asked, taking her cue from Eileen but earning a frown from her husband.

'Yes,' Julia said.

'We're hurrying back for lunch,' said Amy. 'It's roast beef today. I must say, I'm quite hungry after looking at all those coffins.' They had been in the museum.

'I'm not going back for lunch,' said Julia. 'There's a taverna along here which does delicious fish dishes.' She hesitated, then added, 'Why don't we all go?'

Amy Finch looked suddenly wistful and touched Harold's sleeve.

'Could we?' she asked. It would make a change.

'I've paid for my lunch on board,' Harold stated.

Julia smiled.

'You'll miss the flavour of Greece,' she said.

'I don't trust that messed-up food,' Harold said. 'It upsets the stomach.'

'The salads are lovely,' Julia said, still looking at Amy.

But Amy knew there was Black Forest gâteau for pudding aboard the ship. Besides, Harold had spoken. The four walked on to the quay.

Amy was dozing, on deck, sated with food, when Julia wandered back. Amy opened heavy eyes and saw the long legs in their pale slacks go past. Julia Fane was still smiling.

Amy had indigestion that evening, but she took some bismuth before dinner and was able to enjoy soup, followed by turbot in creamy sauce, and pork chops. She'd slip back to the cabin afterwards for another dose before joining the others for the ship's company's cabaret, which was the evening's entertainment.

Julia ordered the wine that night. Taking his cue from Harold, Paul had paid for the table's wine in rotation with him and the First Officer, and Julia had accepted a glass or two each night. Paul and Eileen, away from the Finches, had wondered if she would try to take her turn but had agreed, without consulting Harold, that they would try to prevent her if she did. Paul was quite old-fashioned in some ways. When it came to the point, though, and Paul began to protest as Julia gave the order, a frown from Harold and a small motion of his hand silenced the younger man. Amy saw the little incident and felt a hot, acid taste rise in her throat. She sipped water to send it away.

Harold drank more than usual that night. The wine steward topped up his glass again and again. On the night when he'd bought it, two bottles of the pleasant light hock had been sufficient, and the same when Paul and the First Officer took their turns. Amy saw the wine steward look enquiringly at Julia when the second bottle was empty; Julia nodded and a third bottle arrived. Amy felt quite ashamed when she saw Julia paying at the end of the meal but she soon forgot about it when the cabaret began. There were songs from the Chief Engineer, who had a fine baritone voice and whose repertoire included *Old Father Thames* and other airs

Amy knew well and the Purser did conjuring tricks. There was dancing, too, and the First Officer and Julia took the floor together several times. They seemed to get on well, though Julia did not sit next to him at meals; the two married ladies did that, with Amy, the senior, on his right. Harold frowned as he watched the pair; it confirmed his suspicions about the young woman. He did not dance, and he did not permit Amy to dance with either the First Officer or Paul, both of whom had asked for the pleasure. Amy, however, quite enjoyed the evening.

The next day was spent at sea. In a corner of the boat deck, protected from the wind, Julia Fane sat painting, working up a sketch made ashore. While she waited for one area to dry, she glanced up and saw Mrs Finch slowly walking up and down the deck ahead. She'd been knocked out of the deck-quoits contest, Julia knew; the fact had been revealed at breakfast.

'Painting?' Mrs Finch said, drawing near, and Julia nodded. 'May I see?'

Julia showed her the half-done work: roofs and white buildings that weren't white but all shades of cream and grey; tamarisk trees and shadows; subtle.

'Oh,' Mrs Finch said. 'You are a real painter, then?'

'I work in graphics,' Julia said.

'Oh,' Mrs Finch said again, smiled vaguely, and wandered on. 'She's clever,' she told Harold later.

Harold knew that. She was also efficient and seemed to manage her life very well on her own. He'd met such women at work, plenty of them, and kept them away from Amy; a woman should be dependent, unquestioningly obedient to the man who was not just her partner but also her master. He didn't hold with this liberated women's self-sufficiency nonsense.

At lunch he and Amy and Paul went through the menu: fruit juice, soup, fish and the lamb, with steamed syrup pudding and biscuits and cheese. Eileen skipped the soup and the pudding. Julia Fane had tomato juice and beef salad; then, carrying an orange from the fruit dish, she left the table. Two days ago she'd asked the steward to serve her promptly so that she need not sit waiting while the others consumed course after course. She made no apology at all and was, this afternoon, on deck with her sketchbook and pencil, her paints put away, when the others appeared. Harold and Paul sat together while Harold told Paul about deals he had made on the stock market. Paul, a long-distance lorry driver, responded with stories of rackets he had seen operated successfully. Presently, both of them slept. The two women talked. As Amy knew, Eileen worked in the hardware department of a large department store; she hoped they'd have children one day, she said, but first they were seeing the world. Amy talked about her grandchildren, but she was sleepy too. Soon the women's eyes closed.

Julia Fane, sketching, saw the quartet at some distance from her, all deeply unconscious.

A small breeze sprang up later, and after a while Amy Finch and Eileen awoke. Their husbands were still asleep, Harold softly snoring, which embarrassed Amy, but Eileen just laughed.

'Like babies, aren't they?' she said, looking fondly at Paul. He'd put on weight, she could see, eyeing the small dome of his stomach. No wonder, the way he'd been eating, and so had she; she patted her own plump form and sighed. Still, it was part of the holiday.

Julia Fane had gone, but on her chair was her sketchbook, sticking out of a woven Greek bag such as they'd seen in the shops in Heraklion, though this one wasn't new.

'Wonder what she's drawing now,' Eileen said idly. 'Paul saw one she'd done of that temple at Delphi. Not up to much, he said.'

'She paints,' Amy said. 'She makes sketches ashore and then paints them later.'

'She hasn't been painting this afternoon,' said Eileen. 'I'm going to have a look.' She got up, glanced around, saw no sign of Julia returning and walked over to where her bag lay on the chair.

'Oh, Eileen, you shouldn't,' Amy protested.

But the younger woman, in mischievous mood, had withdrawn the pad from the woven bag and was turning the pages. She giggled, then looked perplexed.

'It's ever so funny,' she said. 'Why, that's Paul. And there's you, Amy, and Harold. Yet it's not.' She frowned.

Sketches of her and of Harold? Amy felt really quite flattered.

'Show me,' she said, too deeply set down in her low deck-chair and too stout to rise with any speed.

Eileen looked worried now.

'No,' she said, turning the pages. 'Better not – she might come back.'

But Amy was curious.

'She won't mind,' she said. 'She let me look at a painting, once.'

'No,' Eileen said again.

Amy, however, was levering herself out of her chair. She crossed to where Eileen stood, still turning the pages of the sketchbook, and took it from her. Amy peered at a page through her bi-focal spectacles.

It depicted a stout woman in an elegant dress, the figure boldly blocked in with heavy pencil lines. The face above the rotund figure was clearly her own, Amy's, yet somehow the nose had become a snout and the hands, in the air, were trotters. Beneath the smart skirt two further trotters in tight shoes were revealed, porcine flesh bulging out above. On another page were Amy and Harold together; their arms, ending in trotters, were linked, and whilst both had pig-like faces, Harold's eyes were much smaller and closer together than Amy's. Above their heads were balloons, and in Harold's balloon were pound signs and dollars. In the balloon over Amy's head was a pretty girl with curly hair on the arm of a tall man in Prince Charming rig; the girl looked exactly as Amy had looked in her youth, and the pig version of Amy, below, wore a yearning, nostalgic expression. A further sketch showed them as two pigs eating at table, knives and

forks held in trotter-like hands. Above Harold's head a
balloon showed a cheque book and a pile of foodstuffs – chops
and cheeses, cakes, and a bottle of wine. Above Amy's head
was a tombstone with RIP inscribed upon it, and beside it a
spade whose blade was strangely composed of human teeth.
There were sketches of other passengers in the book: a man
with a bushy moustache drawn as a walrus; and the First
Officer, with his plump, beaky face like a genial penguin. The
walrus's wife was portrayed as a sprightly young heifer. There
was a fox, too, just like another man Mrs Finch had observed
on board, small and red-haired, sharp-featured. His wife
seemed to be a sheep in tight trousers. Eileen was there, as
well, disguised as a spaniel with anxious large eyes, and Paul,
with his sloping forehead and earnest expression, was a boxer
dog. There were more: horses, cats, giraffes, geese, ducks and
chickens, all bearing strong resemblances to passengers or
crew. Even the Captain was not spared; he was a turkey-
cock.

Amy snapped the book shut.

'Put it back,' she said. 'They mustn't see,' and she glanced
at Harold and Paul.

The two women went back to their seats. Amy felt sick and
dizzy. She wasn't quite sure if she'd understood all the points
in the sketches.

'She's laughing at us,' she said.

'They're clever,' said Eileen. 'And I don't think she is. Not
really.' Some of the animals had worn friendly expressions.

Julia had been to fetch a coat. When she returned, all four
of her table companions seemed to be still asleep.

That night, on the menu, whitebait featured, and curry;
there were chocolate éclairs and strawberry flan – a difficult
choice. Mrs Finch, in the end, had both.

What else was there for her to do?

MOUNTAIN
FEVER

Mrs Harper always went along to the travel agency to arrange their holidays. At first, Mr Harper had gone too, sitting meekly beside her as she insisted on twin beds and a balcony with a sea view, but as his opinions were never consulted, nor his preferences indulged, it was a waste of time. These days, he merely wrote the cheque – though even that Nora could nowadays do, from the profits of her hairdressing salon. In winter, the Harpers went to the West Indies – though once they had been to the Seychelles and Nora was talking of Australia next year – and in summer to Spain or Greece.

Mr Harper yearned for the mountains, but Nora insisted on sun. She liked oiling her lean, leathery body, cooking it thoroughly, toasting first one side, then the other under the grilling rays while Mr Harper perspired under a beach umbrella with the latest Dick Francis in paperback. The heat made him lethargic; soon he would doze, dreaming of well-done steak.

Things had not always been like this. When they married, Nora's skin was white and soft and she had a long slender neck which was revealed below her upswept bouffant hair. He'd nuzzled her neck under the lacquered, brightly rinsed coiffure as he'd walked her home after a dance. That was nearly forty years ago, in what seemed like another life, when he was doing his National Service in the RAF. Nora worked in a shop. She had long fingernails, carefully enamelled red. He thought of them now as talons. She was a predator.

It wasn't so bad at first. They were parted soon after their marriage when Bob was posted abroad, and Nora was left to enjoy her new bridal status. It didn't stop her from going to dances or the cinema with other men friends. She'd got what at the time so many girls wanted – a ring on her finger – and she'd had a lovely wedding, wearing a satin dress with a huge stiffened skirt and a train, made by her mother. Bob had smiled proudly in his uniform; his fresh face looked scrubbed as a schoolboy's in the photograph which was now banished to a box in the attic.

There had been no children. Both of them were disappointed, but Nora's feelings changed when she saw her friends tired and disgruntled, exhausted by crying babies and piles of washing. There were no claims on her. Bob had become a garage mechanic after his demobilisation; he'd been a fitter in the Air Force. Now he filled up the spare time that might have been occupied with a family by buying a clapped-out old Morris Eight for five pounds, renovating it and selling it for sixty. Next, he picked up an old Chrysler; his profit on that was higher. His boss let him work after hours behind the garage where he was employed, for there was no space in the tiny garden of Nora's parents' house, where at first they lived. After a while they found a flat, and as things grew easier Bob opened a garage of his own. Soon, because of his growing reputation, he had so much work that he had to take on an apprentice. Since then he had trained over twenty lads, watched them mature, marry, have families. Even though some moved away from him, they never lost touch and many were still working in one of his chain of garages.

Nora would not even do the books. She liked nothing about the car trade. She didn't like Bob's dirty oily overalls; she didn't like his dirty oily smell. She'd always liked things nice, she said, arranging bought flowers on the dresser.

Soon Bob was providing everything she wanted: pretty clothes, gadgets for the house. He worked all hours and prospered. His customers trusted him, judging by results, and recommended him to their friends. He saw very little of Nora. For some time she had had a job in a café, sitting in a little booth taking the money. When the café changed hands and the new owners expected her to become a waitress, Nora left.

By now she had lost her youthful plumpness and had

developed a confident manner which only became shrill at
home; she got a job as a receptionist at a hairdresser's, and
soon began having lunch at the Crown Hotel on half-closing
day with Mr André, the owner. People did not gossip, because
they thought Mr André was gay (though the word was not
used in that context in those days) but he was not: after
lunching, he and Nora would drive out of the town on those
long afternoons to his flat in Hove. When he died, rather
suddenly, of a heart attack, he left Nora the business which
was now thriving, concentrating on its middle-class, middle-
aged clientèle with their regular appointments. Nora grew
even cleaner, more fragrant, tougher: her own hair, now, was
cropped close to her skull and rinsed to a metallic dark copper
colour.

Bob had changed, too. He sold his original garage and
workshop to a development company which was acquiring
property in the area to build a shopping complex, with offices
on the upper floors. Bob opened new premises on the edge of
town where, as well as servicing them, he began dealing in
new and used cars. He employed a smart young man to
manage the showroom and spent most of his own time in the
workshop. He became a member of the town's Chamber of
Commerce but was still happiest in his overalls, tinkering
with engines. Machinery never talked back at you; if it
rebelled or was intransigent it could usually be gentled and
coaxed into an improved performance; at worst, worn parts
could be replaced.

It never occurred to him to replace Nora. She was his
responsibility. If there had been kiddies, he would think –
well, things might have been different. Her shop was her
baby. Now they lived in a large house with half an acre of
garden which kept Bob out of Nora's way at weekends. He
had a workshop at White Lodge, an elderly Bentley, and an
old Invicta which he was rebuilding, so he had plenty of
excuses for avoiding entering the house except at meal-times.
He did not want to lie on a foreign beach when he had plenty
to do at home, but it was his duty to escort Nora for these few

weeks each year. He'd given up, now, asking to go to the mountains. He simply dreamed of them instead, reading books about them and watching any climbing programmes that came on television. He had his own study, which he used in the winter when it was too dark to work outside. When he was stationed in Germany, he had spent some weekend leaves in the mountains and had been fascinated by the majesty of the mighty towering peaks. Craftily, he'd tried to tempt Nora by describing how they could drive out, stay in comfortable hotels on the way, like some of her clients who toured France or Italy, but she would not be won round. She craved the sun, she declared; did he begrudge her so little a thing, when she worked so hard for the rest of the year?

He knew that she liked to return deeply tanned; it was some sort of symbol, a suntan, Bob thought, unable to fathom its appeal.

Nora had a new head coiffeur now in the business, known as Andreas – following in the footsteps of the original André – and allegedly Cypriot, though in fact he was a Cockney whose real name was Ted. He followed André's pattern in other ways, too, and on half-closing day, after the cleaning woman had gone home, returned with Nora to White Lodge. Ted went willingly. He did not bother too much about something that could be treated as routine and would one day pay dividends of one sort or another. His wife in Tonbridge never knew.

Bob had tried to interest Nora in the Himalayas. The prestige of such a trip might appeal to her.

'What – and get dysentery – or worse?' A client of Nora's had returned from some eastern trip with hepatitis and been really ill. 'Certainly not.' Nora liked reasonable assurances of pure water and clean food; she had had a stomach upset in Marrakesh and that area was now off the map.

Nora needed Bob. Without him, she could not live in the large house at the edge of the Downs; without him, there would be no tame chauffeur. She could not drive – she had never wanted to learn when he had been eager to teach her

– and he dealt with all the maintenance of the house. Alone, she could live well, but must fend for herself in every sphere and, inevitably, lose the status that mattered so much to her now. The house was large enough for them to avoid each other most of the time.

This year, Crete was to be the Harpers' destination. They had been there before and met some very nice people. Nora had spent hours on the beach, and Bob had hired a car and visited some of the archaeological sites. Crete, at least, contained a mountain; so did Cyprus. Nora was always tired by the time they went away. She would never admit it, but being able to let go – not have to be bright and alert in the salon, remember the potted biographies of long-term clients and ask the right interested questions – was an immense relief. And her ageing body needed a rest from Ted, who was only thirty-three. Sometimes she found it hard to match his energy, yet she longed for it and could not do without him. Bob had never been much use in that respect; no wonder they had no children, she often thought, and once, even, had taunted him with it; he'd gone quite white and begun to tremble in a way she had never seen. That barb had gone home.

When the travel agent telephoned to say that their tickets were ready, Bob sent the apprentice, Joe, to fetch them. Joe loved driving and snatched any chance of an errand; he was always willing to pick up parts, deliver new cars, drive customers home while their cars were serviced. While Joe was out, Bob opened the drawer of his office desk and drew out a folder. It was a travel wallet from a different agent. He looked inside, checked the tickets and hotel vouchers, then replaced it, smiling.

The Harpers were leaving for Crete on a Thursday. Joe usually took them to Gatwick and collected them on their return, in the Bentley. This time, when he arrived at White Lodge on his motor-cycle, early in the morning, Bob told him that one of their most valued clients had just telephoned about a breakdown. He always left home soon after seven to reach his office by eight, and today his Rover refused to start.

'Go over there, Joe, and find the trouble. Get him to work first,' said Bob. 'I've ordered a taxi.'

Joe skittered off on his motor-cycle; he'd go over to the client's in a car from the workshop which the client could use. He met a taxi approaching White Lodge as he went down the road.

On Saturday evening Bob arrived at Bergen airport. He collected his suitcase and went by bus to the terminal in the town. Contrary to his expectations, no line of taxis waited for airline passengers leaving the bus, but the telephone number of a taxi firm was prominently displayed above a row of public telephones. A rather bossy-looking middle-aged woman, who had been on the same flight, reached the pay-phone before Bob and said, hearing where he was going, that they might as well share a taxi since their destinations were not far apart.

Bob submitted. He sat in the taxi peering eagerly out of the window, an ageing man with sparse grey hair and a florid face. The woman was leaving the next day on the coastal steamer bound for the North Cape, a trip she'd planned for years.

'Oh yes?' said Bob.

She told him about the small steamers that sail daily along the Norwegian coast delivering stores, mail and passengers to the small ports on the way.

'Where are you going?' she asked.

He turned a beaming face towards her.

'To the mountains,' he said.

'Perhaps we'll meet on the way home,' said the woman. 'Then we can compare notes.' She padded off, a sturdy self-reliant figure in trousers and anorak, into her hotel, while Bob continued to his.

In the morning, he collected a hire car and set off to the north.

He had planned his route carefully, and had booked in for a night on the way to his mountain hotel. The twisting roads might make travelling slow; there were ferries to cross; he did not want to hurry.

The journey surpassed his expectations. Often, flying to some beach or other, he had peered from the plane's window at the Alps or the Apennines, fascinated by the tall peaks coated in crystalline snow like icing sugar, bare of humans. Now he drove past peaks still snow-clad, and through beautiful scenery where lakes split the valleys and waterfalls tumbled down the steep granite slopes of the lower mountains.

In the fortnight that followed, every day was perfect. The weather was fine and Bob woke to blue skies and sunshine; indeed, the sun scarcely set, although he was not far enough north for the Midnight Sun. Instead of a balcony breakfast with Nora, he went down each day to the hotel restaurant where a vast table was spread with an amazing array of dishes – fish, cheese, cold meat, eggs – even salmon. Bob tried them all in turn, and learned to say '*Tak*' to the fair-haired waitress who filled up his coffee-cup. There were no other English visitors to this mountain hotel and Bob was glad; he did not have to answer questions about where he lived and why he was there alone. In the evenings the television set was turned on in the lounge and he watched old British and American programmes with Norwegian subtitles, sometimes talking to Norwegian visitors, all of whom spoke at least some English. But most nights he went early to bed, tired after walking up mountain trails with his lunch in a pack on his back. He went out in the car every day to a different range.

On Midsummer's Eve, after dinner, a bonfire was lit in a meadow below the hotel and three fiddlers played cheerful music while the guests danced round. Bob joined in, partnering a cheerful grey-haired Norwegian lady who spoke very little English. His holiday was nearly over.

He needn't go back at all. He could just disappear over here, he thought: face up to nothing. But he'd need some money. He hadn't thought of that. He could have brought enough to tide him over for quite some time. He fell asleep wishing he had arranged for a longer absence, and woke in the early hours suffering from mild indigestion. That was what dancing did for you at his age, he thought.

But in the morning he was quite himself again. He was fitter now, after days spent in the open, and able to tackle steeper paths. He had walked on a glacier – reached by an ordinary trail, no climbing needed – and not met a soul. He had pretended to be a real mountaineer, drawing into his lungs the pure air that held the chill of ice.

On Midsummer's Day he ate his lunch by a stream at the foot of a grassy slope. Kingcups bordered the water; the sun was hot and bees buzzed in the burgeoning heather. He felt rather sleepy after his disturbed night, and dozed off for a while, waking with a start. He glanced at his watch; he'd slept for over an hour.

Bob got clumsily to his feet and began packing up his picnic things, settling them into his bag. For a moment he was tempted to turn back, walk down the mountainside to his car. But he'd planned to go higher, to discover what lay beyond the summit of this ascent; he hoped to see, on the other side, seven giant peaks still white with snow.

The adder struck him as he climbed through the close-matted heather. He saw it rearing up before him, and he felt its bite. He did not collapse at once, walking on for a time, wondering what he should do.

When the English visitor was not in promptly for dinner, the hotel staff were concerned. He had always been punctual. His key was still at the desk, and when dinner was over he had neither returned nor telephoned. He had not said where he was going, despite requests in the hotel literature that visitors should do this.

The duty clerk asked various guests if they knew where he had planned to go. He always went off in the car, but he walked, everyone was aware. He must have heard the golden rule: *If you lose the path, turn back.* It was better to retrace one's steps than to get lost.

At ten o'clock a search began and a helicopter pilot saw the car parked at the side of a mountain road. He flew lower, looking at the slope, and he saw Bob lying amongst the heather.

He had died of a heart attack, the autopsy showed; his heart was not in a good state and it could have happened at any time. The adder, by the time Bob was found, had slithered away, and snakes were rare in that area; the bite, not suspected, remained undetected. A good way to go, people said, hearing about it at home, but where was Nora?

A puzzled cleaning woman told the police that Mr and Mrs Harper had left for Crete, but she hadn't received her usual postcard from Mrs Harper, who always wrote when she was away. What could Mr Harper be doing in Norway?

They found Nora in the inspection pit in Bob's workshop at home, the Bentley parked above her. Perhaps he had planned to dispose of her elsewhere on his return, with a tale to cover her disappearance, but there was not much doubt about what had happened. Her skull had been shattered with a large spanner which also lay in the inspection pit, wrapped in a rag.

Whoever would have thought it of him? It was the wonder of the week in the district. Ted, at the salon, joined aloud in the general amazement, but he knew the truth. He'd always quite liked old Bob and sympathised with his wish for a different holiday.

'I don't know why you and Nora don't go your own ways,' he'd said, over a beer with Bob after he brought Nora home one closing day. Bob thought they'd been doing the books. Ted spoke in his normal Cockney voice; the Greek accent was kept for the salon. Ted, himself, was beginning to wonder how much longer he could keep his affair with Nora going. At first it had been a challenge, and the material benefits were considerable – often cheques on the side. But there was a new girl, now, at the salon, called Loraine, who was not in awe of him, and who was trim and pert; he was drawn to her, and they'd had a couple of dates already. Nora would be furious if she found out, and she hadn't yet made him a partner, a promise she had been dangling for over two years now.

She had told Ted that she had left him the business in her will.

'What about Bob?' Ted had said.

'He's never needed it – or me – not really,' Nora had answered. 'All he ever thinks about are cars and his mountains.'

After his talk with Ted, Bob had brooded. He could go off on his own. He suggested it, but Nora said people would think it most odd.

'Even if I came away with you later?' Bob had argued.

'Even so.'

She'd turned from him then, presenting the nape of her neck, and he'd thought how easy it would be. He'd do it the last evening before they were due to leave for Crete. If he lost his nerve, or an opportunity didn't occur when she wasn't looking – he didn't want her to see the blow coming or to feel pain – nothing would be lost except his travel tickets.

As it was, after pointing out that the lilacs were spreading too widely and needed trimming – she liked everything neat – Nora had, on that last day, bent to examine some mud on her shoe. Bob was holding the spanner; she'd dragged him out from the workshop to complain about the lilacs. It was done in a second.

He hadn't decided what to do afterwards. He'd dump her somewhere, probably. Somehow that didn't matter. Not now. Not now that he had his chance of the mountains.

When everything was settled, Ted duly inherited the salon. He left his dull wife and in time he married Loraine. The motor business went to a distant cousin of Bob's, for he had not made a will and it was obvious Nora had died before him. Tracking down the legitimate heir was quite a task for the lawyers.

Occasionally the bossy woman Bob had met in Bergen wondered how the man with the red face had enjoyed the mountains. Then she forgot about him.

THE
WRATH
OF
ZEUS

The gods indeed were angry, Mr Dunn thought as he sat on the hotel balcony, a towel wrapped ruglike round his bare, skinny shanks, for it was chilly in the storm. He still wore his blue cotton holiday shorts, though the warm weather had been replaced by a day that would have seemed normal in an English September. Beyond the oleanders and orange trees that edged the hotel garden and bordered the swimming pool, the Ionian Sea raged grey, dotted with whitecaps, and the beach, once fringed with golden sand, was now drab-brown, riven where torrents of rainwater had poured down from the hills and into the sea. The water, once so clear, was muddied with stirred-up sand.

Poseidon, Mr Dunn decided as he observed the scene through his binoculars, was demonstrating his power to goad the sea into a wild warning to mere humans.

Earlier, before the storm, the air had been still, heavy with humidity, the sky full of dense purple clouds massing over the mountains across the bay. Then the sky had been rent by bright bars of vivid forked lightning, followed instantly by deafening thunder. Zeus, in his majesty, was displaying his authority beneath which mortal man must quail.

Henry and Mavis Dunn were spending a fortnight on this Greek island, which could be reached only by ferry from a larger one with an airport – though the term 'airport' seemed a grandiloquent description for the minimal hutted buildings serving the runway. Each summer the Dunns went abroad, always to somewhere new, and the choice was usually made by Mavis. This year, however, Henry's wishes had prevailed. For years he'd longed to visit this island, steeped in myth and legend. Now it had a large hotel and he had pointed out to his wife that soon it would be fashionable. By visiting it now, they could boast they'd been there before it became part of the regular tourist run. The argument had persuaded Mavis.

Henry woke early each morning and went out on to the balcony of their hotel room to watch the sky grow light under the beneficence of Aurora. As the sky grew brighter, gradually, in all his glory, Apollo would preside over the heavens while the sun shone burningly down. And in the evening the sunsets were magnificent. Even Mavis, drinking duty-free gin on the balcony before dinner, marvelled as the huge, fiery orb dropped rapidly behind the distant mountain, taking only just over two minutes from the time its rim touched the mountaintop. For a few more minutes, streaks of orange and gold would light the sky – then it was dark. There was no dusk in those waters.

When the sun went down, Mavis would go into the bedroom and begin her evening toilet, which even on holiday included much grimacing in the mirror as she examined her wrinkles; the patting of cream into her thin cheeks; then the painting of brows on the pale ridge of skin over her small, button-brown eyes. It took time to select which dress to wear before she was ready to go down to the bar to meet their new holiday friends, Eileen and Bill, with whom they now dined each night, to Henry's relief. It helped with conversation.

Mavis had been a pretty girl when Henry first met her, long ago. She'd worked as a typist for a firm for which he was a traveller – representatives, they were all called these days. His nymph, he had christened her then. Even as a young man, Henry had enjoyed reading about ancient times – a schoolmaster had caught his imagination with tales of Mycenae and that had begun it all. 'Your silly old books,' Mavis would say, referring to the rows of volumes he had acquired from secondhand booksellers over the years.

The first time he took her out they went to a concert, but during the interval he discovered that the music bored her so they left. Their next date, and those that followed, had been at the cinema; he'd held her hand in the conspiring darkness, and she'd giggled and squirmed.

They married quickly when war was declared, for Henry was in the Territorial Army and was called up at once. Their brief honeymoon was a disappointment to both, but for the next six years they met rarely. Things would improve after the war, Henry told himself, clasping her resisting body on the station platform before he left for service abroad.

When he returned after four years, Mavis was no longer the plump, curly-haired girl whose photograph he had carried through the western desert and up the leg of Italy and whose rare, stiff letters he knew by heart. But she'd had a tough time, he reminded himself then. Food had been scarce at home; there had been bombs and doodlebugs – though, to be truthful, few had fallen near Mavis, who had found a job in a government department whose offices were moved, for safety, to Wales. It had been dull for her there, though, Henry allowed, and he was grateful that she'd stayed faithful, for so many of his comrades had returned to find that their wives had failed them.

The first years after the war were not easy. Henry had to make up for lost time. He wanted to succeed in the world, and he knew that he must be able to give Mavis the good things of life to preserve their marriage – possessions were important to her.

'I have certain standards, Henry,' she'd said, turning down the first flat he'd found – a dark basement one, but cheap.

It would be better when babies arrived, he'd felt. She'd alter then – be warmer, fulfilled. But no babies came, and he seemed to lack the secret of making her content. Her mouth grew thin and hard. She never laughed. He often thought of her girlish giggle, now gone, and sighed.

In time they had a small house, and later a larger one. Since there were no children, Mavis had kept on her job, transferring from one department to another as time went on, and only recently she had retired from a senior position. Henry had done well himself – he'd had to, to keep up with her. He became a keen gardener, thus keeping out of Mavis's way on summer evenings and weekends, and in winter he read a great deal. His little library steadily grew and his interest in Greek mythology revived.

Now he realised Mavis was not a nymph and never had been. Watching her as she painted her face, her hair tinted dark brown and permed into frizzy corkscrew curls, he thought she was more like Medusa, with her hard expression and with snakes for hair. He was a frightened man, for he himself would retire at Christmas and after that there would be no escape from Mavis. Now she devoted to the house the energy that had been channelled into her work. She'd always been neat and house-proud, but now she was fanatical. How would he manage at home all day, Henry wondered bleakly, and what would he do for company without the daily colleagues he had spent more time with than with Mavis?

Years ago Mavis had turned the small guest bedroom in their house into what she called his den. There he kept his books and his record player and a transistor radio – she didn't want that sort of rubbish cluttering up her living-room, she had said. Henry knew he would be spending much of his time in his den in future. All these years, by avoiding each other during the day, they'd managed to maintain brief conversations over the evening meal and even Sunday lunch, but holidays had been difficult until they learned to diffuse their intimacy by making friends with another couple. (It was Henry who always found the holiday friends. He'd get talking in the bar the first evening to someone he'd already picked out on the plane as looking likely. He was aware they weren't the only pair with a problem.)

He'd take up bowling, he thought. It was a pity he'd never played golf, but perhaps it wasn't too late to learn – then he could spend every day at the club. Still, he preferred the idea of adult education classes. He might learn to paint, or even to speak Greek. But, inevitably there would still be hours at home and when he thought about the future, Henry panicked.

***

Among the holiday visitors on the island, there were some happy couples. Henry looked wistfully at a pair, not young at all, strolling arm-in-arm down the road to the little town past orchards of pomegranates and swathes of lush bougainvillea, bright hibiscus, and trails of brilliant morning glory. Nature approved of passion, he sighed, knowing little about it. There were nymphs to be seen, too: lovely young girls who lay, almost naked, stretched out on the beach, their oiled limbs surrendering to the sun. When he went into the sea for his swim he met others emerging, long hair wet against small, neat skulls, curving bodies full of promise. He would watch them covertly, like a schoolboy, for he knew he had missed something wonderful in the arid years of his marriage.

Zeus had had his way with any maiden he fancied, Henry thought enviously. Age was no handicap to a god. Henry's own chest bore a light tufting of grey hair and his legs were still pale despite several days in the sun. Zeus – older than time – would simply transform himself into some irresistible figure before conquering the maiden of his choice. Henry picked out a maiden – well, a damsel – for himself and dreamed of appearing before her in the guise of a Greek hero, with golden curls and muscled torso, to carry her off to a cave, where he would ravish her to their mutual delight. His choice was a fair girl who toasted herself on a sunbed close to the spot where, early every morning, Henry laid out his own and Mavis's towels under a plaited straw shelter on the beach. Here, between the swims which punctuated his day, he could watch the girl from behind the cover of his book.

Eileen and Bill shared the shade of their shelter. Occasionally the two women splashed in the shallows. Mavis was a poor swimmer and Eileen could manage only a gasping breast-stroke. Bill would coast up and down with some style but short breath. But Henry swam across the wide sweep of the bay each morning to the headland opposite, almost half a mile. There he would haul himself on to a rock, wary of sea urchins hiding under the seaweed, rest for a while, and swim back, escaping from his companions and occupying time in a manner that was not only good for him but pleasant. Some of the way he would power himself on with a vigorous crawl, but for much of the distance he would swim slowly on his side, gazing at the scenery. Above the rocky hilltops was the vivid blue sky and below were the olive trees on which much of the island's prosperity was founded, silvery grey in the sunlight.

The day before the storm, Eileen and Mavis had spent some hours poking about in the little town while Henry and Bill took a taxi out to a ruined monastery. Eileen, who kept a dress shop in Sussex, didn't care for ruins, and neither did Mavis. The women had enjoyed their day, returning with several parcels. The men had had an agreeable time, too.

Eileen and Bill had an air-bed on which Eileen would paddle herself for some distance on the calm blue water. Mavis, encouraged to take her turn on the bed, paddled too, and found it was easy enough to move the light mattress and guide it with the movement of her hands. Henry supposed it was safe enough out here where the sea was so calm, though he knew such beds were dangerous in British waters.

Each afternoon, however, no matter how calm and still the sea was in the morning, a sharp breeze blew up and the sailboard riders would come out, their little craft dancing like ballerinas on the small waves. And now there was a storm.

It would pass, Henry thought as he watched the lightning stab the sky and heard the thunder overhead. Calm would return when the gods were appeased. Did they demand a sacrifice, he wondered.

The next day, the storm had died down and the sky was washed clear of cloud. The swimming-pool, filled with twigs and sand swept down by the rain, was drained and cleaned. The tourists went down to the beach again to resume their sybaritic routine.

For three more days it was calm and sunny, but then the air grew still and humid once more. The sea was like glass and Henry went off for his morning swim while the good weather held. He struck out strongly across the bay towards his landmark at the tip of the headland and scrambled out for his rest. But he stayed a shorter time than usual when he saw the sky grow darker. As he swam back, a slight swell caught him half-way across the bay. It was like the wash from a boat. He glanced round, expecting to see a waterskier, though he had heard no motor boat. He saw no craft near enough to have caused the movement of the water, which was odd.

He swam on towards the straw-topped shades on the distant beach, putting his head down and going into a powerful crawl that moved him fast through the water, looking up from time to time to make sure his direction was correct. Some way ahead, a good distance from the shore, he saw an air-bed, and just as he noticed it a big wave came up behind him, wrapping itself around him. Henry, a good and confident swimmer, rode the wave safely, but he saw it sweep on towards the air-bed. The mattress bobbed up with the wave and Henry wondered who was on it and if it was Eileen's bed. He swam on and made out the bright colour of Mavis's cerise two-piece swimsuit.

Then another wave caught him, a much bigger one than its forerunner. It engulfed him totally, and when he had swum through it he saw it roll towards the air-bed.

Poseidon he pleaded, Poseidon – great god of the sea – free me of her. And, as he willed the elements, he saw the air-bed, caught by the wave, tip up and throw the woman on it into the water.

As he swam towards the spot, Henry understood what had caused the waves. An earthquake had struck this island years ago, and the area was subject to earth tremors. A tremor somewhere out at sea had made the wave. Drawing nearer, Henry could see a head bobbing in the water. Mavis would panic. She wouldn't be able to swim to the shore and he thought it unlikely that she'd be able to clamber back on to the mattress. He swam powerfully on, and as he drew near another wave came. There was no time to reflect. Poseidon had answered his prayer. Henry took a deep breath and dived into the wave as it bore down on the bobbing head. He grabbed the woman and dragged her beneath the wave with him, forcing her head down and holding it submerged, fighting the natural buoyancy of the salt water to keep her under long enough to make of her the sacrificial offering demanded by the gods, his own lungs bursting with the effort. She struggled and kicked, then finally went limp. At last he surfaced, still holding her. Then he felt Zeus, in vengeance, send a shaft of agony through his own chest.

A man swimming with a snorkel mask and flippers fished the woman's body from the water. Henry was pulled out later, hauled aboard the dinghy that shepherded the sailboard riders.

His death was ruled a massive heart attack while attempting to save a friend – for the woman's body was Eileen's. She had been wearing a cerise swimsuit she had borrowed from the victim's wife. Perhaps, it was conjectured, he had mistaken her for his wife, had been attempting to save his wife.

Mavis received a good deal of sympathy, together with Henry's insurances, which brought with them a very comfortable pension, so that she was able to continue to live up to the considerable standards she had set for them both.

A
SORT
OF
PRIDE

Mandy enjoyed her work as a representative for Gladways Holidays until the night Mrs Featherstone disappeared in the Aegean Sea.

The Featherstones had given no trouble during their stay at the Korona Beach Hotel. They had not complained about the noise from the discothèque, unlike Miss Jeffs and Miss Dawes who had protested so vigorously that even Mr Salonides, the manager, agreed that they must be moved to a quiet room overlooking the oleander grove on the far side of the hotel; it was obvious that otherwise there would be telephone calls to London and perhaps the intervention of the Managing Director of Gladways Tours himself. Mr Salonides did not want to risk losing the company's block booking for next season.

The Featherstones had made friends with the Barkers, and met on the Barkers' balcony each evening before dinner for drinks from everyone's duty-free bottles. The Barkers' room overlooked the sea but the Featherstones, in one above the hotel entrance, were disturbed not only by the disco, which was situated in a building higher up the hillside, but also by the arrival and departure of tour coaches, the bus which shuttled to and from the local town, and staff and guests coming and going on scooters.

The two couples were by far the oldest guests in the hotel, and Mandy had been relieved to note that they seemed physically spry though all, as she knew from their passport details, were well into their seventies. Mrs Featherstone was conspicuous because of her bright orange hair, sparsely arranged over her pink skull and curled around her ears in which she always wore large earrings, even in the sea. Her make-up was vivid, and she took care not to get sunburned, preserving a pink-and-white look accentuated with rouge, eye-liner – the lot. She carried a parasol, and, when forced to lay that down to swim, put on a shady straw hat.

Denis Barker thought her a game old thing. In her day she must have been quite a girl and he wished that he had known her then. His own wife, Hazel, thought Dolly Featherstone looked ridiculous but then they were none of them getting any younger. Hazel, in the sea, wore a severe black one-piece costume and a blue rubber cap; she swam briskly several times a day while Dolly wallowed in the shallows or, with uneven breast-stroke, tried to match Tommy Featherstone's steady progress parallel to the shore.

Tommy had been on the island during the war. He had told Mandy this when he briefed her group of guests the morning after their arrival. He wanted to hire a car and visit the hill village where he had hidden in a cave, with a small band of men, until they were betrayed to the occupying troops and captured. He had spent the rest of the war in a prison camp while Dolly performed with ENSA, entertaining the forces with song and dance routines. With two other girls, none of them related, she formed a singing trio, The Glitter Sisters, and glitter they did, in sequinned dresses; men needed glamour then and they needed it still, so Dolly did her best to retain hers. During the war years, despite many propositions and even some temptation, Dolly had remained faithful to Tommy, writing to him regularly and knitting socks and sweaters for him.

After the war she had given up show business to settle down and raise a family. Unspoken was the possibility that it might otherwise give her up, since though she had charm and vitality, her talent was not large. She soon acquired domestic skills, but motherhood eluded Dolly as the years went by. Tommy rose in the bank, to which he had returned as soon as he was demobilised, and their first flat was exchanged for a small house, then a larger one in a better neighbourhood, and so it went on. When he retired, Tommy took up bowls and Dolly became stage manager for the local dramatic society, but she never performed. She would not accept the dowager roles that would have been her lot.

Holidays were spent in various places, often France, and even other parts of Greece, but until this year they had never visited the island. Tommy had not wanted to, and Dolly had decided that this was because his memories of hardships endured there and his final capture were too painful.

Tommy had been anxious in case he was considered too old to hire a car: this had happened to him in Dublin recently; but such strictures did not apply here and Mandy was able to arrange a small Fiat for his use. They'd both laughed over the unsuitability of a Mini Moke, though he'd thought it looked Jeep-like and rather fun. Mandy found it difficult to imagine him as a dashing soldier; the whole pilgrimage seemed to her to be romantic.

He made several expeditions into the hills, always alone, leaving Dolly beneath a canopy beside the pool, or under a straw shade on the beach. When Mandy came to the hotel for her evening visit she seldom met the two couples, but one night she saw Dolly sitting alone on the terrace, drinking ouzo. The old woman's painted face looked blotchy in spite of her make-up, and she wore dark glasses. Mandy had the distinct impression that she had been crying. But why? What had she to cry about, for heaven's sake? Except that you could say her life was almost over.

Mandy did not realise until later just how accurate that judgement was.

'Well, Mrs Featherstone, everything all right?' she asked brightly, pausing by Dolly's chair. Apart from the Barkers and Featherstones, Mandy called all her clients by their Christian names, but she sensed that they would think such intimacy presumptuous.

Dolly, with an effort, turned her gaze from the dark sea beyond the hotel grounds towards the girl, who was small, with pointed features and neat elfin ears. Dolly had once been rather like her.

'Ah, my dear, come and have a drink,' she invited, and called out to a passing waiter.

Mandy was anxious to hurry back to the flat she shared with Spiros, a jealous man who worked on one of the island ferries, but her time of being available at the hotel was not yet up.

'Just an orange juice, then,' she accepted. 'Thanks.'

The waiter fetched it, and Mrs Featherstone signed the chit. She had ordered another large ouzo for herself.

'*Yia sou*,' said Dolly, falsely cheery, and then asked Mandy why she had taken the island job.

'Was it a love affair with Greece? Or with a Greek?' she asked.

'You're too clever,' Mandy answered, almost blushing beneath her tan. 'A bit of both, really. I got bored with being a typist in the city. I came for a holiday and didn't fancy going back.'

She'd met Dimitri, in fact. After a winter in her office she'd come out again, rented a room and learned a little of the language. That was four years ago. Dimitri had married his Greek fiancée and acquired her dowry, a practice that still obtained in parts of Greece, and she'd found a job with Gladways. Eventually she'd been sent to this island and had met Spiros. Some of this she now told Dolly, who listened intently.

'Will it work out? You and Spiros?' Dolly asked.

'I don't know,' admitted Mandy.

'They're strong on duty, aren't they? Family first – all that,' said Dolly. 'Tommy's told me. A family hid him here during the war.'

'So he said,' Mandy answered. 'Did he ever find them? That's why he wanted the car, wasn't it? To go and look for them?'

'Yes, he found them,' Dolly said.

He'd been to the mountain village so often that Denis Barker had become intrigued. In the end, he too had hired a car, packed Dolly into it with Hazel and himself, and followed.

They'd found Tommy's car parked outside a small white-washed cottage, where purple bougainvillea tumbled over a low wall and two thin cats lay in the sun. The trio approached, and as they drew level with the cottage they saw that on the rough track in front of it, a boy was playing with a ball, while beneath a eucalyptus in the cottage garden, a woman sat talking to Tommy.

The boy looked up at the new arrivals and smiled shyly. He had fair hair and large blue eyes, not unknown in Greece but rare on this island.

'Good morning,' he said. 'Hullo.'

'Good morning and hullo to you,' said Denis heartily. 'I see you speak English. What's your name?'

'*Thomas*,' said the child, pronouncing it the Greek way, the *th* sound thick.

Tommy, Dolly's husband, had risen to his feet and was staring at her fearfully across the space, filled with bright geraniums, that separated them. His features seemed to crumple, but then he stood up and spoke firmly.

'This is Ilena, the boy's mother,' he said, indicating the short, dark woman, dressed in black, who now stood, hands clasped before her, stout, smiling uncomprehendingly, a handkerchief tied around her head, her face lined and weatherbeaten. 'She's the daughter of an English soldier,' Tommy said, his voice harsh, rasping in the clear, still air.

'A wartime romance, eh?' said Denis, nodding.

'They weren't married,' Tommy said. 'She was only seventeen, but he was frightened and she comforted him. The man she was to marry betrayed him and his companions to the Germans. Eight villagers were shot for hiding the British soldiers, but she was spared. Later, she had a daughter – Ilena.' He looked at the bent woman beside him, prematurely aged by the strong sun and a life of hard peasant work: his daughter.

And Dolly knew. With ice-cold certainty, she understood.

'What happened to the mother?' she whispered.

'She died when Ilena was born,' Tommy answered. He laid his hand on Ilena's arm and she smiled up at him, bewildered by the conversation. 'The family took care of Ilena. She's a

widow now, but she has two older sons. One of them is a
waiter in a hotel in Athens. The other works at the airport
here. Her daughter is a maid at one of the hotels – not ours,'
he added. 'They work the land, too. They own a lot of olive
trees.'

'Quite a story,' said Denis, eyeing Tommy Featherstone
speculatively.

'Yes,' said Tommy flatly. Misery showed on his face as he
looked across at Dolly, but it was mixed with another
emotion, and Hazel identified it as the old man's eyes began
to shine and he glanced at the boy: it was a sort of pride.

'We'll go,' she decided. 'Come on, Dolly. See you later,
Tommy,' and she took Dolly's arm to lead her back to their
car.

'Sorry to intrude, old man,' said Denis, still uncertain if his
conclusions were the right ones.

Dolly did not tell Mandy any of this.

'Greek family solidarity is very strong, my dear. It's difficult
for outsiders to understand it – to accept it,' she said.

'Mixed marriages can be a great success,' said Mandy
stubbornly, but she thought about Spiros's jealousy, his
questions about male guests she met, the way he sometimes
turned up unexpectedly during folk dance sessions and other
evening activities arranged by Gladways for their clients.

'I wish you luck,' said Dolly, sighing.

Before it was light next morning, Dolly slipped out of bed
without disturbing Tommy, who was snoring gently, as he
always did. She put on her white swimsuit with the sprawling
emerald flowers and arranged its matching wrap around her
shoulders, but she did not paint her face. Carrying her
espadrilles, she opened the door carefully while Tommy slept
on. She stepped into the passage where lights burned all
night, and the door made a tiny click as she closed it, not
pushing the button that would lock it as then it would not
shut without a bang. She tiptoed along the corridor and down
the winding stairs into the hall. The duty clerk was in the
office, dozing. No one saw Dolly open the glass door to the

terrace where she had talked to Mandy the previous evening, and no one watched her walk past the swimming pool over the garden to the beach.

The sea was glassy still, and the moon shone down, painting a swathe of silver on the blackness of the water.

Dolly dropped her espadrilles and wrap on the sand. She had not brought a towel: she would not need one. She walked into the water, shivering as she felt its chill clutch on her thin old limbs. As she began her unsteady breast-stroke, heading out along the moonlight's track towards the horizon, she remembered the letters Tommy had written her from the prison camp, his mention of her flaming hair and tender, ivory skin. She had always tried to stay beautiful for Tommy and all the time there had been this secret. Of course, he hadn't known about the daughter.

She was a feeble swimmer, but she should be able to keep going long enough to leave the beach far behind her. Perhaps the cold, or cramp, would get her first. Her legs and arms sent her slowly but inexorably onward. What would Tommy do? Would he know what she had intended? She had left no note. Perhaps he would always wonder what was in her mind. She was not altogether sure that she knew herself, except that it seemed as if her whole life had been a pretence.

Without her, Tommy might sell up and come out here to live. He'd been able to talk in Greek to that woman who turned out to be his daughter. He'd picked up quite a lot, all those years ago, and had enjoyed using it to the hotel staff and people in the town. She'd be about fifty, that woman: Ilena. Living here was cheap, and Tommy might be able to help the youngest boy – see that he had an education – and perhaps set the daughter up in a tourist shop, or at least provide a dowry.

They hadn't talked about it. She'd pleaded a headache and gone straight to bed after dinner. Tommy had stayed for a nightcap with the Barkers and when he came up, she had pretended to be asleep. It was the first time in the long years of their marriage that she had resorted to deceit.

Poor Tommy, was her last thought as the water closed over her head and she surrendered her body to the wine-dark sea.

No one mentioned to the police that Dolly had been rather quiet that night and had missed the usual session on the Barkers' balcony, and Mandy decided to keep to herself her theory about the dead woman's blotched complexion. It was probably caused by sunburn, after all. No one spoke of Tommy's visits to the hillside village. It was best to keep things simple so that the formalities could be swiftly dealt with; it wasn't as though foul play were suspected.

The absence of a towel left on the beach was never queried.

It was all a dreadful accident. Wasn't it?

GIFTS FROM THE BRIDEGROOM

O nly ten more days to go!
  'Are you nervous?' Wendy asked, meeting him by
  chance in the lunch hour. He had gone into town to
buy toothpaste; there never seemed to be time at weekends for
such mundane shopping, for every moment had to be spent
buying the things Hazel decreed essential to their future
married life.

'Why should I be?' Alan answered. He'd known Hazel for
over two years; they'd been to Torremolinos together, and
had often made love in his bed-sitter. Once, when her parents
were away, he'd even stayed overnight at The Elms, giggling
with Hazel as they clung together in her narrow bed in the
room where a row of stuffed teddy bears gazed down at their
transports.

'It's going to be quite a do, isn't it?' Wendy said. 'How many
bridesmaids are you having?'

'Three. Hazel's niece, and her friends Linda and Maeve.' He
sighed. All three had to be given presents. He'd thought of
gold bracelets, but it seemed Maeve wanted a pearl on a
chain, and Linda favoured dangly earrings. This problem had
yet to be resolved and the gifts purchased.

'Well, I'm sure it will be a great production,' said Wendy.
'Best of luck,' she added. 'I'll be thinking of you on the big
day,' and she hurried off to her office.

Her words echoed in his head as he returned to his own,
where a pile of papers waited for his attention. If he worked
hard and was never made redundant, in forty-two years' time
– nearly twice as long as he had lived already – he might be
head of a department and retiring with his graduated
pension.

Retiring to what?

Why, to Hazel of course.

Through Alan's mind ran images of Hazel as she was now: small, pert and pretty, a bank clerk with the Midland. He saw also a mental picture of her mother, hair rinsed brassy gold, figure trimly girdled, neat ankles twinkly as, high-heeled on short legs, she stepped about her day, ordaining the lives of her family. Her husband was a civil servant employed by the local authority and they moved in ever rising circles. Hazel's mother had planned the wedding to the last detail; she had vetted the guest list, not permitting him to include Wendy, with whom he had been at school, because her father ran a betting shop.

A production, Wendy had called the wedding, and it was: like some sort of pageant, Alan thought.

Would Hazel choose his future friends? Alan's mind ranged over the years ahead, past the freedom to make love at will and the honeymoon in Corfu. At first, due to a hold-up in arrangements over the small first-time buyer's home for which they were negotiating, they would be living in his bed-sitter, to Hazel's mother's great chagrin; but later there would be the house, then a bigger one when their finances improved. One day there would be children. He foresaw their regimented lives, their freshly laundered, spotless white socks and shirts, their well-scrubbed faces, their diligently completed homework, all firmly supervised by Hazel. He thought of the comforts he would enjoy: the well-cooked food, the tastefully furnished home for which even now he was committed to paying by instalments. The previous weekend they had chosen an expensive three-piece suite. The salesman at Fisher's Furnishings had said it had been made by one of the foremost firms in the world. Testing its suedette comfort, Alan had wondered; he had wondered, too, about the cooker Hazel had selected, split-level hob and all, which would take up so much space in their tiny kitchen. He thought of the money in his building society account, all pledged in advance for coping with the down payment on the house, and with an effort he turned his mind's eye to Hazel in her bikini, spread out on a Corfiote beach. As he stood, eyes closed, on the marble flooring of the town's new shopping arcade, he felt her soft, responsive body in his arms. All that would be wonderful, he knew; it already was when they had the chance.

But first there was the wedding, that performance which must be enacted to please Hazel and her mother. There would be Hazel's progress on her father's arm up the aisle of the local church, which Hazel herself had visited only once to hear the banns read, and her mother on the other two occasions to show willing to the vicar. There had been half an hour's talk in his study with the vicar himself, when Alan and Hazel were advised to show tolerance to one another throughout their lives, expect from each other not perfection, but simply kindness, and adjured not to give up at the first sign of trouble but to work through storms into harbour.

Standing there while the shoppers eddied about him, Alan knew panic. What had he done in his twenty-three years? Where had he been? What could he look forward to, except routine?

He'd gone straight from school into his first job with the firm which still employed him. He had been to Spain and Ibiza. He had spent a day in Boulogne.

There was a whole world beyond this town – a world beyond Spain and Corfu. There were Australia, Siam and India. There was China, too, and he'd see none of them, for Hazel and their children would have to be fed and the rates must be paid.

As he went back to his office, Alan knew that Wendy's words had changed his life for ever.

Five days later – it took him that long to work out a plan – Mrs Doreen Groves, whose husband managed the bank where Hazel worked, was just washing up the breakfast things when the telephone rang.

'Mrs Groves?' asked a voice, male, and carefully articulating.

Mrs Groves owned to her identity.

'I'm afraid I have bad news for you,' said the caller, and went on to tell her that Mr Groves, driving to the bank earlier that morning, had had a serious accident and was on his way to hospital by ambulance. Because of the grave nature of his injuries he was being taken, not to the local hospital, but to the regional one twenty miles away where all facilities were to hand. There was no answer when she asked for more details.

For some seconds Mrs Groves was made immobile by shock. Then she attempted to dial the bank to find out if the assistant manager could give her more information, but the telephone was dead.

Alan had not cut the line. In the nearby call-box, from which he had rung Mrs Groves, he had inserted enough coins to keep the connection for several minutes, and he left the receiver off the hook while he hurried round to the Groves' house. He slipped into the garden through the fence, and under cover of the shrubbery went up to the side of the building where, on an earlier reconnaissance, he had observed that the telephone line was attached, and snipped the cable neatly. He waited, hidden behind some laurels, while Mrs Groves reversed her Mini out of the garage and sped off. Then he returned to the telephone-box, replaced the receiver, and made a call to the bank.

He asked to speak to the manager. It was an urgent matter, he said, concerning Mrs Groves. To the girl answering the telephone he said he was a police officer, and gave his name as Sergeant Thomas from the local headquarters.

When Mr Groves came on the line, sounding worried as he asked what was wrong, Alan held a scarf to his mouth and spoke in a false voice. His heart beat fast with excitement as he told the manager, 'We've got your wife. Bring fifty thousand pounds in used notes, fives and tens, to Heathrow Airport by twelve noon. More instructions will wait for you at the information desk in Terminal Two.' Alan had intended to ask for twenty thousand; he was quite surprised to hear himself name the larger sum. 'And don't get in touch with the police or it will be the worse for your wife,' he remembered to add, in menacing tones.

He rang off before Mr Groves could reply. Would it work? He'd read somewhere that bank managers were instructed to pay up at such times – to risk no one's life – although certain alarm routines had to be followed. It was a pity he'd never asked Hazel more about security measures; he knew that she was not meant to disclose what precautions were operated and until now he hadn't been interested. He had tried to turn the conversation that way at the weekend, but she'd wanted to talk only about the wedding.

Alan had already telephoned his own firm to say he wouldn't be coming in, pleading a stomach upset. There were jokes and quips about first-night nerves.

After making the call, Alan got straight into his ramshackle old Fiat, which Hazel had long since condemned, and drove to Heathrow. He left the car in the short-stay park and crossed to Terminal Two, where he noticed a boy wandering around without apparent purpose. Alan said he was late for his flight and asked the lad to deliver a note to the information desk. He gave the boy a pound and, skulking among the shifting people, watched to see his commission executed. Inside an envelope addressed in capital letters to Mr Groves were instructions to place the bag beside the nearest newspaper stand. Alan intended to walk rapidly by, collecting it as he passed and vanishing into the crowd before he could be detected. He felt certain that by now the police would have been alerted in some manner. As soon as she reached the hospital, Mrs Groves would have discovered that her husband had not been admitted, but she was sure to be confused. She might telephone the bank, but by then Mr Groves would have left with the ransom if he were to reach the airport by noon. He would have had no problem in finding the actual cash; now Alan wondered with misgiving whether there might not be some bugging device attached to its container. If Mrs Groves was known to be safe, the police might be close behind her husband, waiting to pounce when Alan claimed the ransom.

He began to feel uneasy. What had seemed a perfect plan now revealed flaws.

Mr Groves was, in fact, almost at Heathrow before his wife learned that the call to her had been a hoax. She spent some time telephoning other hospitals before she rang the bank, and in the interval Mr Groves had parked his car in the short-stay park near a small, shabby Fiat which looked very like one he had seen outside his own house that morning.

Awaiting his prey, but with waning confidence, Alan tapped his pocket. The previous day, he had withdrawn all the money that stood to his credit with the building society. It was not fifty thousand pounds, but it was enough to keep him for some time and it was all rightfully his own. He had his passport, and a small case in which he had planned to transport his booty out of the country.

As suddenly as Wendy's words had earlier opened his eyes to the future, Alan saw that if he went ahead with his plan he would never be free from fear of detection. Here was another moment of decision, and there was no need for any theft; he could simply walk away from the rendezvous and disappear. No one would connect him with a dumped case of bank notes.

Alan went to the Air France desk, where he bought a ticket to Paris. His original plan had been to drive to Dover, sell his car there for whatever it would fetch, and catch the ferry to Calais. He had been afraid, if he flew, that the security inspection at the airport would reveal the wads of money in the case, but now he had nothing to dread.

He'd spend a few days in Paris, then hitch south, maybe to Rome. Perhaps he could pick up some work as he went along. He'd stay away at least while his money lasted, possibly for good, depending on what opportunities arose.

At the airport post office Alan mailed, second-class, a package to Hazel. It contained the tickets for the honeymoon in Corfu; she could still use them, taking Linda or Maeve with her. He attempted no explanation beyond a note saying he was sorry to upset her but he wasn't ready to settle down just yet and it was better to find that out now rather than when it was too late. Luckily, he hadn't bought the bridesmaids' presents.

Alan sat in the plane waiting for take-off. To the other

passengers he was just a young man on a business trip with the minimal luggage of a small bag and his raincoat; only he knew that at last he was starting to live. He could always come back one day; even if the hoax telephone calls were attributed to him, such a minor offence wouldn't merit much of a punishment. At the moment he felt that a journey to freedom now was worth a few months in jail later on.

In another area of the same plane sat an older man on his way to adventure.

Mr Groves was six months short of retiring. He did not look forward to spending more time with his wife, who was one of life's cosseters and would fuss over him much too tenderly, making him old before his time. She had turned down his suggestion that they should go on a trip to Australia; even a cruise did not appeal to her. A stay-at-home girl was Doreen, and their holidays, apart from a weekend in Venice, had been spent in either Scotland or Cornwall. She'd made him into her child, perhaps because they had none of their own.

If they had, he couldn't have done what he was doing now. On the way to Heathrow he had called in at his home. The cleaning woman did not come today, and it had been odd to find the breakfast dishes still in the sink. There were, however, no signs of struggle.

Poor Doreen! How terrified she must have been, he had thought, and, on impulse, collected his passport from his desk; who knew where the trail might lead?

On the way to the information desk in the main concourse at Terminal Two, another impulse had turned Mr Groves towards a telephone, from which he had called the bank. They might as well know he had arrived. The police might have some instructions for him – if they were shadowing him, they could not come forward now, just as he was about to 'make the drop', wasn't it called?

Mr Groves had been told that his wife had telephoned and, though distressed, was unharmed. She had been to look for him at the hospital as the result of a hoax telephone call; the whole thing was some prank.

Mr Groves had replaced the receiver, relieved beyond measure to know that Doreen was safe. Then he had realised that here he was, as the result of someone's idea of a joke, with fifty thousand pounds of the bank's money.

What a chance! But the police would be watching him and he mustn't waste time.

He had collected the envelope left for him at the desk – there had been one; the hoaxer had clearly meant business – opened it and read the message. Then he had turned and gone, as if instructed, to the Air France counter where he had bought a ticket to Paris. The police would reason that, having discovered his wife was safe, he intended to lead them to the perpetrator of the hoax kidnap. It would be some time before they would suspect him of having fled himself. Interpol might have to be invoked, and by then he would be on his way to Australia. If he were to be traced, he could be extradited from there but there might be time, before he was apprehended, to move on to Spain, where barons of crime still lived in safety, although he thought plans were afoot to end that.

Mr Groves mingled confidently with the other travellers at Charles de Gaulle Airport. He noticed a pretty woman, perhaps thirty-five years old, walking ahead towards Passport Control. The world was full of pretty young women with broader views than those of his wife. Hitherto a strictly moral man, Mr Groves' thoughts dwelt happily on the delights that might lie ahead.

Thus enjoying his future, he saw a young man who seemed vaguely familiar going through customs. He carried only a case and a raincoat, and he looked eagerly confident, the world at his feet. Ah, youth, reflected Mr Groves, and his mind turned to Doreen. She would be very upset and she would never forgive him. No matter what happened now, he could not go home because he had stolen the bank's money. Well, at his age it was easy to resolve that he would not be caught alive. He would seek present pleasure, and if capture threatened he would take the final escape.

* * *

Hazel wept when the holiday tickets arrived. How dreadful of Alan to behave like this! She could not understand what had got into him; it was all so humiliating.

Her mother was furious, but it seemed that Hazel had, in the nick of time, been saved from wrecking her life. To think that that quiet young man could be so deceitful!

She drew comfort from the troubles of others, however, when she learned that Mr Groves at the bank had apparently set up a fake kidnap to lure his wife from home, then pretended to receive a ransom demand so that he could obtain a large sum of money and flee the country. The police had found his car at Heathrow. Oddly enough, Alan's car was found there too, in the very next bay. It was almost as though the two had conspired.

ANNIVERSARY

It was a special day.

Mrs Frobisher had made careful preparations. A bottle of champagne was on ice and she had bought smoked salmon, asparagus, and a plump partridge.

In the living-room of her comfortable flat all was arranged. The table was laid with the best silver and cut glass. There were spring flowers in a small vase.

She would celebrate alone, for next to the money her tranquil solitude was, after so long, a prize. For three years she had steadfastly carried out her daily duties – fetching and carrying, wheeling Matthew out in his chair, placing his tweed hat tenderly on his pale bald head, wrapping his soft wool scarf round his throat (though she longed to pull it tight against his windpipe), tucking a mohair rug round his knees and his bony old ankles. Because of her his last years had been spent in great comfort – and, indeed, he owed them to her nursing skill.

They met when the agency sent her as his special nurse to the nursing home where Matthew was recovering from a stroke. She was accustomed to caring for the elderly, and she had found him an easy patient. He was light to lift and determined to regain his powers of speech and movement. Aiding his rehabilitation had been a challenge to her skills. After months in the nursing home, he was well enough to leave but required full-time home care, and he suggested to her that she should become his permanent attendant.

This might be her only chance: she had resolved not to let it pass. She was a plain, sturdy woman with a sallow complexion and glasses. Her legs were stout and her ankles thick – though her feet were small, and often, for this reason, ached as they carried her heavy body about her duties. Mr

Frobisher was a widower, and wealthy. His visitors at the nursing home had been his former business associates – he had retired from active work before his illness but was still on the board of several companies. He had no children.

Once home in the flat overlooking the esplanade he became demanding, and she worked hard complying with his wishes. She kept him physically spruce and arranged bridge evenings for him with former cronies, for he had recovered enough to enjoy a few rubbers once or twice a week. She would slip out, then, for a couple of hours at the cinema, returning in time to serve drinks and sandwiches to the men. Otherwise, apart from shopping and trips to the library, she went out only with Matthew, pushing him in his chair along the esplanade when the weather allowed.

She had expected it to be for just a few months – a year at the most – for Mr Frobisher was old. The excitement of marriage, she had thought, when it came (as she knew it would) would hasten his end.

'You must be cared for, my dear,' he told her, patting her hand. 'You care for me so well.'

When they were married he no longer paid her a salary. He was mean with money. She had discovered this in the nursing home and had known he would think of marriage because it would cost him less, though why he guarded his funds so carefully when he had no one to leave his fortune to was hard to explain. It was characteristic of the elderly rich, she had noticed before. Now she had to account for every penny she spent when shopping, and Matthew saw no reason to keep the woman who had come twice a week to do the cleaning.

As the months went by, Mrs Frobisher was instructed to practise still more thrift by frugal catering. He ordered her to serve mince, rice pudding, and custard instead of salmon, crème caramel, and fruit out of season. She began to adjust her housekeeping accounts to extract enough money for splurges in cafés when she was shopping. Then she would drink coffee or chocolate topped with rich cream and eat cakes and pastries before hurrying home to Matthew, who would be reading the *Financial Times*.

The doctor, who called regularly, praised her care of her elderly husband. He'd got rather difficult, Mrs Frobisher once confessed, but she knew it was simply his health that made him pernickety about details.

'A trust fund, my dear,' Mr Frobisher had suddenly said one day. 'You are not used to handling money. You'll be at the mercy of fortune hunters when I'm gone. I must protect you.'

Mrs Frobisher was dismayed. She wanted her fortune, when she received it, to be her own, to handle as she desired. She had earned it, after all. She would travel. She planned to go on a cruise round the world, perhaps meet romance on a boat deck under the moon. She secretly read brochures, picked up on her shopping trips, and daydreamed over them when Matthew slept. She was still only forty-six years old and she had never known love. A young man resembling a god, she romanced, might woo her in Greece. An Italian with deep brown eyes, perhaps, would serenade her in Venice.

While her husband slumbered, Mrs Frobisher escaped to a world of dreams. She read magazines, and romantic novels she borrowed from the library without Mr Frobisher's knowledge. And she watched television, too, until late at night. She had formed an attachment in her mind to a handsome middle-aged actor who featured in many plays. He often played rather sinister roles and was suave. Mrs Frobisher, alone in her bed while Matthew snored nearby in his, would imagine the actor whispering to her, his lips on her neck, herself at last responding to physical passion, something that had eluded her in her life thus far.

Mr Frobisher, after their marriage, had requested intimate contact. He was capable only of touch, and that, he indicated, was his right now that they were husband and wife.

'It's not good for you, dear. You'll send up your blood pressure,' Mrs Frobisher had said, avoiding compliance, promising it as a treat for one day in the future when he was better. But his hands, increasingly, reached for her as she dealt with his needs; he would watch her with narrowed eyes as she moved about their bedroom.

Mrs Frobisher had grown to hate her husband before he threatened to curtail her future liberty by means of a trust and acted in time to prevent him.

It had been carefully planned.

At first she had thought of demanding money for personal spending, making him angry, and leaving his physical wants untended so that bedsores and other problems developed, but pride in her profession, finally, would not permit the use of these means to make his blood pressure rise and bring on another stroke – which he might have at any time. Though again, since his heart was strong, he might survive.

In the end, she had been more subtle. She had done it with frozen chicken, thawing it imperfectly and ceasing its cooking too soon, leaving it in the warm kitchen where it could begin to go off even if there were no risk of salmonella. It didn't work the first time, but the second attempt, when she'd made a chicken risotto and added lamb from the weekend joint which she had kept exposed until it started to smell rather nasty, did the trick.

She ate a little herself, so she could tell the doctor, truthfully, that she too had felt ill, but she disposed of all that was left down the lavatory, flushing it thoroughly.

He had lingered for twenty-four hours after the dreadful vomiting, his breathing harsh in the quiet room. She would not have him taken to the hospital. 'I am a nurse,' she said with pride.

For some hours she had feared he would recover again. She was tempted to lay a pillow over his face or pinch his nostrils, but suppose betraying signs resulted? She could wipe away any froth that might be exuded, but she couldn't disperse petechial haemorrhages if they occurred, and the doctor might observe them. He would look at his patient's eyes.

But such action was not needed.

Just before he died, Matthew opened his eyes and glared at her, seeing her clearly.

He knew. She and the doctor had discussed the possible

cause of his food-poisoning while Matthew lay there, and perhaps he had understood their conversation. He had known how careful she was in the kitchen, how unlikely the chance of contaminated food being served under her charge.

Well, he could do nothing now: it was too late. She stared back at him until it was over.

She had affected grief for a year, only slowly emerging in becoming, elegant clothes – in muted hues as first the executors advanced her funds and finally the estate, which was in perfect order, was settled. And tomorrow she was leaving on a world cruise. Her bags were packed and labelled. The porter in the block of flats knew of her plans. She had no intimate friends, but she told her few acquaintances that she was going away.

During her year of widowhood, Mrs Frobisher had put on weight, for she had made amends for the years of rice pudding and mince – but she could carry it off, she thought, regarding herself in the mirror. She had had her hair rinsed a rich honey blonde and had bought a mink coat. Her spectacles had been exchanged for contact lenses. She felt sure she would find romance on her voyage, though perhaps not of a durable kind. When she returned, she would open an expensive eventide home where rich elderly people could end their days in her experienced care and be off the hands of their families.

That evening, after her celebratory meal, a further treat awaited Mrs Frobisher – the perfect way to round off the day. The final instalment of a television drama series in which her actor hero played a leading role. She had arranged her cruise for after the end of the series, not willing to miss any appearance he might make. And now, in this last episode, the chain of spellbinding events would be tied off.

Mrs Frobisher ate her smoked salmon with wafer-thin brown bread and butter. She had learned to cut it like that for her patients. She ate her succulent partridge, and to follow she had two chocolate éclairs bought at the new patisserie in town.

She piled the crockery into the dishwasher. She would turn

it on in the morning after breakfast, before the taxi arrived to take her to the airport from which she was due to fly to join her cruise. She made coffee and poured out the last of the champagne to drink while she watched her play.

In the warm luxurious room, Mrs Frobisher sat in her deep armchair and gazed at the screen while her hero, captured by terrorists planning to kill him, sought to evade what seemed an inevitable fate. The camera cut to his wife (middle-aged and careworn) and his mistress (young and curvaceous). The background was Spanish, the countryside burnt brown, baking in shimmering heat. Shots of a bullfight were briefly, irrelevantly, shown.

Mrs Frobisher's hero, bound and gagged, watched water entering his prison cell in the dungeon of an old castle. It lapped about his feet. The terrorists, on the ramparts, watched for the helicopter that would take them to safety.

The telephone rang in Mrs Frobisher's hall.

The sound startled her. She received few calls apart from an occasional message from the porter.

Could it be the shipping line? They had her number in case, as the booking clerk had explained, there were last-minute changes of plan, alterations to flights due to weather or other conditions.

She had better answer. She'd be quick, missing only moments of the play's approaching dénouement.

She brusquely gave her own number, and added, 'Mrs Frobisher speaking.'

'Mavis – at last! I've had such a trouble to find you,' a female voice said. 'It's Beatrice. I've only just heard you'd got married. I'm so sorry to hear you've lost your husband.'

'Beatrice!' Mrs Frobisher echoed.

'Yes. I traced you through the nursing agency,' the voice of her younger sister declared.

Mrs Frobisher was too shocked to answer. From the living-room came the sound of gunfire and the clattering noise of helicopter blades. Mrs Frobisher replaced the telephone receiver, ignoring the voice that continued to speak, and returned to the living-room. She poured herself out a small brandy and was sipping it when the telephone started to ring again.

Mrs Frobisher sat watching the screen, letting it ring. The blood pounded in her temples. She had not heard from Beatrice for years. Her sister had married young and had four children – she lived in Wales with her farmer husband. What had happened to make Beatrice seek her out?

She wanted money, Mrs Frobisher thought. She must have discovered that Matthew had been a rich man.

Mrs Frobisher gazed at the screen, pouring a second brandy. While she was out of the room, her hero had somehow freed himself from his bonds and was now driving a car across a desert while shots were fired at him from a helicopter overhead.

The telephone went on ringing.

Mrs Frobisher rose, went into the hall, and took the receiver off the hook. Her hero, now wounded, was staggering on foot across a small river when she returned to her seat. On the far bank, his mistress was waiting, holding a chestnut horse by the bridle. The camera cut to the helicopter from which guns protruded.

Beatrice had always been a nuisance. She'd been cleverer than Mavis – and prettier, too, with boys hanging about her since she was fourteen. She'd got herself pregnant and had to get married, but hadn't seemed to mind the loss of her chances for betterment. Beatrice, who had not wanted one, had been assured of a university place, while Mavis, who sought advancement, had struggled to pass her nursing exams. She'd crossed swords more than once with ward sisters. Private nursing had been a haven, for she'd soon discovered which patients would pay with gifts for extra attention and which would accept good care as merely their right, so that it was not worth taking trouble for them.

Beatrice, getting in touch with her like this, must want something. It could only be money, for what else had Mavis that Beatrice might envy?

The hero, on her screen, struggled out of the river towards the outstretched hand of his mistress. Guns in the helicopter fired, and at that moment the screen flickered and went black.

It was not a power failure. The soft light from the table lamp beside Mrs Frobisher's chair burnt on. She rose and pressed various buttons on the set. She hit it and swore, but it remained dark.

The play had ten more minutes to run. Her hero was far from safe. She felt sure that in the end he would escape, but would his mistress survive, too, and how? Were the terrorists caught? The interruption, at such a tense time in the story, enraged Mrs Frobisher. It was Beatrice's fault – if she hadn't telephoned, the set would not have gone wrong. All their lives, Beatrice had frustrated her sister and taken what was Mavis's due – her looks, her ability to do well at school, the attention, before he died, of their father. And now she had spoiled the perfection of Mrs Frobisher's special evening.

Mavis stood in front of the television set shaking her fists. Her face went red. The pounding continued inside her head.

As the picture, after a short break due to a transmitter fault, returned to her set, Mrs Frobisher was unable to see it, for she lay unconscious on the floor.

She lay there all night.

In the morning, the taxi that was to take her to the airport arrived. When the hall porter telephoned to tell her and there was no reply, he came up himself to knock at her door. In the end, he opened it with his master key.

Mrs Frobisher's blood pressure, never tested, had, unknown to her, long been high. She had eaten and drunk too well in her year as a widow, and rage and frustration had caused it to soar, bringing on a stroke.

Her eyes opened as she was lifted to a stretcher. She opened her mouth to speak, but no sound emerged. She tried to sit up, but she could not move.

Two days later, Beatrice came to the hospital where Mrs

Frobisher, unable to ask for private attention, lay in a public ward. Though it was years since they had met, Mrs Frobisher recognised her at once, despite greying hair and a red weatherbeaten complexion. There was that something about her – an aura. Mrs Frobisher knew the word as she stared at the hated face. It was joy. Beatrice was a happy woman.

'Poor Mavis. How terribly sad,' Beatrice said, taking Mrs Frobisher's unresponsive hand which lay neatly on top of the sheet, convenient for the nurse who would take her pulse. 'No wonder you couldn't answer the telephone after we were cut off. If only I'd realised, you'd have been found much sooner. Fancy the television still on in the morning, making a terrible noise. But don't worry. I'll see that you're taken care of. I was trying to find you to tell you that Hugh – my eldest son – that his wife has had twins. You're a great-aunt, Mavis. Isn't that nice?' She squeezed Mavis's hand. 'I'm sure you can understand what I'm saying,' her voice went on. 'We've been out of touch too long. Families should stick together. You were hard to trace. You're moved about a lot since you did your training.'

Mavis's eyes looked up at the ceiling. She heard and understood every word, but she could not reply.

'Still, you're not short of money, are you? The doctor thinks you have a good chance of getting much better, but you'll always need looking after. I'll take you home with me when you can travel.' Again, Beatrice patted the motionless hand. 'I'm your next-of-kin, after all.'

THE
MOUSE
WILL
PLAY

Mrs Bellew surveyed her neighbours through the large picture window of her living-room at Number 17 Windsor Crescent. Across the road, the fair young man with the beard was getting into his Sierra, briefcase already placed in the rear. Two small children and their mother watched him leave, all waving. Up and down the street, other morning rituals were taking place. Some husbands sprang into their cars and drove away without a visible farewell; at several houses both partners – you could not be certain they were married nowadays – left home daily. Soon the Crescent would settle into its weekday mode as the children left for school, the younger ones with their mothers, others alone, a few in groups. Then the toddlers would come out to play – a few, to Mrs Bellew's horror, in the street. Mrs Bellew's own son had never played in the street.

She was, as far as she could tell, the only senior resident on the estate, and she had been accustomed to a very different life.

Mrs Bellew's husband had died a year ago, suddenly, of a heart attack while in Singapore on business. Until then, hers had been a busy, fulfilling existence, acting as his hostess as his own business expanded. Frequently, guests who were in fact his customers were entertained at Springhill Lodge to dinner, or even for an entire weekend, with a round of golf or a swim in the Bellews' kidney-shaped azure pool. Deals were mooted and concluded around the Bellews' mahogany dining-table while Mrs Bellew and the visiting wife chatted of this and that in the drawing-room and the hired Cordon Bleu cook cleared up in the kitchen. Mrs Bellew planned the menus but never prepared them.

Occasionally, in her turn, Mrs Bellew travelled abroad with

Sam and was, herself, entertained, but not on that last journey.

And now it had ended, with Sam heavily in debt.

After his death their son had decided that his mother must be resettled in a small, easy-to-manage house on a bus route and within walking distance of a general store, for she would not be able to afford a car. Thus it was that she had been uprooted from her large house with its two acres of garden in Surrey and despatched to this commuter village where she knew no one.

She could catch the train to London easily, her son had pointed out, to visit him and her grandchildren, and it was not far from his own weekend cottage in the Cotswolds.

Mrs Bellew would have agreed that the distance was not great if she could have been whisked there in Sam's Rover, or even in her own Polo, but there was no way of getting to Fettingham from Windsor Crescent by public transport without two changes of bus involving a long wait between them, so she stayed away. Giles had said he would often fetch her for a visit, and this had happened once, but Mrs Bellew had not enjoyed the weekend spent in the damp stone cottage which Giles and his wife were renovating. While they spent their time decorating or in the pub, Mrs Bellew was expected to mind the children and to cook the lunch. Chilled and miserable, Mrs Bellew was thankful to return to 17 Windsor Crescent, with its central heating.

But her days were long and solitary. She kept to a routine of housework, as she had done throughout her life before she had anyone to help her with it, but she could not dust and polish all day long. Meals were dull. She missed not Sam so much as what went with him – the bustle of his life and its purpose, as well as the comforts she had now grown used to, which his money bought; and she felt bitter anger at his failure to leave her properly provided for. Now she was no one, just an elderly woman living in a modern house – one of the smallest on the estate – among other anonymous houses in an area where there was no sense of community. Mrs

Bellew did not require the services of Meals on Wheels or the old people's day centre. It did not occur to her that she could have usefully lent her aid and experience to either of these organisations.

When Sam died, the deal that he had been negotiating had been intended to put his business back in profit, but meanwhile his credit was extended, funds borrowed and despatched, like Antonio's argosies, to earn reward, and like those, some were lost. He had pledged his main insurance on this last project.

'You've got to face it, Mother. Father was a speculator and his gamble came unstuck,' Giles had told her sternly. 'If he hadn't died, he'd have been in serious trouble.' It had taken all Giles's own considerable ingenuity to rescue what he had from the collapse of his father's ventures, and he had been unable to spare his mother the discovery that the old man had died as he had lived, dangerously, in bed with a young Chinese woman.

Now, nothing broke the monotony of Mrs Bellew's days. No Sam, red-faced and cheerful, returned with tales of successfully concluded deals.

How many of such stories had been lies? Like his protests that he missed her when he went abroad?

These thoughts were unendurable. Mrs Bellew would not entertain them and instead she concentrated on her neighbours. Which of them, superficially so self-satisfied and smug, with their rising incomes and, in many cases, their second car and salary, were living lies?

Wondering about them, Mrs Bellew began to notice things. There was the dark blue Audi which left Number 32 each morning at half-past seven and was sometimes absent for several days at a time. One day she saw the owner, a man in his late thirties, carrying an overnight bag to the car. Like Sam's, his job obviously involved travel. She watched the house while he was gone and saw a green Porsche parked outside it until very late at night. Mrs Bellew soon identified the driver, a young man with fair curly hair.

The cat's away, she thought, and that mouse is playing.

She noticed other things: an impatient, angry mother cuffing her small son about the head as they walked along the road bound for the nursery school; older children on roller-skates who swung on trees that overhung the pavement, breaking branches and skating off, giggling, before they were discovered. She began to keep a record, writing down the habits of her neighbours in a notebook. She knew no one's name, but within the compass of her vision from her window she observed which wife was visited by her mother every Tuesday; who was called on by a man in a Triumph Spitfire every Wednesday afternoon; who cleaned and polished – such women were seen in pinafores cleaning windows – and who employed someone to help them. She recognised her neighbours in the supermarket in the local town and saw how they laid out their money: who bought frozen food in bulk; who spent vast sums on pet food; who was frugal. Walking along the street on winter afternoons, she could see through the large lighted windows into rooms where women spent hours eating chocolates and watching television.

Some of them had secrets, and she began to learn them.

Mrs Bellew prepared the letters carefully, cutting the words from a magazine and pasting them on to plain sheets of Basildon Bond. She planned every operation with the same meticulousness that had made her dinner parties so success-ful, choosing each victim when she was confident of her facts, and finding out their names from the voters' list.

She wrote to the social security office about the child she saw cuffed in the street, and soon had the satisfaction of seeing an official-looking woman calling at the house. Later the child's mother went away. The window-cleaner – almost her only contact apart from the postman and the milkman – told her that the father, left alone with the child and a job to do, could not cope and the small boy had been taken into care.

'A shame, I call it,' said the window-cleaner. 'Been knock-ing the kid about, it seems – the mother had. Girls don't know they're born, these days. But I don't know – poor little lad. It makes you think.'

Mrs Bellew agreed that indeed it did. She was surprised at the outcome of her intervention; still, the boy would be looked after now.

She did not fear discovery; the recipients of her letters would not broadcast their own guilt. On trips to London, which were cheap because she used her old person's rail card though she did not like to think that she looked old, Mrs Bellew mailed her serpent missives. Then she would indulge herself in tea at Harrods before catching her train home. She would prepare the next offensive whilst awaiting the outcome of the last.

One Wednesday, the husband of the woman visited by the Triumph Spitfire driver came home unexpectedly. He caught his wife *in flagrante* with the young man from the estate agent's who had sold the house to them, and went straight round to see the young man's wife who had also been ignorant of what was going on. Eventually, both couples separated. Four school-age children were involved, two in each family.

Mrs Bellew soon had the interest of watching new neighbours move into Number 25.

The window-cleaner expressed dismay that there had been so much unhappiness on the estate lately. He'd heard that Mrs Fisher's mother, who came to see her daughter every Tuesday, had been asked by her son-in-law to restrict her visits because it was time Mary Fisher pulled herself together and stood on her own feet after her fourth miscarriage. She ought to get a job, her husband had told her, and stop brooding. She'd told the window-cleaner all about it when he went round and found her weeping bitterly.

Mrs Bellew was surprised to hear about the miscarriages. Her letter to Mr Fisher had mentioned his wife's childlike dependency on her mother and suggested she was idle. To the window-cleaner, she opined that sitting about indulging in self-pity was not constructive.

Mrs Bellew went on a summer visit to her son and his family in their cottage. This began as a better experience than the last; she sat in a deckchair for an hour reading *Good Housekeeping*, but was expected to cook the Sunday lunch while her son and his wife met their friends, fellow weekenders, in the local pub. The children were delighted as their grandmother had been left a leg of lamb to roast; on other Sundays a precooked pie, bought from the local butcher, was their lot. It was a grandmother's pleasure to cherish her family, Giles's wife stated firmly; her own mother liked nothing better than to cook for any number.

'Get her to do it, then,' said Mrs Bellew, demanding to be taken home early.

She was in time to see an ambulance drawn up outside the Fishers' house, but she did not learn what had happened until the next visit of the window-cleaner. He told her without any prompting.

Mrs Fisher had tried to kill herself. She had swallowed various pills, drunk a lot of sherry, and gone to bed with a plastic bag over her head. Woozy with the sherry and the drugs, she had used a bag already perforated for safety and so she had survived, though she was deeply unconscious when discovered by her next-door neighbour. Mary's mother had known that Tim Fisher, an enthusiastic golfer, was playing a double round that day. Unable to reach her daughter on the telephone, she called the neighbour. Tim had come back from the golf course grumbling about neurotic women.

There was a satisfactory amount of coming and going to please Mrs Bellew for several days after this. She knew that Tim Fisher would never show her original letter to a soul, and she did not make the mistake of following it with a second. She had a new target lined up in her sights now.

In the local supermarket, she had noticed the woman from Number 43 buying gin and sherry – such a lot of it, several bottles every week. The woman's face was flushed; she was one of those who watched television in the afternoons.

Neatly and painstakingly, Mrs Bellew cut the words from

Home and Gardens. The paper was pleasanter to work with than ordinary newsprint, which made one's fingers inky.

Does your wife take her empty gin bottles to the bottle bank? Mrs Bellew enquired, in careful composition. Her messages were always terse, just enough to sow disquiet.

Dick Pearson showed his wife the letter when he tackled her. There were tears and recriminations as Barbara confessed to feeling useless and lonely while the children, both now teenagers, were at school all day. Dick didn't want her to go to work; his was an income adequate for their needs and a mother's place was in the home; besides, she had no proper qualifications.

Now he felt shame. Busy chasing orders for his firm, which dealt in manufacturing equipment, he had failed to think of her, even to talk to her when he was at home. But for the anonymous letter, he was thinking, she could have ended up like Mary Fisher.

Had there been a letter there?

He could not ask, but both he and Barbara wondered.

Mary Fisher left the hospital at last. When she came home, her mother resumed her visits, and Barbara Pearson, trying to redeem herself, also took to calling round. The two women began to discuss launching a joint enterprise, catering for private parties – even, perhaps, business lunches in the local town. Both were skilful cooks.

The idea burgeoned. They had cards printed and put notices in the local paper. Then they distributed leaflets.

'That woman at Number 17,' said Barbara. 'She always looks so elegant, but she must be getting on. I wouldn't mind betting she'd appreciate a bit of help when she entertains. And she might have well-off friends who'd use us, too. Let's go and see her.'

Mary, wrapped in her own misery, had barely noticed Mrs Bellew. She thought she looked stuck-up.

She went to call, with Barbara.

Mrs Bellew, unaccustomed, now, to company, recognised them both and at first she did not want to let them in. But

Barbara said they needed her advice, and so, reluctantly, she admitted them.

In her elegant living-room, Barbara described their plan.

Mrs Bellew said she never entertained now, but had done a lot during her husband's lifetime. She waxed eloquent about *milles feuilles* and chicken suprême.

'You should join us,' Barbara enthused. 'Your experience would be invaluable.'

Six months ago, Mrs Bellew might have considered it; she knew all about well-chosen, balanced menus. But now she was already wondering how she could bring them down, for she had learned to hate success.

Mary had problems concentrating these days. Her attention wandered, and she picked up a magazine from the coffee table in front of her, leafing idly through it. Mrs Bellew saw what she was doing, rose swiftly and removed the magazine from her grasp as if she was a child touching a forbidden object. Without a word of explanation, she put it in a drawer and soon the interview had ended.

'Wasn't that odd of her?' said Mary as they left. 'But it was rude of me, I suppose, to look at it when we were meant to be talking. Sorry.'

'She was ruder,' Barbara said.

'There were holes in it,' said Mary.

'Holes?'

'Sort of like windows. Pieces cut from different pages.'

'Recipes cut out?'

'No. Bits in the middle of a story,' Mary said.

Barbara had seen the letter sent to Dick. He alone of all the recipients in Windsor Crescent had shown it to its subject.

Next Friday, Mrs Bellew went, as usual, to the supermarket in the local town. Barbara was also there. She had often seen the older woman buying her one packet of butter, her small portion of frozen food, and had vaguely pitied her. Now, she was curious; she'd thought a lot about the mutilated magazine. Whoever had written that letter to Dick had either seen her buying drink or disposing of her empties and so was local, though the letter had had a London postmark. So many small tragedies had happened lately in the area; other people might have been receiving letters too.

Watching Mrs Bellew study prices on some chops, Barbara selected two pairs of tights she did not want. She scarcely thought about it as she passed behind Mrs Bellew who was stooping forward, peering into the freezer chest, her wicker basket gaping on her arm. Barbara, not even worrying in case she was observed herself, dropped the tights into it, and moved on.

They might not be discovered. Nothing might be done about it if they were, especially if Mrs Bellew proclaimed her ignorance of how they got there.

Far off among the cereals, Barbara missed the small commotion at the door as Mrs Bellew was led away for questioning.

THE
BREASTS
OF
APHRODITE

A group of tamarisk trees clustered together in the coarse grass between the bungalow block and the sea, which today was whipped into small stiff waves with narrow white crests. At sunset, the sturdy pollarded trunks of the trees stood out black against the pinky-gold sky and the shining water, their branches entwined like interwoven limbs topped with feathery foliage. Several hundred yards from the grey pebbled shore a fishing boat trawled its nets, the vessel pitching and tossing among the hollows of the vivid blue sea. There was not a cloud in the wide pale sky, and today the humped outline of the Turkish coast, only ten miles distant, was just a grey haze on the horizon.

On loungers outside the low white building where each apartment tapered off from its neighbour to give an illusion of privacy, Lionel and Eileen Blunt lay toasting in the sun, Lionel in shorts, Eileen in a trim one-piece suit which to some extent restrained her generous curves. Behind them their bungalow was orderly, all trace of their picnic lunch tidied away, no clutter of possessions strewn about the cool bedroom where the twin beds reposed pristine, their fresh white sheets undisturbed since the maid's earlier attentions.

'Fancy! No blankets!' Eileen had marvelled when they arrived two days ago.

'Too hot, dear. You'll not need one,' said Lionel in a worldly way.

Before making the reservation he'd closely questioned colleagues at work, taking every precaution against booking them into an unsuitable hotel: you heard dire tales of holiday disaster, and Eileen would not take in her stride any imperfection in the arrangements. Why should she? A holiday was for pleasure and refreshment.

The Blunts usually went to the Lake District or Cornwall each September. As their circumstances improved over the years, with Lionel secure though no longer rising in the hierarchy at the bank, and Eileen safe in the county planning office, they had progressed from the bed-and-breakfast accommodation of early years to comfortable three-star hotels with bathrooms en suite and usually tea-making facilities too. Eileen had resisted the lure of foreign travel: something to do with their honeymoon in Majorca where she had not liked the plumbing nor the night-club in their hotel, which on their one visit after dinner had given her a headache.

They'd married late, both thirty-five at the time. Lionel, until then, had been the support of a widowed and delicate mother, and Eileen, one way and the other, had somehow missed out on marriage. They'd met, prosaically enough, when Eileen had enquired about opening a high interest deposit account at the bank and Lionel had taken immense pains to advise her wisely.

Now they had been married ten years, and Lionel, to surprise her, had come home one February day with a bundle of brochures and a tentative booking made for two weeks in a Greek holiday paradise where, in your own private bungalow, you could forget the world amid palm trees and bougainvillea. The hotel had been recommended by the assistant branch manager at the bank, who had been there the year before and had allayed Lionel's fears about any defects Eileen might not enjoy.

'I'd thought St Mawes this year,' had been Eileen's response. There were palm trees there, if Lionel was so set on them.

'We should go abroad, while we're in our prime,' said Lionel stoutly. 'One day we'll be too old.' And won't have been anywhere, he added, silently. 'We'd be sure of the sun,' he told her. 'That would set you up before winter, dear. You know you've been peaky lately.'

They'd both had flu, a nasty variety leaving them coughing and aching for weeks afterwards.

'Well, if you'd like it, dear, then of course we'll go,' said Eileen. She was fond of Lionel, who had caused her not a moment's anxiety since he rescued her from spinsterhood.

The decision made, she applied herself to preparations for their expedition with her usual efficiency, laying in extra supplies of anti-mosquito lotion, antiseptic cream, sting remedies and bismuth mixture.

'You'd think we were going to Timbuctoo,' said Lionel at work, feeling a trifle disloyal as he revealed that the spare room bed at 3, The Crescent was already neatly covered in travel necessities laid out for packing. Eileen had made herself two new sundresses; she liked sewing and did *gros point* tapestry in the evenings while Lionel watched television. His mother had knitted a lot; he liked to see a woman work creatively with her hands.

There were no little Blunts. None had arrived, and since Eileen never referred to the matter, Lionel concealed his own disappointment. They never discussed such subjects and even now, after moments of intimacy, were both embarrassed by the inevitable loss of dignity involved. Eileen, in particular, attached great importance to outward appearances and was always so neat; there was never a thing out of place at home, everything washed up immediately after use and put away, cushions plumped up and newspaper tidily folded. So that now even the holiday bungalow was in apple-pie trim.

It wasn't like that at the Dawsons.

You could have knocked Lionel down with a feather when there, in the queue at Gatwick, stood Bill and June Dawson, he in jeans and anorak, she in a pink cotton jumpsuit, her unruly mane of curly, copper-coloured hair cascading down her back.

The Dawsons, with their three children, had moved to The Crescent two years ago. Their furniture was a hotch-potch collection acquired from junk shops over the years; watching them unload it from a self-drive hired van one Saturday, Eileen had felt quite ashamed on their behalf of its shoddiness. The children, who usually had dirty faces and often snivelling noses, were plump, happy and confident; never shy.

'Their manners are atrocious,' Eileen had said, when, after debating the matter because the newcomers were so shabby and down-at-heel in appearance, she had gone over to speak words of welcome as became the senior wife in the group of six identical houses. She found the children all sitting round the kitchen table eating bread and jam with no plates, just in their fingers, which were grubby to say the least.

Lionel, an only child, thought it sounded rather fun. As time went on he had made friends with the young Dawsons, mended their bicycles – all bought third, fourth, or fifth hand and not checked for safety before use – and, when they went on holiday or to see their grandparents, he looked after their hamsters and rabbits. The Dawsons had gone camping in France every year since their marriage – sheer folly, Eileen thought, when they still lacked a decent three-piece suite and the children wore clothes bought at jumble sales. Eileen was an excellent cook and she often baked jam tarts or ginger-bread men especially for the Dawson children, whom she suspected of being fed solely on chips and baked beans. She had wondered if June would be offended if she were to make the small girl a dress as a Christmas present; the child, who was four, always wore her brothers' outgrown and patched trousers and old felted sweaters. Lionel's main recreation was making models of men o'war throughout the ages, and both the small boys were intrigued by his work though their sister was too young to show much interest. They often came round to examine the construction in progress, leaving behind a considerable trail of dropped sweet papers and, it seemed to Lionel, an echo of laughter.

But now here the Dawsons stood, in line for the flight the Blunts were catching, and alone, without their children!

'That is who I think it is, isn't it?' Eileen whispered, fumbling for her spectacles.

'Oh yes,' Lionel said. No one but June could have hair that colour, tumbling in such sweet disorder down her back.

'They never said!' Eileen's tone was accusing.

'Where are the children?' wondered Lionel.

'Well, they won't be going to the Bella Vista,' said Eileen dismissively. It was far too expensive for the impecunious Dawsons. Bill was a freelance photographer and how they managed to keep up their payments on the house in The Crescent Eileen did not know.

But indeed they were! Lionel could make out the labels hung on Bill's camera bag.

'Surprise, surprise!' said June, who detected no reservation in the tone of either Blunt neighbour as they uttered cries of greeting and recognition.

It seemed that her father had won the holiday in a sweepstake on the Derby and had presented it to them for a second honeymoon. By coincidence, the hotel allotted as the prize was this one so carefully researched by Lionel months before, and the only date for which it was available was now.

'We can lose each other out there,' Eileen decided as they checked in their luggage and were given adjacent seats across the aisle of the plane.

But it hadn't worked out like that. Their bungalows adjoined, and much time was spent spread out among the oleanders and hibiscus bushes soaking up the sun within a few yards of one another.

And June lay there topless!

Eileen was appalled. Apart from themselves, there was the gnarled old gardener who moved about adjusting the range of the sprinklers which daily soaked all the vegetation. Even Lionel did not know where to look when June spoke to him, as she often did. He tried not to notice her small, high breasts with the amazing, huge dark nipples. You'd think with all those kids they'd be different somehow. He began dreaming about them at night, even moaning once in his sleep.

Eileen woke him at once.

'Sh, Lionel,' she admonished. 'You were making a noise. Bill and June will think—' but she would not say what they would think if they heard these abandoned sounds through their wide-open windows. She pressed her own lips tightly together when Lionel was overwhelmed with ardour. It would never do for Bill and June even to think they'd heard anything remotely 'like that', and she hid her own head in the pillow when it became clear that the other couple were turning to good account June's father's gift.

'There'll be another mouth to feed next year, you mark my words,' Eileen declared, and even Lionel thought that would be excessive, costs being what they were.

'Why don't you strip off too?' said June on the third morning.

'I'd be ashamed,' said Eileen austerely.

'Why be coy about your body?' said June. 'You'll feel so free, and it's only natural, after all.'

Eileen blushed furiously.

'I'm not slim like you,' she answered.

It was true. Looking at them, you would think Eileen was the mother of three, not the lithe young woman whose skin was already the colour of honey. Eileen suspected she lay about half-naked in their untidy garden whenever the summer sun shone instead of cleaning the house or preparing a wholesome meal. Still, in spite of her disapproval, even Eileen could not help warming to the girl whose fecklessness was in such contrast to her own capability.

That first night the two couples entered the restaurant together and were placed at neighbouring tables by wide windows which were open to the terrace on these balmy nights. Subsequently, the Blunts ate early after a drink in the bar which overlooked the huge blue-tiled swimming-pool. The Dawsons had brought their own duty-free liquor which they consumed on their bungalow verandah. The Blunts had usually almost finished their meal by the time the younger couple arrived, both rather tiddly by this time and with June's appearance drawing warm smiles of welcome from Spiro, their waiter.

It was Bill who suggested that for part of the holiday they should share the hire of a car. In that way they could explore the island properly without being herded along on a tour.

There were archaeological sites to inspect and natural beau-
ties too, valleys and gorges of renown; and they could seek out
hidden isolated beaches. Lionel, who was apprehensive about
driving on the wrong side of the road since he had never done
it, leaped at the idea, aware of how such freedom could
enlarge their explorations. The costs for a week, shared out,
would not be enormous, and Bill could do all the driving.

In their rented Fiat they visited an ancient excavated city
set on a hill amid pines and fragrant herbs. They entered tiny
white-washed churches whose ornate interiors were redolent
with the scent of incense. In one village an old lady beckoned
them into her house and displayed photographs of seaman
sons and indicated her own bed, high against one wall. She
gave them sprigs of myrtle and offered them bottles of oil, and
they left her three crumpled fifty-drachmae notes, Lionel
wondering if they had given her enough. They ate at tavernas
by the sea or had picnic lunches on the beach, buying huge
tomatoes, fresh cucumbers and fruit and rather dry rolls,
drinking the rough local wine. And they found deserted coves
where June stripped off all her clothes and hedonistically
bathed naked in the warm sea.

Eileen, by this time, had begun to slip the straps of her
bathing dress over her broad, fleshy shoulders as she lay on
the sand, a straw hat over her face, sleeping off the wine
which seemed to pack a hidden punch, or perhaps it was the
air that made her feel as if she was floating away; she hadn't
slept so much and so deeply for years. When the others were
all in the sea, she at last daringly pulled her top right down
and June was correct: she did feel a sense of liberation. She
intended to restore herself to decency before the swimmers
returned, but she dozed off. Waking, blushing, she heard
Bill's camera click.

'You shouldn't, Bill,' Lionel rebuked.

'Why not? Eileen's got breasts like Aphrodite,' said Bill.
'What's it matter between friends?'

But Lionel was worried and fell silent. He was sure that Bill
would display his holidays snaps around The Crescent when

they returned; Eileen's nakedness would be revealed to all their neighbours. What he did about June was his own affair; she was a pagan soul, and shameless; but Eileen was different.

She altered, however, after that episode, and in the evening suggested they should invite June and Bill to drinks on their patio before dinner. She made Lionel go with her to the small supermarket near the hotel and they bought beer, ouzo and cheese biscuits, although until now she had refused even to sample ouzo.

'Aphrodite was the goddess of love, you know,' Bill said, toasting her.

Eileen simpered. Yes, that was the word; and Lionel shuddered as he drank his beer – he liked to know where he was with his drinks – and proffered peanuts.

They all dined at the same time that night, and afterwards strolled on the shingly beach. June led Lionel down to the water's edge and began throwing stones out to sea, shaking back her mane after each toss, dabbling her toes in the phosphorescence at the water's edge, her sandals kicked off and abandoned, bare feet impervious to the pebbles. When they turned at last the other pair were nowhere to be seen.

'Bill's seducing Eileen,' June said, giggling. 'He fancies her something rotten, you know. He'll be calling on Bacchus for help.'

'You shouldn't talk like that,' Lionel reproved, 'I know you're only joking, but some people might think you meant it.'

'Believe me, it's true,' said June. 'Why shouldn't they have some fun? And why shouldn't we?'

Lionel knew about wife-swapping, of course; it had even been alleged to take place on the estate where The Crescent was situated; keys were flung into some central pool and general post was played. But such activities were not for him and Eileen and he was shocked.

'What nonsense you talk,' he said, and walked off along the beach. 'Come on, June,' he called.

He was anxious to return to his wife in case June's incredible words should somehow prove to be true, but he did not want to leave her alone and it took him some time to persuade her. She was in a silly mood and clung to him, pressing her slim shape against him, hanging on to his arm. Her hair floated against his face and across his mouth; it smelled fragrantly of lemon shampoo. When at last they reached the bungalow block and he left her on her own verandah, she still clung to him and fastened her mouth to his; she was insatiable. Lionel hoped he had no grass stains on his trousers; they had moved off the hard stony beach into the shelter of a clump of hibiscus. He had to unwind her arms from around his neck and push her towards her own room. Where the light was on, no doubt attracting mosquitoes.

Eileen, more sensibly, had turned theirs off; he could hear her evenly breathing as, freshly showered, she lay beneath the sheet. He showered too; June's scent was all over him.

He did not see the footprints until the next morning. Clear and sharp, in talcum powder, they led one way, from the Dawsons' verandah on to his and Eileen's, and they were made by his wife's size six feet; June's feet were several sizes smaller.

Lionel did not, at first, accept the message. He knew that June spread chaos wherever she went and no doubt talcum powder too: but Eileen didn't. He brooded about the trail as they drove to Lindos after breakfast. Bill's camera lay on the back seat of the car; what other exposures had he made?

They parked as near to the beach as they could, then trudged through the busy streets of the small town to the citadel. June toyed with the idea of riding a donkey but it cost money, and Eileen, who would have liked to avoid the climb, felt she could not be the only one to do so.

'We'll swim later,' Bill said. The beach was already filling with exposed bodies beneath umbrellas. They'd have lunch, they decided, at one of the tavernas where vines shaded the tables.

The ascent was steep, past white-washed buildings and

importunate shop-keepers, and, higher up, vendors of embroidered tablecloths and lace mats whose wares were spread at the side of the high, narrow path. Eileen stopped to admire some fine examples and was subjected to a tirade of sales patter in Greek and fragmented English.

'Your work is as fine as that,' Lionel declared loyally. His own lapse had to be erased, and so must all evidence of anything Eileen had done, which would not be easy since proof lay in Bill's expensive camera. His mind closed on a vision of what might have passed between the pair while June kept him occupied; had the Dawsons colluded to lead him and Eileen astray or was June just seeking vengeance of her own? And what about Eileen herself? How to account for her actions? Of course, she was drunk on not only ouzo and wine but also the diet of myth and legend they had absorbed, and it was all his fault, for it was he who had wished to forsake safe St Mawes and seek the Aegean sun.

At the entrance to the site they paid their fee, took their tickets and began the final climb. June went first, her long slim legs, tanned brown now, scissoring their way. Eileen, panting a little in the heat, followed, and then Bill, who wore his camera slung round his neck. Lionel came last in the file of modern pilgrims.

'Be careful,' called Lionel, for the steps were steep and there was no barrier to protect you from the sheer drop at the side.

As he spoke, Bill unhooked his camera to fiddle with some adjustment of the lens. He was going to use it, snap poor Eileen's fat rump as she lumbered upwards.

Lionel spoke to him sharply, distracting him, and the moment passed, but in that instant he made a plan and his chance to carry it out came when they descended. Bill had taken several exposures on the acropolis; he had photographed the bay where allegedly St Paul had landed, and the town below. As they went down the path again, in the same order, Bill, as if to plan, was holding the camera in his hands. Lionel reached out to jerk it from his grasp; one twitch was all it would need to send the thing hurtling down to the rocks below, where it would smash and the film inside would be destroyed.

But Bill's reactions were quick to protect his precious possession. Saving it, he stumbled, and his left hand shot out towards Eileen. She lost her balance straight away, gave one shrill cry and, in a second, had taken the fall Lionel had intended for the camera.

'Oh, my God!' Bill was the first to scramble down the rest of the stairs and make his way to the mewing heap that was Eileen as she lay, legs twisted beneath her, in the shadow of the citadel.

The shock was too much for her. She died of that, not her injuries.

After the funeral Bill gave Lionel the photographs he had taken of her that last night, a sheet draped round her like a chiton, Aphrodite garbed.

Was that all that had happened between them? Now Lionel would never know. He hoped that decency alone would prevent Bill from showing any of the other exposures round The Crescent, but in any case, as soon as it was possible, he sold the house and asked the bank to arrange a transfer.

He moved to Manchester, where two years later he married a widow he met on a cruise.

THE
LUCK
OF
THE
DRAW

She'd been looking forward to it for weeks, ever since the letter arrived.

She'd bought the two raffle tickets, one for herself and one for Micky, from a woman who came to the door when she was staying with him. Ten pence each, they'd been, and now she'd won the first prize, a cruise to the Mediterranean. The ticket and other documents would follow, said the letter, and she must be in possession of a passport. No special inoculations or vaccinations were necessary, and cheques could be cashed on board.

She'd rung Micky at once to see if he'd also won a prize, but he hadn't. He couldn't have gone, anyway, he said; business was too demanding. Micky was her nephew who ran a used car business outside Glasgow and lived in a small grey bungalow overlooking the Clyde. His wife had departed some years ago, taking the children, and this saddened Carmen for they were the only family she ever saw. Micky's father, her elder brother, was dead, and her own sons had left long ago, one for Australia and the other for Singapore. She never heard from either, which was hard to accept after all she had done to bring them up alone. Things hadn't been easy for widows then, not like it was for single mothers today when the best way to get your own place was to become pregnant and be housed by the council.

Micky didn't seem to have any regrets. He was out a lot and had a series of women friends, some of whom Carmen had met. He took her out to dinner at least once during her annual visit, and last time they'd had lunch one Sunday at a grand granite hotel where he seemed to know most of the other clients. Carmen managed to make them laugh at the jokes she told; she'd always been the life and soul of the party.

215

'What a character,' she'd hear them say, and would smile. She liked attention.

It seemed that Micky was used to the high life, but for Carmen such occasions were treats to remember when she went back to the council flat in Southampton where she had lived for years.

She liked the sea. She'd spent all her life near it, so going on a cruise was certain to be a success, and it was free! She planned her wardrobe with care, for there would be smart dinners, all that: it would be like old times when she used to dress up to go to the palais.

That was where she met Tom, in a Paul Jones. They didn't have such things these days; you grabbed whoever you fancied to dance with but then didn't touch them at all which seemed to Carmen a funny way of going about things. Tom wasn't her first, by any means, though he never knew that, but he was different because he wanted to marry her and in those days to be married was very important. It conferred status, meant you wouldn't have been passed over if all the men got killed like they did last time, leaving so many girls on the shelf. Tom was so smart in his bell-bottoms and square rig. He was thin and fair, with blue eyes, and he was twenty-two when his ship was torpedoed on convoy duty in the Mediterranean.

Billy was born two weeks after she had heard that he was dead.

Things were tough then. Carmen was still living with her mother, and she soon got a factory job, working shifts, so that one of them was always there with the baby. When Billy was two she met Jock, who was Stuart's father. They couldn't get married because he had a wife in Aberdeen, or so he said.

That was the beginning of the black days. Her mother was killed, not by a bomb but by slipping on an icy road and being run over by a bus whose driver had no chance to stop. After that it was a struggle to keep the boys, but she'd done it, working nights in a club, and she'd always done a bit on the side. She'd been choosy, though, and over the years some of the men became regulars, real pals, bringing her presents from their trips and being fatherly to the boys before they were packed off to bed when it was time for business. She'd been soft enough to get really fond of one of them, Stavros, who called whenever his ship was in port. She'd woven a dream about him, imagining herself wafted to one of those Greek islands he'd told her about, where the sun always shone and the sea was blue and olives hung heavy on ancient trees.

He was married, of course. He showed her snaps of his wife and his sons, first two, then a third, then four. He was generous to her, though, and for nearly ten years looked nowhere else for the comforts of shore. She missed him when he stopped coming, and for a while worked as a maid in a hotel, living in. The boys had left home by then and Carmen saw no point in keeping a place on just for herself. But after she entertained one man friend too many in the hotel she lost her job. For some years she rented a room and found what work she could: bar-maiding, selling sweets in a cinema, helping out at a newsagent's, picking up employment here and there, and also men.

Carmen's real name was Doris Watkins, but she became Carmen when she started in the clubs. It suited her dark looks and she said that she came from Brazil and was the illegitimate daughter of a diplomat, though the truth was that her father had been a travelling salesman who had left her mother when Doris was five. Doris had adored him and she wept for him for years. It was only after her mother's death that she discovered he had had several wives and had been sent to prison for bigamy. Since then, she had told her invented story so often that she had begun to believe it.

It was difficult, these days, to find company but occasionally, even now, there was someone she met in a pub who came home with her. Mostly, though, she had to be satisfied with having an occasional drink bought for her. She went to bingo because there were prizes, but too many of the players were women; she did like a man or two about the place. She'd enjoy telling her fellow bingo players about the cruise when she returned; some of them were quite spiteful in their remarks – jealous, of course, because she so often won – but now they'd really have something to gripe about.

Carmen had never before been further south than the Isle of Wight, but she admitted to no fears as she set off with a new suitcase, larger than the one she used for her trips to Scotland. She went by taxi to the station to catch her train for the port of embarkation and several neighbours watched her go. She waved triumphantly, then inserted her stout body into the comfortable seat. She used taxis when she returned from the pub a bit worse for wear, but otherwise, except during her visits to Micky, she never went in a car.

This was the life!

'Of course I've travelled a lot,' she told the driver, practising what she would say on board. Carmen's method of compensating for her own inadequacies was to attack. She asked a man on the platform to lift her case into the train for her, and another to take it down when she reached her destination, and both instantly obeyed. A second taxi swept her to the dock and there a friendly man bore her luggage away as she joined a short queue at passport control, handing over her new passport. A smiling young woman directed her to a bus which took her out to the ship and Carmen stepped confidently up the gangway. She'd been aboard ships before, though usually clandestinely.

Her cabin was on a lower deck. It was very small, with two bunks and a tiny cubicle containing a shower and lavatory. There was no porthole. That was a pity; she would have liked to look at the sea. Carmen felt a cool breeze on her head: the air-conditioning. She picked the further bunk and began spreading her clothes about; there was plenty of room.

Then she set off to explore.

The ship seemed vast. She went along corridors and up and down companionways and eventually found an enormous lounge where tea was being served. Carmen would have liked a slug of something in hers, but there seemed no chance of that so she slurped it down as it was, and secured three slices of iced sponge cake, looking about at the other passengers who seemed to be mainly elderly couples. There was head after head of grey hair. Carmen's was rinsed jet black, and her eyebrows were dyed. She'd never given up on her appearance.

When she went back to her cabin to change for dinner she received a shock, for her belongings had been moved to make space for others: an alien toothbrush was slotted into the bathroom holder and a sparse array of clothes shared the hanging space. The things that Carmen had left draped over the second bunk had been gathered together and deposited neatly on the one where her nightdress already lay.

Was she to share?

Such a thought had never occurred to Carmen. She picked up the telephone and asked for the purser whose assistant, to whom she made known this fact, replied that yes, indeed, she was sharing with Mrs Ford and no other arrangement was possible.

Carmen shrugged. She was a sound sleeper; it would not worry her.

She had a shower, put on her black satin pants and gold lamé top – you must start as you mean to go on and she intended to create an impression straight off – and was sitting on her bunk buckling her high-heeled sandals when Frances Ford came in, blinked at the moist atmosphere for the cabin was full of steam, and smiled anxiously at Carmen.

'I do hope you didn't mind my moving some of your things,' she said in a soft, nervous voice. She was a tall, thin woman with stringy brown hair and Carmen later learned that she came from Rye and was a widow with no children. She had a black poodle called Hetty whom it had been a wrench to deposit in kennels.

'I didn't reckon to be sharing,' Carmen told her bluntly.

'But it's so expensive having a cabin to oneself,' said Frances. 'Of course, if you've paid for that, there must be some mistake.'

'I didn't,' said Carmen. 'I won the trip in a raffle and I just thought it meant a single cabin. Not to worry – Frances, was it, you said?'

'That's right.' Frances wrinkled her nose at the damp air. 'How thoughtful of you to get changed early so that we weren't both wanting the bathroom at once,' she said. 'I wonder if the air-conditioning will cope with this steam?'

'Give it an hour or two and it will,' said Carmen, now busy applying petunia lipstick to her mouth.

'Are you having first sitting dinner?' asked Frances.

'Yes.' Carmen pouted, blotted her lips and gave them another wipe with the shiny lipstick.

'Ah – I'm second. That will make things easier, won't it?' Frances peered at her companion through the opaque air.

'If you say so,' said Carmen and picked up her handbag. 'I'll see you, then,' and she swung out of the cabin leaving Frances in possession. She was ready for a nip, and there would be company in the bar, if she could find one. There were at least three on board, according to the plan of the ship she'd received with her ticket.

Sipping a double gin, Carmen stoked up on dutch courage to face the ordeal of dinner where she would be among strangers. Looking around, she noticed that everyone else was plainly attired, though most were tidy, the men wearing ties, the women in skirts and blouses or simple dresses. She'd expected to see dinner suits and long gowns. Ten minutes before the meal was due to start she moved towards the restaurant and found a queue had already formed leading down the stairs.

'Greedy lot,' muttered Carmen under her breath, and heard a woman remark that some people were overdressed as it was not customary to change on the first night at sea.

'Stuff you.' Carmen tossed her head, scarcely shifting the crisp cap of her new perm. You could carry anything off if you had the nerve, and how was she to know that? Far worse if she'd just worn her old jersey slacks and sweater and everyone else had been in satin.

She was shown to a round table for eight where her companions were two couples whom she at once labelled as stuffed shirts, one pair from Ealing and the other from Tunbridge Wells; a lone man with a hearing aid; and two elderly widows who were sisters and lived in Bath. They all hid their faces behind the long menus handed to them by a waiter and Carmen, studying her copy, was at a loss. How could you choose? It was all written in French. However, it seemed to be for information only, for without consulting anyone, the meal was served. When a plate of soup was placed before her, Carmen began to behave as she always did when insecure, by complaining that it was too cold. She found the pasta which followed it too sticky and the beef too rare. Used to small, snacky meals, she soon felt full and messed her plate about, pushing the vegetables around with her knife and fork and grumbling. One of the widows raised a pained brow during these displays and exchanged a sad glance with her sister. You found all sorts on cruises: they knew that, having travelled in other ships before this one. The deaf man bought two bottles of claret for the table, and one of the other men, thanking him, declared that it would be his turn tomorrow. Carmen accepted her share; no one would expect her, a widow, to stand treat.

Their table waiter, a Greek, who wore his name, Giorgio, on a badge pinned to the lapel of his green monkey jacket, bore no resemblance to Stavros but Carmen had remembered a little of the language and the pale, thickset, tired man, who had finished clearing ship of the last lot of passengers only hours before the embarkation of the present company, was moved. He forgave her crude complaints and wished her *Kalynikta* when everyone left the restaurant.

Carmen laid a hand on his arm and, as one of the sisters later commented, positively leered at him.

'*Agapo*,' she stated. '*Agapo* all Greeks.'

Giorgio patted her hand.

'*Oraia*,' he replied, and she took it to mean that he thought she was beautiful for that was what Stavros had told her many years ago.

Some of the passengers went on deck to watch the lights of shore fade away as the SS *Aphrodite* put to sea but Carmen went to the lounge where bingo was on the programme.

She enjoyed herself, though she won nothing. A friendly couple at her table bought her a drink. She had dipped heavily into her savings for the trip, buying not only the suitcase but a purple kaftan on which she'd stitched several packets of sequins, her lamé blouse and satin pants, a purple taffeta skirt and a low-necked velvet top, and she had very little spare cash. Moving about, attaching herself to different people, should make it possible for her to accept drinks from others most nights, she decided. The second couple at her table bought another round before the cabaret and Carmen made sure that hers was a double. People were generous, she'd always found, if you were lively company and hadn't let yourself go to pieces.

The lounge filled up when the second sitting of diners arrived in time for the show. Carmen, in a good seat, enjoyed it all, especially the comics, and stayed on to watch the dancing. Maybe someone would ask her to dance.

But nobody did.

Afterwards there was supper in an upper lounge. Carmen felt quite hungry by this time and was able to put away a hearty snack. When she teetered on her high heels back to the cabin, Frances was asleep, neat under the duvet, her face to the wall.

She woke up as Carmen clattered round, bumping into the furniture, tittering drunkenly, making noises in the tiny bathroom, and sighed, drawing the covers tight round her ears. Quiet came at last, broken only by Carmen's light snores. Frances inserted ear plugs; she never travelled without them.

In the morning she had gone to breakfast by the time Carmen woke up, and that was the pattern of the days that followed. Breakfast was a serve-yourself affair and quite a scramble, with a splendid buffet laid out to tempt the greedy. After that, it was up on deck and into a deck-chair to pass the morning until coffee and biscuits were served.

Carmen took her crochet with her to a chair on the main deck. She crocheted beautifully and was making a shawl which later she would sell. It was a skill she had learned in hospital after Billy was born; a girl in the next bed had taught her. There was a boutique owner who would buy anything she made and it was something to do in winter, watching television.

People kept themselves to themselves, Carmen found. No one seemed to want to talk. Passengers were reading or sleeping. A brisk man in a pork pie hat walked round the deck. Ping-pong was played by some energetic younger people and deck-quoits was available, as she learned when she tried to start a conversation with a woman sitting next to her.

Her neighbour had an appointment to play on an upper deck and left after a minimal exchange.

Luncheon could be taken either in the restaurant or from a buffet on deck. Carmen decided not to face the prim people from her table again until she must, at dinner, and went to the buffet where she loaded two plates with every morsel that took her fancy. After that, she went below for a nap.

Frances, immersed in the latest Catherine Cookson, saw her go and resigned herself to snoozing on deck, well tucked up in the blanket she had had the foresight to bring from the cabin. It was cold in the fresh westerly wind but soon it should get warmer as they proceeded southwards.

That night the Captain's welcome aboard party was held and Carmen, in her purple skirt and low top, was photographed shaking the hand of the handsome dark-haired man with the neat beard. She'd have to buy a print of that as a souvenir.

She managed to lower quite a few free drinks during the party.

At dinner, she and Giorgio exchanged witticisms in Greek. Giorgio assumed she knew more of the language than was the case, and he wanted to please her. Many women passengers required all sorts of services from the stewards or crew, and, used to reading signals that were seldom subtle, Giorgio took to resting his hand heavily on Carmen's shoulder as he took away her plate, hiding his weary revulsion at the messed-up food she always left. She flirted with him, archly, in the manner that had been effective when she was young but now disgusted her table companions.

The two sisters asked to be moved to another table but were told it was not possible. The deaf man, one of nature's victims, found himself sitting next to Carmen every night, but the place on her other side always remained vacant for the last comer. Sometimes one of the sisters was her neighbour, and whoever drew her made no effort so that she sat in an island of neglect as they spoke across her.

People soon discovered that Frances was Carmen's cabin-mate, and her restrained accounts of washing hung from every corner of the cabin, half-eaten oranges left about, steamy use of the shower, snoring and other anti-social practices earned her sympathy from her own table companions and anyone else who heard her soft comments, which were never forceful enough to be complaints.

'You run risks, sharing with someone you don't know,' was the general opinion, and those other passengers who had chanced the same thing counted their blessings if they had been luckier.

Carmen came to bed later and later – or rather, earlier and earlier in the small hours.

Frances mentioned this, ashore in Lisbon, to the Major and his wife from Surrey at whose table she sat.

'I wonder where she goes?' she said. 'Is the bar open all night?'

'Hardly,' opined the Major's wife.

'She's got very little money,' Frances said. 'She won the cruise in a raffle.'

'Bully for her,' said the Major, the man who, in his pork pie hat, walked a mile on deck every day. 'Probably running a line on the side,' he added, and earned a reproving frown from his wife.

'What, at her age?' Frances was shocked. 'She must be nearly seventy.'

'It's never too late for some,' was the Major's sage reply.

Carmen went on none of the organised shore excursions. She had been sent vouchers for several with her ticket, but she had discovered that she could surrender them and receive a refund. This helped finance her gambling in the casino where once or twice she won small sums, and her bingo, and the drinks she was forced to buy for herself.

At Agadir she walked round the town until her arthritic joints ached. Recognising some people from the ship, including the Major and his wife, she followed behind them and entered a carpet factory where they all sat on the rolled-up rugs and were given mint tea while a handsome young man in robes and a fez described how the carpets were made. Afterwards, they were encouraged to buy not only rugs but handbags and leather coats. Carmen tried on several jackets, causing a good deal of commotion while she searched for her size and demanded different colours, but as she could not afford to buy anything, she left empty-handed. The Major and his wife took a taxi back to the ship, leaving her standing on the pavement.

It was the deaf man from her table who took pity on Carmen. He was escorting the widowed sisters, and they saw her limping along towards the harbour.

'She'll never make it,' he murmured. 'We must stop for her.'

'You're a nice man,' said the elder sister, truthfully, but he did not hear her as he alighted from the cab to rescue Carmen. He put her in the front seat beside the driver and she was noisily grateful.

On her wrist she wore a gold bracelet which the sisters had not noticed before. Had she bought it, or had she managed to steal it when no one was looking? They could believe anything of Carmen.

Approaching Gibraltar, the cruise two-thirds over and the voyage homewards about to begin, Carmen stared at the steep grey rock and thought how forbidding it looked. Tom had been there during the war, and so a tear came to her eye as the ship berthed.

She'd mentioned him to no one. No one had wanted to know her history, though she'd told plenty of people whom she found herself sitting next to on deck while she crocheted about her diplomat father and her sons in important overseas posts. It was strange how restless people were: no one stayed sitting next to her long, moving off on some mission without a word of apology.

She saw the deaf man and the sisters going down the gangway and went ashore after them, tagging along, aiming to scrounge a lift into town in their taxi. They were doing a tour of the island which did not interest her. Who wanted to gaze at Barbary apes? The passengers themselves were apes enough.

She knew there were pubs in the town and she wanted to visit one, for she was homesick for what was familiar.

'Drop me off in the main street,' she instructed, and was soon pushing her way along the crowded pavement.

Inside a pub, which could have been one in any town in England, she had several gins and began to feel better, though she couldn't get the thought of Tom quite out of her mind, which was silly. He'd been dead more than forty-five years, after all. Maybe food was what she needed. If she returned to the ship there would be lunch provided; ashore, she would have to pay.

She began the trudge back to the harbour and met Frances coming out of Marks and Spencer's, carrying one of their green bags.

'You can go to Marks at home,' she remarked. 'Why bother here?'

'I needed a nightie and a few other things,' said Frances. 'There's so little space in the cabin, I can't get my washing dry.'

'Shall we share a cab back to the ship?' Carmen suggested airily, not rising to this taunt. She'd been lucky to run into someone she knew; it was a fair walk back to the quayside.

Frances accepted the inevitable, and was not surprised when Carmen sprang out of the cab with remarkable speed, leaving her to pay the driver.

'Ta,' Carmen said, heading up the gangplank. 'That was ever so kind.' A nice thank-you went a long way in life.

Africa lay to the south as they sailed through the Straits of Gibraltar, land visible only a few miles distant on either side. The Germans had strung nets under the water across this narrow space to trap submarines during the war, the Major told his table companions, and Frances listened as he went on to talk about his days as a Desert Rat. Earlier at her table, Carmen had staged diversions while the others discussed their day ashore. She dropped a roll on the floor, asked for more butter, put the skeleton of her trout on the side plate of her neighbour, the deaf man. In only a few days now they would be steaming up the Channel, bidding one another farewell, exchanging addresses and promises to keep in touch that would remain unfulfilled. Carmen dreaded her return to solitude.

The weather grew colder every day. Thick jerseys and trousers replaced sundresses and shorts, and red sunburned skin was shrouded. Passengers with peeling faces paced the deck while oily fumes from the funnel streamed out like a pennant behind the ship as she sailed northwards with no land in sight. Funny how you missed it after a day or so, thought Carmen. Once they saw whales, spouting; another time, a school of porpoises followed the ship. An occasional cargo vessel would be left astern as the Captain hurried on, anxious to beat bad weather heading in from the west before he made landfall and held his farewell parties.

Carmen knew the drill now. You could go to both and have two lots of free drinks, slipping into the lounge by a side door to dodge the reception line the second time.

On the last evening, the deaf man bought three bottles of wine to celebrate the end of the cruise and Carmen remarked that he'd been too quick for her when it should have been her treat.

'You can say that again,' said the elder widow, and her sister nodded in agreement. They'd insisted on standing their turns.

The lights dimmed and the waiters bore in trays of flaming Baked Alaska. Carmen received a generous helping from Giorgio, whose manner towards her had become aloof and correct since the deaf man, not expecting much response from her, had begun talking to her at dinner. When she spoke, he had difficulty in hearing what she said, so he adopted the tactic which he found worked well in any social circumstance: he did the talking. He spoke to her of his golf club and his grandchildren, his garden and his Vauxhall car, of his past career as a tax inspector and of the china he mended as a hobby. Carmen let his words wash over her as she tried to picture him before age and deafness took their toll. Maybe she'd have fancied him then, but now his neck was wrinkled and his cheeks were gaunt. His thin old hands had brown spots on their backs but were steady as he poured the wine.

He bade her good night very formally after the final cabaret, to which he escorted her, not wanting her to sit alone on the last night. He felt pity for her, out of her depth in every way as she was and, like a child, craving attention. He had seen her smile and had realised that she had once been a very pretty girl. Together, now, they watched the lively young dancers who by day ran the library and the bingo, and the comedian who supervised trap shooting on deck.

'It's been lovely,' Carmen said. 'A real treat to remember in the winter.'

'Yes,' said the deaf man, who was returning to his lonely retirement bungalow in Essex.

Overnight, the ship berthed, and in the morning the crew dashed ashore as soon as the baggage had been unloaded. In groups, the passengers disembarked to claim their luggage.

Carmen had bought only her duty-free allowance of spirits and cigarettes – she didn't smoke but she could sell those at a profit – and the gold bracelet, her one souvenir. She went through the green channel and was asked to stop.

The Major and his wife, passing blamelessly by, saw Carmen's possessions disposed about the table, her shabby underwear displayed, her lamé blouse and her shiny kaftan, and, among them, little mounds of the sealed butter and jam cartons put out for breakfast. She had secreted dozens of them, and packs of cracker biscuits, too, even cheese, anything that could be hoarded for the weeks ahead.

There was another packet: a small one wrapped in brown paper which, undone, proved to contain a thick plastic bag filled with white powder. Carmen stared at it. Where had that come from? It looked like sugar.

Protesting loudly, not understanding, she was led away by two customs officers.

Frances went through the red channel and declared her purchase of a small oriental carpet. No one looked inside her jacket, where some much bigger packs of cocaine were stitched into the lining. It had been simple to plant the decoy in Carmen's suitcase, where, in the baggage hall, a trained dog had sniffed it out, just as she had planned when Micky, whom she'd got to know when he began handling stolen cars for her brother, had mentioned his aunt. It had been easy to set the old woman up, go to his place when he was at work and sell Carmen the raffle tickets. She'd worn a wig and tinted glasses, and a wool cap pulled low over her forehead, an adequate disguise.

She'd collected the stuff from her contact in Gib, exchanging carrier bags in Marks and Spencer's without a word passing between them. The cost of Carmen's cruise ticket scarcely dented the huge profit she would make when she passed it on, and after all, what was a year or two in gaol to Carmen? She'd have her travels to remember.

And it might have been missed altogether: it was just the luck of the draw.

MEANS
TO
MURDER

In my brown Jaeger dressing-gown and striped viyella pyjamas, I knelt on the landing, watching between the banisters as, below, the guests arrived. I recognised Dr Pitt, who often came to see Mother. The small plump lady with him must be Mrs Pitt. She took off her fur coat and handed it to Trotter, the parlourmaid, who was helping Fitch admit them. Outside, John was in charge of parking the cars, directing them into position with the aid of a torch. Each lady was dropped at the door before the car drove on to its space.

Lady White had a chauffeur and her car was a Daimler. I knew this because I had discussed the arrangements with John earlier in the day while he was polishing my father's Invicta. Among his duties was that of maintaining the car and even, sometimes, driving it, if Mother, who did not drive, had to be fetched from the station after a day in town, or wanted to pay a call on a neighbour.

It was New Year's Eve.

An enormous Christmas tree stood in the hall, its topmost branches level with the banister rail, and opposite me was one of the bright painted birds with feathery tails clipped to its boughs. Dozens of brilliant baubles hung on the tree, and fairy lights, but I liked the birds best; there were three of them, one blue, one red and one green. The red one was on a low branch and I had been allowed to put it there when Mother, helped by Fitch, who stood on a ladder, was dressing the tree.

Fitch was the butler. He was bald, and very thin, with creases all over his face, and he was good at card tricks. If he wasn't too busy, he would entertain me with them when I visited him in his pantry. Sometimes I helped him clean the silver, and he said if I kept on with it I'd get a butler's thumb, which would be a great help with the spoons. His own right thumb was smooth and flat, much broader than the one on his left hand.

Fitch had been at the Manor for ever, even when Mother was young, for this had been her home until she and Father married. They met when he was on leave from the Indian Army, and they returned there together after the wedding. I was born in India, and I had a good life there with a kind ayah and other children to play with, but the climate didn't suit Mother, who often felt faint and ill. When I was seven my grandfather, who owned the Manor, died of pneumonia, and Mother and I came home to be with my grandmother for a time, but we never went back because my grandmother, pining, soon died, too, and after that Father sent in his papers and left the Army.

It seemed rather strange. Was it copies of *The Times* he had sent to Colonel Swethington, or a series of notebooks or letters? I hadn't understood what papers they were, but it meant we could all be together and I wouldn't be sent home alone to boarding-school, like the other children older than me.

At my post on the landing, I sighed with happiness. On Christmas morning a gleaming new bicycle was waiting for me at the foot of the tree. I had ridden it round and round on the frozen lawn, and I'd soon learn to balance without hands and do tricks, like Peter, the garden boy, whom I'd seen riding along with his hands in his pockets, swaying from side to side and whistling. His mother had been my mother's nanny and they lived in a cottage in the village.

Now the Manor belonged to Mother and Father, and we should live there always, and though I was sad about my grandparents, after all, they were old.

Mother was looking beautiful tonight in a shimmering dress of gold, which matched her hair. For a year she'd worn black or grey, in mourning, but now that was over. In India, she had always been pale and tired; here, she was different, and though she was still sometimes unwell, she wasn't so thin and her cheeks were often quite pink. I watched as she led the way in to dinner, crossing the hall on the arm of a tall man with white hair whose name I didn't know. How wonderful they all looked, the men in dinner jackets with gleaming white shirts and the women in long dresses of every hue.

One woman wore black. That was Mrs Fox, from Summer Cottage. We had known her in India, where her husband, Captain Fox, had been killed during some riots, or so I was told. I wasn't sure what had happened, exactly, but as a result, Maxwell Fox was an orphan.

Tom Swethington said he couldn't be an orphan as his mother was still alive; you were only an orphan if both your parents died; but whether he was right or not, it was sad. Max had stayed with us for a time while his father, who did not die at once, was in hospital. I heard one of the servants telling Ayah that the Captain's horse had fallen, throwing Captain Fox to the ground, and he had been trampled on. This didn't sound quite the glorious death in battle that Max had seemed to believe was his father's fate, and Tom Swethington muttered that there was some talk of the girth having broken, causing the saddle to swing, but I didn't really understand what that meant.

Tom said that we mustn't talk about it to Max. He believed his father had died a hero's death, and that was how it should be.

'He'll probably get a medal,' said Tom, confident of his own father's ability to arrange such rewards.

Mrs Fox and Max remained in India for some months after we left, and then they returned to stay with relations in Kent while looking for somewhere permanent. Three weeks before Christmas they had come to Summer Cottage, when its lease was up.

'It's cheap and convenient, and it will be a kindness to tell her about it,' Father had said one day at breakfast, and Mother had agreed.

'It will be nice for the boys,' she said.

I wasn't so pleased. I didn't like Max, though I knew I must be sorry for him and allow him to play with my toys. He was a year older than me, tall and thin, with straight dark hair like his mother's, and he would bend my arm behind my back to make me do as he wished, if I didn't agree at once. He'd do Chinese burns, too, twisting his hands round my wrist till it hurt and I yelled, and then he'd call me a cry-baby.

I hadn't seen much of him since they arrived, to my relief, as he had been sent to boarding-school, but he'd come with his mother that morning when she called to ask if she could help prepare for the party. She'd brought an apron in a holdall and offered to arrange flowers, but Mother had done them the day before, so Mrs Fox didn't stay long and I didn't have to let Maxwell try my bike.

I didn't go to school. I had lessons at the Vicarage from Mr Hastings, the vicar, and his daughter Jane, who looked after him. His wife was dead. This worried me a little; neither she nor Captain Fox had reached three score years and ten, which was man's allotted span, I knew.

When the dining-room door closed behind the last guest, Daisy, the housemaid who looked after me when Mother was busy – thank goodness it had been decided that I was too old to have Ayah replaced by a nanny or governess – came bustling along to put me to bed. I had seen Father take in Lady White, and Mrs Fox had entered the dining-room on the arm of the curate from Little Marpleton, a pale young man, a bachelor. She, too, was pale, in her long black velvet dress with sleeves to her wrist and a single-strand pearl necklace.

I had been asleep for some time when the music woke me. It was faint, a reedy sound, not the same as when Mother played the piano. Sometimes we sang rousing ditties like *Clementine*, and sentimental ballads, and in the weeks before Christmas it had been carols, even Father joining in with his deep voice for *Good King Wenceslas* while Mother and I were the page.

Gradually, the music grew louder, the strain taken up by some harsher instrument than the first. I lay for a while and listened, until a jiggy little tune made my feet twitch and want to dance. Who was playing?

I got out of bed, found dressing-gown and slippers, put them on and slipped out on to the landing again. As I did so, Trotter opened the drawing-room door to let Fitch go in with a tray of drinks and the music swelled up more strongly. Trotter went off through the green baize door that led to the kitchen regions, and I ran down the stairs and crouched behind the big Christmas tree in a position that would let me peep round the branches and look through the door when Fitch emerged, as he must in time. If he saw me, he wouldn't be cross, though he might send me back to bed. He wouldn't tell Father; I could trust Fitch.

It was a little while before the door opened and I caught a glimpse of some men in fancy dress, with coloured frock coats and knee breeches, like George III in my history books. They sat before music stands, and the gleam of brass caught my eye. I knew it came from a French horn; I'd heard the military band often enough to recognise some instruments.

I must have dozed off, tucked there behind the tree, waking at intervals when the drawing-room door opened to let someone in or out, usually a man on his way to the cloakroom. I saw Dr Pitt, and the curate, and I saw Mrs Fox come out and go into the study.

I drowsed and woke, drowsed and woke. Then I saw the ghost. A figure in a green frock coat, ruffles at throat and wrists, and wearing pale breeches and black shoes, came down the stairs and disappeared into the study. That frightened me, and as soon as the door had closed I hurried upstairs and jumped back into bed, only then realising that it must have been one of the musicians. After that night, I never saw my mother again.

The day after the party, Daisy's face was all blotched, as if she'd been crying, but she told me it was only a cold. She set me to tidy my toys in the morning, and in the afternoon she took me for a walk in the village. We went to the smithy, where Bob Pearce was shoeing a carthorse, and I was allowed to pump the bellows to fan the coals as the huge shoes were heated and shaped. There was a strong smell as the hot iron was placed on the horse's hooves and hammered into place. Surely it must hurt the horse, having nails driven into its feet like that? The smith assured me that the hoof felt no more than a human fingernail, and I was mollified.

Mr Giles, the farmer, asked Daisy and me back to tea at the farm, and let me ride on the back of the big gentle animal. Clip, clop, went the new shoes on the big hooves with the long feathers of silky hair hanging over them. I clutched a hank of the horse's mane to keep my balance.

'I'm surprised you haven't got a pony to ride, young fellow,' said Mr Giles.

I'd ridden in India, and Father had talked about getting me a pony soon, but I wasn't keen.

'A bike's more in my line, Mr Giles,' I replied.

We stabled the horse, shutting him into a stall with a bale of sweet-smelling hay hooked in the corner, and Mr Giles left Daisy and me to find our own way into the house while he went to help his son, Fred, with the milking. I could hear the spurt of the milk hitting the pail as we passed the long shed, and a cow uttered a low, soft moo. Daisy said she wouldn't mind working on a farm, among beasts.

Soon we were in the warm kitchen and Mrs Giles was giving me home-made scones with butter and strawberry jam, and milk fresh from the cow, still warm.

'Poor lamb, what a start to the New Year,' she said, and then, 'When's the ...?' but Daisy cut in before she could finish, and I wondered what had happened to the lamb to render it pitiful. I'd seen no lambs on the farm.

It was dark when we reached home, and I wanted to know where Mother was, but when I asked Daisy, she didn't answer. There was no sign of Father. I had my bath, then milk and biscuits and a game of Racing Demon with Daisy. I was tired after so much fresh air, and fell asleep as soon as I was tucked into bed.

Next morning Father was at breakfast, but he showed no interest when I told him about my visit to the forge. He ate quickly, glancing at *The Times* as he drank his coffee, and he left the table before I had finished. Mother would be having her breakfast in bed, as she often did. I decided to go and see her.

She and Father had separate bedrooms. She sometimes spent a day in bed, but she was never too ill to welcome a visit, and we would play Battleships, or Hangman, or she would read to me, so I set off confidently and tapped on her door. When there was no answer, I opened it and went in. The room was very tidy, the bed made, and all her things were gone: there were no brushes, pots, or books to be seen, not even the photograph of me with Ayah which she kept on her dressing-table. Everything had vanished, and so had she.

Father found me standing there, bewildered.

'What are you doing here, Dick?' he demanded, and I said I was looking for Mother.

'She's gone away,' he told me. 'And she won't be coming back. You'd better forget her as soon as you can. I don't want to hear you mention her ever again. Out, now,' and he chivvied me from the room, locking the door after me.

I cried, of course, running along the passage to my own room and flinging myself on the bed in misery, but soon Daisy came and cuddled me against her soft apron, crying too.

'But where is she?' I wailed. 'And why didn't she say goodbye?'

'She couldn't,' said Daisy. 'Of course you're sad, Master Dick. So am I – so's Cook, and Fitch and Trotter and John – we all are – but the master has said no one's to talk about it, and that's that. You'll get over it in time, my lovey, and you're to go off to school, so that'll be exciting, won't it? You're going to Pitcairn House with young Maxwell Fox, and there's all your clothes and things to get.'

I'd expected to go to school next year, when I'd be nine, but not as soon as this, and at first I didn't like the idea much, but without Mother things weren't the same. Father was out a lot – something to do with business, he said – and I had no one to play with, though Daisy spent a lot of time with me and there was still my bike to enjoy. We went to the farm again, and Mr Giles gave me a calf to look after and said that it could be mine. Before term began, the flooded water meadows froze and I slid on the ice, a novelty after India.

Then came a trip to London with Father to buy my uniform.

We went to Harrods, where we met Mrs Fox and Maxwell in

the boys' outfitting department. It seemed he needed things too, and we bought shirts, shorts, socks and football boots. I quite enjoyed the day, especially the large lunch we had at the Hyde Park Hotel, where I drank ginger beer and Maxwell had cider. Father and Mrs Fox shared a bottle of champagne and were in a very cheerful mood, which I thought strange after Mother had only just gone away, but it was true that for a while I had forgotten about her, bearing out Daisy's prophecy. I felt bad about it, and cried in bed later.

Mrs Fox and Maxwell had travelled up by train, but we all came home in the Invicta, and when Father jumped out of the car to open the door for her I heard him say, 'The time will soon pass, Lois. June, I think.'

What could he mean? What would happen in June?

When it arrived, I understood, for in June Father and Mrs Fox were married, and she and Maxwell came to live at the Manor, which seemed to belong entirely to Father, now that Mother had gone.

Things changed again. During the summer holidays Father and Mrs Fox, as I still thought of her though I had been told to call her Aunt Lois, went touring in Europe, and Maxwell stayed with his grandparents in Cornwall. I remained at the Manor, for I had neither grandparents nor uncles and aunts, but there were plenty of people to look after me. I spent a lot of time at the farm, where my calf was growing, and I began riding Mr Giles's old cob, a quiet creature. She was too big for me, but I grew bold and imagined myself to be a cowboy taming a bronco. I went to the forge, too, and Bob Pearce helped me make a trivet for Mrs Giles to rest her kettle on.

Maxwell came back after a month, and he wanted to come to the farm. He rode the cob, galloping her about the fields, whipping her with a stick cut from the hedge until Mr Giles told him he would not be allowed to ride again.

'Let your mother pay for you to have lessons at the stables,' he said. 'She can afford it now,' and he stormed off while Maxwell shouted after him that he was not be spoken to in that tone.

Daisy became silent and grim, and the atmosphere in the house altered as Maxwell demanded special dishes from Cook, and complained, unjustly, that John had not cleaned his shoes properly. I remonstrated with Maxwell, but timidly, because at school he was a hero, admired because he was good at games and cared nothing for discipline, daring other boys to carry out deeds requiring courage. I noticed that he never did them himself. He called me a little squit, and his friends commiserated with him for having such a poor object as myself as his stepbrother, while my own contemporaries envied what they saw as my good fortune.

Father and Mrs Fox – Aunt Lois – returned, and she slept in what had been my mother's room. While I was away at school it had been repapered and painted, equipped with new curtains and different furniture, but to me it was still Mother's room, and Father was in there, too. His own room was now called the dressing-room.

Then Daisy said she was leaving; she wouldn't be there when I came home for the Christmas holidays.

I clung to her, sobbing that I'd never see her again and she laughed and hugged me, telling me not to be a silly boy, that she was only marrying Bob Pearce, the smith, and would be in the village where I could come and see her as much as I liked. 'I shan't be dead, like your poor mother,' she said.

'Dead? Is she dead?' I stared at Daisy.

'Why, didn't you know?' Daisy exclaimed. 'Didn't anyone ever tell you?' she cried, then reminded herself, aloud, that Father had forbidden everyone to discuss what had happened, thinking least said, soonest mended. 'But I thought he'd told you something,' she said, and she took me to the churchyard, where beside my grandparents' grave was another, with a simple headstone bearing my mother's name and the dates of her birth and death.

'We'll pick her some flowers,' said Daisy. 'You'll feel better then,' and she explained that the old illness my mother had suffered from so badly in India had returned, to prove fatal, the night of the New Year's Eve party. The funeral had been on the day we spent at the farm, when Mr Giles gave me the calf.

In the years that followed I often went to the churchyard with roses or sweet peas, or sometimes just flowers from the hedgerows, primroses, or poppies, and wild scabious, and Daisy was right: to do so made me feel better. Even now, more than fifty years later, I can still recall the sweet smell of newly-mown grass and the scent of the flowers I had brought.

Today, I took daffodils and iris, bought on my way from the airport, and after my visit to the grave I called to see Daisy, who is still alive. Indeed, it is because of her that I have returned after all this time.

I did well at school, and was separated from Maxwell when we left Pitcairn House, for he went to Harrow while I was sent to a lesser establishment. After my war service, as there was nothing to keep me in England I emigrated to Australia, where I did well from sheep and bought into mines. Now I am a rich man. My father died in 1972, leaving the Manor and everything else to his widow, and some time after that Maxwell joined her there, with his painter friend, Trevor. Trevor, eventually, had died, but the other two were still living in what had originally been my mother's house. Lois must be nearly ninety by now.

It seemed that they had run out of money. Daisy had written to me through the years, and I knew that Maxwell had tried several methods of raising funds, investing in various ventures and speculating on the Stock Exchange, but the upkeep of the place had drained the available cash, and his attempt at marriage had ended in an expensive divorce on account of Trevor. Now he intended to sell the estate to a development company which planned to build an entire town with schools, shops and even light industry in a beautiful piece of country, destroying for ever the water meadows, which would be filled in and the flood water presumably diverted elsewhere, into, perhaps, the village. How could an ageing, childless man be so greedy?

Daisy, a widow now with three children of her own and

seven grandchildren, lived with her elder son and his wife in the old forge, which had been renovated, extended and modernised. Her son was a smith, like his father, but he made wrought ironwork, gates, weathervanes and the like. The other son was an accountant, and the daughter was a doctor. They had moved up the social scale. Daisy herself had white curls and the same deep blue eyes in a face that still smiled though it was wrinkled. She gave me a hug as warm and as welcome as when I was a lad.

I had offered to buy the estate from Maxwell, but he would not accept my bid. He would make millions from the developer if it went through. Now I was going to see him, to make a final appeal.

Sitting by Daisy's fireside, I asked her to tell me all that she knew or could remember about my mother's death.

Daisy screwed up her face and touched her eyes with a handkerchief, moved, still, by that experience when, on New Year's morning, she had taken in my mother's breakfast tray and found her still asleep, as she thought. But the sleep was the sleep of death.

'It was diabetes she had, poor lady,' said Daisy. 'She'd been ill in India, but when she came home Dr Pitt found out what was wrong and she gave herself injections every day. She must have forgotten her dose, that night, or perhaps something went wrong because she had eaten things she shouldn't have had. Dr Pitt said anything like that could have happened. There'd been a big party that night. You'd been watching the guests arrive. Then I put you to bed.'

'I got up again,' I told her. 'I heard the music and crept down to the hall to see the musicians when Fitch opened the drawing-room door. I fell asleep down there, hidden behind the Christmas tree. But I saw them, in their silk coats and their breeches and their white wigs. Regency minstrels.' I could conjure them up, even now. 'One of them went through the hall alone – he went into the study – to have a quick nip of my father's brandy, I suppose. He had come down the stairs.'

'Funny you should have remembered that,' Daisy said.

'There was a whole suit of those fancy clothes, and a wig, pushed under the big leather chair in there when I went in to clean in the morning. I took them upstairs and put them away, meaning to mention them to my poor lady.'

'What happened to them?' I asked. 'Were they reclaimed?'

'No, they weren't. I think they may have been all packed up with your mother's things,' said Daisy. 'It was odd, though, I thought at the time, because the musicians all got dressed in one of the bedrooms, and changed there again before leaving. Why should one of them leave his clothes in the study?'

'Was it a green coat?' I asked.

'Yes,' said Daisy, surprised.

I'd seen Mrs Fox go into the study, too, but I must have been asleep when she and the musician came out, for surely, I thought now with hindsight, they must have had a rendezvous there? But why was the suit left behind?

'What happened to all my mother's things?' I asked.

'They're here, in the attic,' said Daisy. 'Your father gave orders that they were to be got rid of, but somehow it didn't seem right to throw them away. They were all that was left of your poor mother, and rightly the whole place should have gone to you, not that Maxwell and his mother. Trotter and I decided to keep everything safely so that you could look through them when you grew up. But the war came, and then you went to Australia. There were papers, photos, diaries. Mrs Giles at the farm kept them first – all packed in trunks, they were – and later we brought them here.'

She paused. 'Trotter and I took a few woollies for ourselves, they'd only have got the moths, otherwise, but nothing's been touched, since. Funny how moths don't seem a problem now, isn't it?'

'I'd like to look at them before I go up to the Manor,' I said. I hadn't announced my visit: I wasn't expected.

First, I telephoned Daisy's daughter, the doctor, and asked her some questions. Her replies made me very thoughtful. Then Daisy's son helped me bring down the trunks and we unpacked them in a bedroom, laying the things we removed carefully on the bed. We found the frock coat, packed in tissue paper, and the breeches and silver-buckled shoes, and the wig. We laid them aside, careful not to disturb them.

'If a murder was done,' I said quietly, 'there might be evidence, even after all this time. The old woman is still alive, after all. Her blood can be tested. I think she wore the suit so that she could move round the house without being recognised. People seeing her would take her for one of the minstrels.'

Daisy's daughter had said that it was possible, if my mother's insulin had been replaced with water, for her to have injected herself and then gone into a coma and died. She might have felt dizzy and thirsty, but as she was alone in her bedroom, no help would be at hand. Without knowing what dosage she was on, and more details, it was impossible to say what the effect might be, perhaps not fatal at once; that would depend on all sorts of things. Such a death might raise no suspicions in a doctor regularly attending; he would assume she had forgotten her medication and if there had been an inquest, accidental death was the likely verdict. These days, stringent rules might make such a means of murder easier to detect, and today there were tests which could prove whether Mrs Fox – Lois – had handled or worn the garments, for she would have left traces – a hair in the wig, perhaps – of herself on them. She could have hidden the suit in the house earlier: suddenly I remembered her call that morning, and how Maxwell had wanted to ride my bike but there wasn't time. She knew her way round; she could have made the opportunity while we boys were having milk and biscuits in the schoolroom.

The law could not permit gain from the result of murder, if it were detected. My mother's will, leaving everything to my father, had been made in London after her marriage, a year before my birth, and she was her parents' outright heir. If Mrs Fox had killed my mother in order to marry my father, her right to his estate must surely be invalidated.

I am waiting at Daisy's for a senior police officer to arrive and accompany me to the Manor. An experienced forensic scientist has already taken away the wig and the garments.

He saw a small bloodstain on the breeches, and muttered something about it possibly being menstrual blood.

'It will be interesting to test it, after so long,' he said with enthusiasm. 'Genetic fingerprinting is making positive proof much easier to obtain.'

Had my father known the truth? Had he been a party to the crime? He and Lois had known each other in India. I remembered the story about Captain Fox's broken girth and wondered if that had really been an accident. In those days divorce meant social disaster and would ruin an army officer's career; she and my father could not have got married without being ostracised and rendered penniless, since neither had private means. As it was, they enjoyed prosperity for many years. During the war they had stayed at the Manor, which had become a convalescent home, with Lois in Red Cross uniform carrying out some administrative function. My father, re-commissioned, had had a desk job at a supply depot nearby. I didn't want to believe that he was her accomplice; only one of her victims. If he'd been involved, he would have made certain that all proof was obliterated – the disguise, for instance, and the bottles of insulin. Three had been found among my mother's things; perhaps all had been tampered with, in case one negative dose was not enough. Lois, however, would not have wanted to draw attention to herself by searching for the clothes or the drug; she must have assumed they were destroyed, perhaps had suggested to my father the very action he had ordered.

Unlike Maxwell, I have children, and one of my sons, daughters, or grandchildren might like to run the Manor estate once the law has returned it to me. For certain, it will not be sold to a speculator, and as there's a nearby motorway already, it shouldn't be subject to compulsory purchase.

I can see a car drawing up outside, a Jaguar with three men in dark suits inside. There's another car, too, with uniformed officers, two of them women.

They may need a doctor. The old lady may die of shock. Still, that won't prevent tests being carried out.

It's too late for vengeance, but it isn't too late for justice.

A
SMALL
EXCITEMENT

I'd forgotten the strong, harsh tang of seaweed, borne inshore on the wind. It smelled of iodine, and I sniffed it sharply, standing on the rocks below the big, gaunt house built like a fortress on a grass patch above the beach. There were no flowers around it; nothing would survive there, unless nurtured tenderly; only some sea-thrift, in summer, grew among the stones on the path to the main door. This had been the holiday residence of a wealthy confectioner from the Midlands and was known irreverently as Candy Castle. Now it had been turned into flats: SEA VIEW HOLIDAY RENTALS proclaimed a notice-board, blue script on white paint, faded by the salty air.

Things had changed since those days long ago when the sweetmaker was in his prime, and I was young. The resort had grown to encompass wind-surfing, even pedaloes, as well as sailing. Then, small boats would stud the bay beyond the house, their blue or red sails dipping to meet the water as they heeled over, steeply tacking. On regatta days, flags flew from the flagstaff beside the Sailing Club's modest headquarters on the headland; no boat here was large enough to be called a yacht. At that time, before the resort's expansion with its caravan parks and small houses built especially for tourists, all the annual visitors whose families could afford some sort of boat sailed, and exclusion from this fraternity meant social oblivion ashore.

When not sailing, the boats were moored in several sheltered coves around the shoreline. I could remember the sound of water slapping against their hulls, the clack of the wind in their stays. That was another life, I thought, as I watched some seagulls swoop down over the rocks. What were they hoping to find? Food of some sort, of course: and what was I seeking here, after so long? A solution? An answer?

It was October, the season over, and nearly all the boats were up, stored away for the winter in local yards or towed home on trailers to rest proudly in suburban gardens, the envy of neighbours, until next year. Today, the sea was grey, riffled with white crests, and further out, beyond the shelter of the cliffs which curved around the bay, the water was really rough, with big waves crashing against the rocks, scattering spray and spume.

This was where Philippa and Hugh had walked together, slipping away from groups, or from houses where their children slept. They had clung to each other in crannies among the rocks, in boathouses, even in her own bed when her unsuspecting husband was away, for though she and the children spent most of August here, he came only for weekends and the final fortnight. Their affair had gone on for years, blossoming every summer and kept alive meanwhile by rare snatched meetings in London or elsewhere. They spoke of permanence when the children were grown up; she had two and he had four. He had not wanted to hurt his wife, who, after all, had done nothing wrong; indeed, she was loyal and affectionate, and an excellent mother. Philippa's husband had a short temper and was a workaholic, but he was generous, and was prospering in a plastics business he had started in an outhouse and which was now housed in a large modern complex among carefully sculptured acres and which did business worldwide.

The children had enjoyed their summers here. For toddlers, the sand was fine and clean, washed by the tide. There were pools in which to catch shrimps, toy boats could be sailed at the water's edge, and young mariners were initiated early into the lore of the sea. Like their parents, their social life was active, with barbecues and sailing picnics when several boats would set off for another bay along the coast. Small children and the food would often go by car, with any spouses who did not like the sea: there were a few and they were teased, but they were useful so their idiosyncrasy was tolerated. Hugh's wife, Marjorie, was among them; she was always willing to look after any number of children at home or to drive them to a spot where bigger boats would drop anchor and their crews row inshore by dinghy, and where smaller ones, centreplates up, would be beached. Hugh and Philippa's affair had begun at such a picnic, when he had helped her haul her little boat ashore and joked about the need to watch the tide lest it be swept away. A sudden glance, an unexpected touch – something very slight was all that was needed to make them first aware of an attraction that soon, with opportunity, turned into a demanding passion.

The fortress on the cliff became his when his father died and he inherited the confectionery empire, but his heart was never in the business; he had wanted to be a painter. This had caused conflict with his father, who said he could paint for pleasure but must follow the family tradition. National Service had brought a reprieve, but at a price: he had been involved in an accident when a rifle was fired in error; his right hand had been badly damaged and he never regained full muscle control, so that he could no longer paint or draw with his former skill.

Unless he made that excuse, I thought now, remembering how awkwardly he had clenched his pen or brush between his thin, weak fingers. Would that have restricted real talent? He had produced pretty seascapes of this bay and had painted other places where he had travelled later, after the house here was sold and he and Marjorie had spent holidays abroad where it was warmer, but the pictures were no more than pleasant; perhaps that had always been the limit of his talent.

His father had been no philistine. He had contributed towards the restoration of a museum in his Midlands neighbourhood and he had taken an interest in an amateur orchestra in which his wife, Hugh's mother, played the violin.

Hugh should have become, in due course, chairman of the firm's board of family directors, but he lacked innovative ideas

as well as drive. His sister's husband, ambitious and discern-
ing, jockeyed for power and eventually out-manoeuvred
Hugh, being appointed in his place. Hugh, fobbed off with the
post of publicity director, was content enough: such a role
suited him; he was spared major decision-making, and could
occupy himself in an area he understood. He enjoyed initiat-
ing advertising drives and redesigning wrappings and packages. He would seek out new artists and copy-writers and use
excursions to meet these people as opportunities to see
Philippa, spicing up his travels with intrigue. She would go
anywhere if there was the promise of a meeting, making
arrangements for her children, setting off in her little car.

Businessmen had to be away from home and Marjorie did
not query Hugh's absences. They lived contentedly enough,
never arguing, discussing differences amicably and making
joint decisions about the children's schooling, their later
studies, the eventual purchase of a holiday cottage in France.
Two of the children continued sailing, joining clubs – one at
a reservoir, the other on an estuary near his university.

Philippa's children grew up too, and then she begged Hugh
to leave his wife. She pressed him, and he kissed her with as
much ardour as ever while requesting further patience. It was
true that over the years they had dreamed of being together
always, often talked of it and fantasised about where they
would live, but that was always safely in the future; now she
wanted her dreams realised. Philippa liked her large house in
Surrey and her comfortable lifestyle, but she did not love her
husband, merely, as she told Hugh, tolerating him. She had
found consolation in her garden, her children – one now
touring Australia, the other in America on a course at
Harvard – and most of all in Hugh, living for their meetings.
He knew she meant it when she said she loved him. Their
affair had endured for more than twelve years, and no one
knew about it, or so they believed. There had been no gossip
because their circles no longer overlapped as Hugh did not go
to the seaside resort where it had begun. Philippa and her
husband went there still; now they owned a new white house

above the bay and quite a splendid boat in which Derek annually won races. They went skiing, too, each winter, spending Christmas at a high mountain village where snow was nearly guaranteed.

Then the letters began arriving.

Lying in Hugh's arms in an impersonal hotel bedroom, Philippa told him about them. Her husband had shown her one at breakfast the previous Saturday, telling her that there had been others which he had destroyed.

'It can't be true,' he'd said, dangling the sheet of ordinary typing paper on which had been pasted accusatory sentences composed of words cut from newspapers. The allegation was that she had been deceiving him for years.

'I denied it, of course,' she told Hugh. 'But what if he decides to have me watched?'

She waited for Hugh's answer. Surely, now, he would declare it didn't matter, that they would, at last, begin to live together.

But Hugh's reaction shocked her.

'He might,' he said. 'We'd better take care – stop meeting for a while.'

She protested, even wept. She would leave home and go with him anywhere he liked.

'I don't care if Derek knows,' she said. 'Now you can tell Marjorie and we can stop pretending.'

But Hugh's elder daughter was getting married in the summer. She was to have an expensive wedding, a marquee on the lawn, all the trimmings. This was no time for scandal.

'Not yet,' he said. 'Please, Philippa. Be patient.'

He looked at her, her face thin now and showing lines around the mouth and eyes; he felt her tense, wiry body pressed against him. He loved her, yes: of course he did, but not enough, now, to interrupt the even pattern of his life, his peaceful time at home, where Marjorie saw that things ran smoothly and still welcomed him into her body with easy familiarity, though Philippa of course did not know this. She assumed, and he had let her, that Marjorie was bored with that side of life.

Of course Philippa made love with Derek too: it was a fact of life, Hugh knew, and something separate from their infrequent secret meetings which made him feel quite youthful. He could give them up, however. The truth was that he loved both women, but one of them was expendable.

'Let's rest it for a while,' he said. 'If we aren't meeting, the letter-writer will give up. Who do you think it is?'

'I don't know. Perhaps someone recognised us somewhere.'

'Or saw you on the train once, followed you out of curiosity – spotted your car that time we went to Oxford when I had that meeting.'

It could have happened anywhere; the surprising thing was that they had not been found out before.

Reluctantly, she consented to an interval with no meetings, at least until after the wedding, and even promised not to ring the office. She did this sometimes, using a code they both understood, pretending that she was speaking from a graphics firm he used.

'It might be someone in your office,' she suggested.

'Wouldn't they write to Marjorie, not Derek?' he said. 'How would they trace you?'

It was logical.

But in spite of their separation, Derek received two more letters, both postmarked London, Philippa told Hugh on the telephone, breaking their agreement. And finally, tired of the pretence, and angry, she had told Derek that the allegations were true, though she had protected his identity.

Derek had left her. There had been a dreadful row. Appalling things were said. Articles were thrown and china broken.

'I'm not sorry,' Philippa declared. 'I'm glad it's in the open.'

Hugh had told her that Derek would cool down and return, but she did not want this reassurance.

'He won't,' she said. 'He's too proud, and I don't want him back.'

Soon after this Derek had told her he had found someone else whom he wished to marry, and he wanted a divorce.

'You don't expect me to be celibate, do you?' he had demanded in a hostile interview on the terrace at their Surrey house, the swimming-pool translucent blue beyond them.

She was young, his woman: someone he had met through work, she learned later, and Hugh, hearing about it, suspected that the affair was not a new romance. Derek obtained his divorce on the grounds of Philippa's admitted adultery with an unnamed individual, and remarried. He was compelled to make provision for Philippa but it was the minimum the law decreed. Her settlement included the seaside house, which she thought she would be forced to sell.

'Letting it could bring you in a useful income,' Derek had remarked, beneficently.

Meanwhile, in a rented flat in Pimlico, Philippa worked in the gift department of a big store while awaiting Hugh's summons, but the time passed and it never came. He would not take her telephone calls, and he did not answer the letters which, in desperation, she wrote to him at home, not caring if in their married intimacy Marjorie should read them.

They met eventually. At last she visited his house and Hugh found her there with Marjorie. They were drinking tea, or Marjorie was. She looked calm, while Philippa had been crying.

'You remember Philippa, don't you, Hugh?' said Marjorie. 'She has had an interesting story to tell me. Would you like some tea?'

Hugh's stomach did a somersault. 'Of course I know Philippa,' he said.

'She tells me that you and she are lovers,' Marjorie remarked. She began pouring tea into a spare cup for Hugh.

Hugh looked from one woman to the other.

'It isn't true,' he said. 'Her husband left her, I believe. Perhaps it's made her fanciful.'

'Do I hear a cock crowing?' Marjorie enquired, head on one side.

'There are no cocks near here.' Hugh did not understand.

'I know you wrote the letters, Marjorie,' said Philippa, jumping to her feet and glaring down at the other woman who sat, plump and placid, very middle-aged, her waved hair flecked with grey. 'You found out and wanted to break us up. You thought if Derek knew, it would spoil things – and it did.' Her voice trailed off into more tears. She was no match for the confident older woman whom she had enjoyed deceiving all this time, mocking her in her mind, deriding her, yet who was the victor now?

'What letters?' asked Marjorie.

'Don't insult me with such a question,' stormed Philippa. 'You knew Hugh was weak, of course. He wouldn't risk the scandal. I've found that out too late. A whole lifetime too late.'

She looked across at Hugh, and as they exchanged glances, Marjorie saw that once there had been love between them. Misery, dismay, and fear showed now, and Hugh was the first to drop his gaze.

'You're contemptible,' Philippa found the courage to tell him, and hurried from the room.

'Go after her,' Marjorie urged him.

'It's best to let her go,' he said. 'It's over. She'll calm down.'

'Don't you owe her something, after all these years?'

'What can I say to her? There's nothing left,' he said, but he went slowly to the door and was in time to see Philippa start her small car and race off in a flurry of gravel.

She reached the gate safely, but in the road outside the big Edwardian house she took the first corner too fast and could not avoid an oncoming bus. Or that was what the police thought had happened. The driver said she drove straight at him.

She was in hospital for months, her face badly cut and permanently scarred despite many operations. Both legs were broken, and an arm, and several ribs, and she had a fractured skull. When she recovered, as much as she ever did, she lived in the seaside house, almost a recluse, disfigured and with one leg shorter than the other, lame for ever and a mental cripple until eventually she had to go into a nursing home.

I made her an allowance. Marjorie insisted, for it was all my fault, and my punishment was to remember that every subsequent day of my life.

'I knew about it, Hugh,' Marjorie told me. 'I'd known all the time. But I didn't write the letters. I made myself content with what I had in life, which was a great deal, as well as your companionship and most of your loyalty. She was your small excitement, and, in a way, I understood. And I remember Derek. He was a selfish, insensitive man, while you are gentle. She deserved some joy.'

Philippa died today. I used to visit her each fortnight, though towards the end she did not know who I was. She was, in the end, relieved of pain and mental anguish by drugs, and I could not bear to see her reduced to such a pitiful piece of wreckage. I snuffed out her life easily enough, with a pillow over her face. She did not struggle, and I left her, tidiness restored, apparently asleep, but the nurses will discover what I did, for they thought that she would live for years. I came here to try to make sense of it all, face my guilt, decide what must be done, and I've concluded that this is not the place for my resolution.

I shall drive inland and stop at a well-known local beauty spot overlooking a spectacular ravine, where a waterfall gushes over rocks forty feet below a viewing point. There has been a lot of rain here in recent weeks, and there will be plenty of water pouring down the mountain. To aid my apparently accidental fall, I may have to break the wooden safety barrier. This may get some official into trouble for neglect, but I do not wish my family to endure the opprobrium of my suicide: as I shall leave no letter, an open verdict of vertigo, even a heart attack, which, if my body is pounded by the rocks, as it will be, obliterating any chance of survival, may not be detectable. An eye for an eye and a tooth for a tooth: a life for a life. I destroyed Philippa long before her death.

I have left a clue for Marjorie. Among my papers she will find an envelope containing words cut out from newspapers, trial efforts at the letters I wrote and sent anonymously when I wanted to extricate myself from my entanglement and sought to do it so despicably. She will understand.

WIDOW'S
MIGHT

Mrs Watson watched as the gardener, high on a ladder, lopped the branches of the tall palm in the hotel garden. Heavy trusses of berries fell to the ground, and the trunk of the tree bore smooth white spherical scars where he made his cuts. So death came, chopping down those who had lived too long or who had flirted with danger, or were doomed.

She sat in a comfortable chair in the shade of a pomegranate, a book on her knee. A gentle breeze stirred the leaves of the red hibiscus and the blue flowers of a plumbago which sprawled on a trellis beside the steps leading to the terrace. Though it was November, the island, warmed by the Gulf Stream, was never cold and seldom uncomfortably hot. Its jagged coastline bore a rash of large hotels, but Mrs Watson's, one of the oldest, was also the most expensive and the most luxurious. Here, the ratio of staff to clients was almost one to one and, lapped in care, the pampered guests felt worries, aches and pains slip away, forgotten.

Mrs Watson and her husband had first visited the island when on a cruise. Their liner had steamed in at daybreak and they had spent an interesting day, visiting the cathedral and driving into the country in a taxi. They had passed banana plantations, waterfalls, and reached mountain areas where the air was fresh, and they had had tea at this hotel where now she sat alone. Her husband had approved it as a suitable place for them to visit in the future: only there had been no future for Mr Watson for that very night, en route to Gibraltar, he had had a heart attack in their cabin on 'A' deck and had died within minutes. Mrs Watson and the coffin had flown home to a well-attended funeral at the local crematorium where representatives of the many organisations with

261

which the deceased had been connected, diluted with members of his staff and several workmen from the current sites he was developing, made up the congregation. There were no children of their union, no son to lead her to her pew, and Mrs Watson proudly walked alone.

Mr Watson had been a property developer, and by the terms of his will, so long as the business prospered, she was well provided for: however, now it was in the hands of his partner. They had amalgamated when both were competing for a particularly desirable site in the centre of a new town: a Dutch auction over it had seemed pointless at the time, and, since then, the two had worked well together. Now the partner was obliged to pay Mrs Watson a large portion annually of his profits. This was satisfactory for several years, until the partner spread himself too far, the banks called in their loans, and the business fell apart.

Mrs Watson was only forty-five years old when she became a widow. She was still trim and shapely, her hair burnished gold, rinsed regularly by Sandra at Bandbox Coiffures, and her complexion smooth. She found life hard alone, for Mr Watson, fifteen years older than she, had cherished her all the twenty-five years of their life together. She had worked in his office as a bookkeeper: she was good at figures, and very pretty, and had soon attracted the attention of the rising Mr Watson, who was looking about for a suitable wife, something he had been too busy to do sooner, for what was the point of amassing a fortune if you had no one to spend it on?

Mrs Watson, then Madge Fraser, had grown up in a semi-detached villa in Luton, where her father was a bank clerk and her mother devotedly kept house, running up frocks for Madge on her Singer machine and cooking nourishing meals, in between keeping the house spotless. In those days women were not expected to strive on all fronts as mothers, wives and wage-earners, and couples who found themselves incompatible or bored with one another usually stayed together in conditions of civilised truce until or unless one of them was tempted away by a new love. However, Madge's parents were fond of each other and of their only child, pinning their ambitions and hopes on her, and when she married her boss, just as happened in the magazines her mother read, their joy and pride were boundless.

Madge went to live in Bletchley, in a new four-bedroomed house with two bathrooms, a study and a utility room as well as a large lounge and dining-room. It stood in nearly an acre of garden, all laid out and planted by a nursery-man. Like her mother, Madge cleaned and baked, and in her spare time did *gros point* as there was no daughter to sew for or take to dancing-class, nor was there an economical reason to dress-make for herself. She went to flower-arranging classes and art lessons to fill up her time, and gradually she became a gardener, rearranging what the nursery-man had planned and devising new corners and grottoes. She joined a gardening club and went with them on excursions to stately homes where she secretly broke off shoots of plants to propagate through cuttings, building up a remarkable collection of shrubs unique in their neighbourhood. Mr Watson was proud of her green fingers and had no notion as to the true source of her acquisitions.

After Madge's father died, her mother stayed on in the house in Luton, but she accompanied the Watsons on their holidays, staying in hotels in Spain and villas in Greece, which she found rather hot. Eventually she expired peacefully in her sleep after a bout of flu, giving in death no more trouble than she had given in life and leaving Madge her worldly possessions, the house now free of its mortgage and her few pieces of jewellery.

Madge sold up and used the money to open a florist's shop which she named Rosa's, where she installed as assistant a woman she met in her flower-arranging class. Mr Watson was amused at the venture and pleased with its success. 'Madge's toy,' he called it, 'her baby, seeing as we've none of our own.' The enterprise flourished and she opened a second shop in another district, then a third. Her foraging trips to alien gardens grew fewer as the business absorbed her surplus

energy and her administrative skills. By the time of Mr
Watson's demise she was prospering in her own right, so that
when his partner went officially bankrupt – though in fact he
had siphoned away considerable funds in the name of his wife
and daughter, enough to enable him to start up again when
his debts were written off – she was able to maintain her
customary standard of living. She continued to reside at
Greenways, which property alone was now worth a considerable sum, enough to fund a comfortable life for Madge if her
florist shops failed. But they did not: they expanded and
throve as Madge took on able managers to whom she paid
bonuses on turnover.

But she did not enjoy being a widow.

It was not simply that she missed the comfort of Mr
Watson's protection, his big warm body, his interest and his
pampering: it was the rest of the condition that irked. She was
unpartnered now, half of what had been a whole, an outcast
in paired society. When travelling, her single state seemed as
if it was a crime. People shunned her. Except in the best
hotels, she was given an inferior room and at far higher cost
than the rate for one half of a couple. Her table in the dining-
room would be near a service door or in a draught, and the
wine waiter would ignore her, although she always ordered
a half bottle of the best local wine available. Sometimes she
would be served rapidly, course following upon course so that
she could be removed swiftly from the scene; at other times
she would be neglected. Mrs Watson never returned to hotels
which treated her in this manner, but here nothing was too
much trouble: she was tended ceremoniously.

Here, it was the guests to whom she seemed invisible, and
Mrs Watson knew the reason: it was fear. The women were
warned of the isolation that would be theirs when they
became widows themselves, as statistically was quite proba-
ble, and the men were reminded of their own mortality.

When she was younger, Mrs Watson had posed a different
threat, though at the time she had been unaware of it because
it had never occurred to her to embark on any sort of affair;

with hindsight, now, she recognised that she had been still pretty, even desirable, when she began to travel alone. At home she had been pursued, to her naïve surprise, by one of her husband's cronies, an untimely widower, but she had soon made her lack of interest plain. She needed no meal ticket for her security, and her energies were directed towards her own business and her garden, where an aged man helped her to keep down the weeds and cut the grass.

She observed the couples who came and went during her visits to various luxurious hotels, and she wondered which would still be together the following year, which parted either by death or by divorce. Because the hotels were expensive, most of the couples she encountered were older guests whose families had grown and flown, but sometimes there were honeymooners, shyly young among their elders and benignly smiled upon, and there were other couples, obviously paired without the formality of a marriage certificate.

Mrs Watson watched an elderly man and his wife cross the lawn and stiffly mount the stairs that led from the garden to the wide verandah where teas were served. The man carried his wife's knitting in its floral bag: Mrs Watson had observed her turning the heel of a warm olive-green sock; her own mother had knitted socks like that when Mrs Watson was herself a schoolgirl, during the war. Her father, myopic and flat-footed, had been spared the call-up but he was an Air Raid Warden and her mother was a member of a knitting-party. Mrs Watson had not realised that people still wore hand-knitted socks. She wondered what work, if any, the husband had done – he was long past retiring age. With them were their son – unmistakable because so like the mother – and a daughter-in-law, a pale, elegant woman who had about her an air of confident distinction. Breeding, thought Mrs Watson, breaking off a spur of the red hibiscus which, if it took, would replace one she had lost in a recent severe winter; breeding gave you that air of quiet arrogance, but would it be of help if your husband was struck down prematurely and you were left alone? Who, then, would open doors for you, carry hand luggage, park the car after dropping you at the door of wherever you were going, complain if a room was unsuitable or the service bad? She would not be left penniless, that elegant woman; there would be insurance if not family wealth, but that was not the only provision she would require.

The younger couple passed Mrs Watson's chair, and the woman saw Mrs Watson drop her hibiscus sprig into her bag.

At dinner, Mrs Watson sat not far from the quartet. Ready to be pleasant, she smiled across at them but was ignored as she consumed her lobster bisque, her gnocchi, her chicken, then her chocolate mousse.

Leaving the dining-room while the four were still eating, passing behind the younger woman's chair, Mrs Watson heard her speak.

'That woman was stealing sprigs from the plants,' she said in a thin, clear voice. 'I saw her do it. An hibiscus shoot today. What will it be tomorrow? A pomegranate, do you suppose? Perhaps she could grow one from the fruit.'

'Charlotte, don't! She'll hear,' shushed the mother, whose own voice was more penetrating than her daughter-in-law's.

'Who cares?' was the answer. 'It should be reported. If every guest did it, there would be nothing left. She's like those people who come to Ferbingham. They've stripped whole sprays from the mulberry, and some of the choicest shrubs are decimated. We've had to put notices up and we may have to employ special patrols.'

Mrs Watson, moving slowly, had heard most of this. So they lived in Ferbingham, did they? She had visited that garden and she had a shoot from the well-known mulberry rooted and beginning to sprout. Ferbingham was a Tudor mansion opened on certain selected dates in the year; Mrs Watson knew that the elder couple had moved to the dower house some years ago, leaving their son to manage the estate.

She made up her mind that night. The supercilious Charlotte should be this year's victim. Every time she went away she chose one, and had been foiled only once when her target had left before she could carry out her plan, leaving no time for a substitute to be picked. Mrs Watson never returned for a second visit to any hotel, however enjoyable her stay; it did not do to retrace one's steps lest a second incident might seem more than coincidence.

Last year, in Montreux, vulgarity had been the trigger. She had felt shame, witnessing the brash conduct of a couple who, as they acquired money and the spurious status it bought, had not acquired manners to match. This year it was an excess of conceit and condescension that were significant.

Last year, near a cable-car station, there had been a fatal fall from a cliff. No one had suspected the white-haired widow – Madge had abandoned her gold rinse years ago – who reported witnessing the fall of being its cause. The man had strayed away from his wife: the side of the mountain was steep and the sudden shove totally unexpected.

This year opportunity and method might be less easy.

Mrs Watson stalked her prey and heard them order a taxi to visit the Botanical Gardens which, she knew, were high on a hillside; she had been there already, herself.

Mrs Watson was there an hour before they arrived. She had walked round seeking possible hazards and admired lilies and orchids, glossy scarlet anthurium which looked waxen, strelitzia – the birds of paradise flowers – the pendulous trumpets of datura, which was a poisonous plant. She leaned on the walking stick she often carried – a versatile accessory – and gazed across the ravine dividing the hills to where the distant sea shone blue. There was no cruise ship in today and, late in the season as it was, there were few visitors to the gardens that day. Then she saw the elderly mother approaching along a side path, pausing to gaze at various plants; she was with her son. Looking about, Mrs Watson saw no sign of Charlotte or her father-in-law. Perhaps they had decided not to come?

It proved to be so. She watched carefully, making sure they were absent: so much the better for her purpose. The old woman and her son – his name was Hugo, Mrs Watson had heard it spoken – consulted the labels attached to various plants, moving slowly to a viewpoint where, protected by a low stone parapet built less than a yard from the sheer drop beyond, one could gaze in safety at the vista. She made an entry in a small red notebook where she had listed plants seen and identified. As she wrote down the name of an unusual cactus – she did not like cacti – fate played into her hands, for Hugo, ahead of his mother and approaching the spot where Mrs Watson was waiting, called out to the old lady.

'There'll be a wonderful view here,' he told her.

'You go ahead,' she replied. 'You know I don't care for heights. I'll wait for you near those lilies we liked. We might note some varieties and see if we can order the bulbs.'

She turned and walked down a cobbled path, vanishing from sight round a bend, and Hugo advanced towards where Mrs Watson stood. She surreptitiously dropped her notebook over the parapet and, before uttering small cries of distress, leaned over to poke at it with her stick till it lodged in a small bush on the edge of the ravine.

Hugo, ever civil, although aware that this was the woman his wife had seen snipping cuttings from plants in the hotel garden, made concerned enquiries as to what was wrong.

'My references,' cried Mrs Watson. 'My check list of names – flowers I've seen and identified, to report to my local flower club. I've dropped it. So silly of me,' and she leaned over the parapet gazing at the spot where, only just out of reach, the small notebook reposed.

'It's important, is it?' asked Hugo.

'Vital. It's the only record I've got,' Mrs Watson declared. 'I have to give a talk to the group when I get home.' She looked at him. 'You're very tall. Couldn't you reach it?'

'Hardly,' said Hugo, with a grimace. 'I might simply knock it over the hillside down the ravine.'

'I'll climb over and get it,' said Mrs Watson. 'Perhaps you'd just hold my arm while I do so, to steady me?'

'I can't let you do that,' exclaimed Hugo, looking aghast at

Mrs Watson, five foot two inches tall, and no longer young. 'I'll have a go. My arms are longer.'

'Oh no!' Hand to mouth, Mrs Watson demurred.

Hugo, carried back to boyhood days of derring-do, swung one leg over the low wall, then the other, crouching, now out of sight of anyone who might come towards them. The ledge was narrow, but though he held the wall at first, he found he could not reach the notebook without releasing his grasp. He had just seized it when he felt a sudden jab in the small of his back. Mrs Watson, pushing with all her might, had feared she would lack the strength to make him lose his balance, but she succeeded, and uttering only a strangled cry, he tore at a bush which broke off in his hand as he hurtled towards the valley.

Mrs Watson held back her piteous cries and shrieks for a few vital seconds, making sure he had fallen satisfactorily and fatally far before raising the alarm. When retrieved, Hugo's body bore a great many bruises, and the sharp round one caused by the ferrule of her walking stick aroused no special interest. She said, with truth, that he had insisted on climbing over the wall to rescue her notebook which most foolishly she had dropped.

'I tried to persuade him it was of no consequence,' she declared, weeping gently. 'But he insisted.'

The notebook was still clutched in his hand. It contained, as she had said, a list of a great many plants but it was not just what she had seen on the island; it was of more significance, for each plant noted was special. The oleander was a memory of Crete, and an accident in a swimming-pool; an agapanthus meant a fall at Lindos. A gentian reminded her of Lausanne and sleeping pills in brandy, followed by a lakeside walk in the dusk. There were others.

The cactus should represent Hugo.

It didn't do to mock at widows. Their ranks increased all the time. Now it was Charlotte's turn.

Who would be next?

THE
LAST
RESORT

Mrs Robinson dressed carefully for the journey up the Rhine. Setting off from Heathrow, she wore her brown and navy check tweed skirt – not an expensive one, although when he gave her the money for it, she had told Roderick that it cost over a hundred pounds. The truth was that she had bought it at a chain store. Roderick liked her to be well-dressed; it was part of her image as his chattel. She understood her role. With the skirt, she wore what looked like a silk blouse, and her pearls. These were genuine, left her by her mother, but now worth very little. A camel-hair jacket covered all these items.

She had to admit that Roderick had never been mean, as long as what was bought could be appreciated by others. For many years he had worked for an organisation with offices in West Africa, Mexico and the Far East, and had spent more time abroad than at home. He had been well paid for his labours, and enjoyed a good pension. While he was away, Mrs Robinson – Lois – had raised two sons and a much younger daughter, Angela, who was now attached, without benefit of marriage, to a guitarist named Barry. They travelled around with other musicians performing in clubs or wherever they could get engagements, to the horror of Angela's father, who condemned her domestic situation as immoral. Angela, renamed Cat, sang with the group, and a photograph of her, wearing a leopard-like catsuit, ornamented their posters and the sleeves of the few records they had made. Roderick had convinced himself that drink or drugs, probably both, provoked the group's noisy energy; he had disowned Angela. Mrs Robinson knew that cheap wine was Barry and Angela's only stimulant, and that in modest amounts. Using cunning, she had visited them in Paris.

After Roderick retired, the Robinsons began travelling in Europe, which he had seldom visited, his business trips taking him much further afield. A habit of restlessness had developed within him, and after a few weeks of playing golf and studying the Stock Exchange, he would fret until he could pack and be off. Now, with no business associates, he required company, and his wife must provide it: who else? They had been to Spain, to Germany, and several times to France, but after a few journeys on their own, they joined escorted tours where ill-chosen hotels or disappointing excursions could be blamed on the organisers, not on Roderick's selection. And there were people to impress, new audiences for his opinions on the day's events or anything else he wished to talk about.

Last year in Paris, Mrs Robinson had found Angela and Barry living in an attic in a cheap area, where they had an outlook across the roofs towards the towers of Notre Dame. The Robinsons' programme for the day had included a visit to Fontainebleau, and that morning Lois had said she felt unwell. Roderick, as she had known he would, went off without her, and she had won her chance to visit Angela.

When she arrived at the flat, she was warmly welcomed by Barry, who had three days' growth of stubble on his chin, but that, Mrs Robinson knew, was current fashion. Nevertheless, it prickled her cheek when he kissed her, and she wondered briefly how Angela felt about it. Her first impression of their one room was of colour: bright cushions, a vivid bedspread thrown over the divan; next, she noticed the cheap furniture, the damp walls. They had rented it from another musician now in America, and would be there for a further fortnight. They had some other bookings, but it was clear that their future was insecure. When they had enough put by, they said, they wanted to open a guest-house of their own in Spain, where Barry would entertain the visitors with songs. Would it ever happen? Mrs Robinson looked at Barry, with his tangled mane of rich brown curls, and saw the kindness in his eyes and their soft expression when he glanced at Angela, whose own blonde hair was cropped to fit like a skull-cap round her small head. Barry's real name was Bartholomew and he was a vicar's son. Mrs Robinson knew that they lived in the hope of realising a dream, but what was wrong with that? Maybe they would achieve it; in the meantime, they had love.

There was no love between her and Roderick; she knew that now, knew also that the illusion of it years ago had been just that: a fantasy. But she had not missed the experience, for she had been married before. Her first husband had been killed soon after the invasion of Normandy. He had stepped on a mine and was blown to pieces. Lois had loved Teddy deeply, but they had had only a week's leave together, which had left her pregnant with Thomas, who was now a plumber in Australia. Occasionally, when subjected to a particularly severe reproof from Roderick about her failure to fulfil one or another of his requirements, Lois would wonder what life with Teddy would have been like. They had scarcely known each other, meeting at a dance in the town where she lived. At the time, she had been a clerk in the local office of the Ministry of Food; it was essential work and exempted her from being called up so that she could live at home and look after her father. Her parents' house had been hit by a bomb in 1942, and her mother was killed. Her father had been badly injured and had lost a leg. The house itself had been shored up and made habitable, and here she had remained, her circumstances little altered until Thomas was born. Her father had made no objections to her hasty marriage; he had married his own wife during the First World War and understood the need to clutch at happiness. It had worked out for them; why should it not work out also for their daughter?

The young widow, her father, and the baby Thomas were happy enough for more than a year, and then Lois's father died suddenly in his sleep. There was not much money left, but mother and baby had a home. After a while, Lois found work at a nearby hospital where there was a crèche arrangement, and there she met the convalescent Roderick, who had had pneumonia. Years later, during a quarrel, she discovered that a girl to whom he had been engaged had married someone else by whom she was already pregnant; at least she hadn't foisted another man's child on him, the furious Roderick had said, when revealing this history.

'I didn't foist Tom on you. You said he was a dear little chap,' wept Lois, but even as she spoke, she recalled how Roderick had laid out Tom's precious little cars – bought second-hand because there were few new toys in those days – in regimented rows for the child to play with. Only with hindsight did she realise that Tom had not been allowed to let them range freely about or be used as tanks and lorries.

'No. They are cars, and must be parked so,' Roderick would say, disciplining Thomas before he was three years old. 'A boy needs a father,' he had declared, offering his hand but never, as she later understood, his heart.

He had assessed the potential value of the property she owned, the bomb-damaged, temporarily repaired small house on the fringe of a south coast town. When they sold it, the money went into Roderick's account and was used to buy another in his name, in a Midland suburb near his new firm's offices. That had appreciated and they had moved again, to a bigger place appropriate to their improved status, and so it had gone on but she was now dependent on Roderick for every penny.

No longer, however, for she had been cheating him for years, building up a nest egg by fraudulent accounting for her clothes and other expenses, and by economical housekeeping. She had milked Roderick of many hundreds of pounds, planning her escape, and she meant to achieve it on this holiday which, after the flight from Heathrow and a night in Cologne, would continue with a trip up the Rhine. Somewhere on the journey she would have an opportunity, and when it came, she must seize it bravely or it would be too late; she was getting old.

Had he been different when he was young, she wondered, watching him across the table in the ship's restaurant. They were travelling with a group of people professing interest in ancient buildings, and they had disembarked to visit cathedrals, churches and occasional castles in the towns through which they passed. With them was their courier, Kay, a trim woman, no longer young, who was adept at defusing friction among her small group. At intervals she also took on the burden of plain Miss Smythe and blowsy Miss Howard, who were each travelling alone and unfortunately had not taken to one another. Roderick ignored them, apart from ostentatiously allowing them to precede him through the doorway. He did not ignore pretty Mrs Clifford, just over five feet tall and as slim as a twelve-year-old girl; he supervised the loading and unloading of her baggage, and nightly included her in the Robinsons' bottle of wine. She lapped all this attention up as though accustomed to it, as, indeed, she was. She had been married three times, divorced once and widowed twice. Now she was looking for someone new, but had not found him on this holiday, for all the men were married and she preferred the unattached. Mrs Robinson could see, in Roderick's manner towards Mrs Clifford, traces of his short-lived concern for her and Thomas; it was all false. Meanwhile, his preoccupation gave her breathing space and she could concentrate on strategy.

Mrs Robinson had been told that Strasbourg would be spectacular, the pierced spires of the cathedral a marvel to behold. Her chance might come there, she thought; she knew they had some distance to walk from their parked coach. Roderick would sit with her in the coach, his bulk uncomfortably close, but he would be watching for Mrs Clifford, waiting to hand her down. Lois would be prepared to slip away, if she could.

That morning, he questioned why she carried her small zipped holdall when the day was warm and dry, but she did not answer. In the bag was a change of underwear, spare tights, a toothbrush, and a fat bundle of travellers' cheques which represented all her savings.

She watched Roderick and Mrs Clifford walking ahead of her along the narrow street towards the cathedral. They had driven round the town, admired the buildings used by the European Parliament, and stood gazing at the timbered houses, so ancient and historic, in the centre of the city. The guide had said that Strasbourg was spared destruction in the war because the United States Command had already decided to have its headquarters there. Forward planning, thought Mrs Robinson, just like Roderick's. And now, her own.

After their marriage, he had not been demobilised for some time and was stationed in Germany, where it was never suggested that she should join him. She and Thomas carried on as before, but she was no longer a widow and there was more money. Soon there was also Julian, now an accountant in Manchester. Mrs Robinson did not like to remember her honeymoon with Roderick, so different from her few nights with Teddy; Julian was the result of that experience.

He's like a tank, running over everything that's in his way, regardless, she thought in the years that followed, and was thankful for his frequent absences overseas. Sometimes he was gone for months, and though wives and families could accompany their husbands on some postings, Roderick, to her great relief, never proposed that his should do so. She was happy while he was away, but when he returned he cross-examined Thomas and Julian about the details of their lives since last he saw them. Thomas never said a lot, but Julian could be led into revelations of maternal mismanagement – running out of eggs, failure to equip him with the right sort of shoes for school, seeing too much of neighbours whom, he sensed, his father disapproved of. Tiny betrayals were easily contrived.

She could not leave Roderick, for she had no money of her own, and there were the two boys to support; in those days, separated mothers were not assured of maintenance or state aid.

The birth of Angela put an end to dreams of a different life, and Mrs Robinson developed a protective shell against the hurts administered verbally by her husband, though she could not always avoid his physical assaults. She had not anticipated having more children, had taken steps to prevent it happening, but had been defeated by Roderick's impatience after a spell overseas. At first the notion of a daughter had intrigued him, but Angela had always been a rebel and she was often in disgrace; small wonder that she, like Thomas, left home as soon as she was old enough.

Thomas had gone to Australia. In those days you could emigrate for very little outlay, and he soon earned enough. In Sydney, he had his own plumbing business which was prospering. He had married, and his daughter Sally, a nurse, had been to England on holiday – a period of delirious joy for the English grandmother whom she had never met before. Her visit coincided with a spell abroad for Roderick; it was easy to pretend that all was well.

Roderick's retirement had meant constant fear, sometimes real terror when he struck her. How many other wives lived in similar dread, she wondered? She had noticed that some widows, after a few months' bereavement, shed years and thrived on their new freedom.

She would not wait till she was widowed. She might have to wait too long; indeed, the time might never come.

The Robinsons now lived in Devon, by the coast, near where they had taken the children for seaside holidays. Mrs Robinson had expected grandchildren to visit them there, but Julian and his smart, sophisticated wife, who was a banker, had no children. Roderick had taken up golf, which kept him out all day; he lunched at the club with his cronies after their morning round, and allegedly played another in the afternoons. On fine days, he did; if it was wet the men sat round drinking, or played snooker. While this went on, Mrs Robinson built up a small network of local activities so that she could escape for at least some evenings in the week. She studied history, she learned to weave, she took up painting. Roderick always made her late for her classes, insisting on her serving dinner first, and he never let her take the car, so she cycled, until people realised what she was doing and began giving her lifts.

Did they suspect anything? Did Elsie Burton, whose husband was one of Roderick's golf partners, notice Lois's bruised cheek, the burn on her hand? No one ever said a word.

Mrs Robinson had known her break must be made while they were away from home, otherwise Roderick would find her before she had properly escaped. Besides, at home she would lack the courage to choose a date and stick to it; on holiday, she briefly bloomed, for Roderick, wanting to impress their fellow travellers with his generosity, would tell her to go off and buy herself a pair of shoes or some trifle, and sit back as if to say she must be indulged. When she returned with her purchase, he would belittle her choice to the company.

Because he already had a passport when they took up travelling, she had obtained her own, though he had intended putting her on his. Foreseeing this, she had already applied. She had decided to visit Tom and her grandchildren in Australia. Roderick had never allowed her to do this; they were not his grandchildren, he had pointed out, so he had no interest in them, and it was her duty to stay at home and look after him.

Mrs Robinson had not planned what would happen when her money ran out. Tom might understand, might suggest she should stay in Sydney, might find her accommodation – she would not live with him and his family, even if they suggested it. She supposed she was too old to find work, though she could cook and clean, and did so every day at home. Perhaps someone would employ her as a housekeeper; latterly, such dreams had given her hope.

She did not know that you had to have a visa for Australia.

On the river cruise, their cabin was small, the space between their beds less than three feet. At home they no longer shared a bedroom; she had moved her things into the small back bedroom when she had a cold, with the excuse of not wanting to infect him, and had never returned. There was a bolt on the door, but so far her privacy had not been challenged. On the boat she lay wakeful, waiting until Roderick's snores began before relaxing. After a few hours he would heave himself out of bed and visit the small closet which held the shower and toilet. He was often noisy in there, but the trip was only for four days; she could endure that. She turned her face to the wall and pulled the duvet round her ears. He left her alone.

Leaving Strasbourg cathedral after admiring the amazing clock, she had begun to walk away from the group when Mrs Clifford called her.

'Lois, we're going to have a cup of tea. Come along,' she cried, in her high, light voice.

She'd left it too late, and next day the voyage, but not the holiday, would end.

After disembarking, they were to travel by coach to a Swiss lakeside hotel for the final two days and nights. Here, the Robinsons had a large room, almost a suite, with a spacious lobby separating the bathroom from the bedroom. There was a balcony overlooking the lake and the mountains, which unfortunately, when they arrived, were shrouded in mist. It would clear by morning, Kay, the courier, said encouragingly, telling them what time dinner would be served in the hotel restaurant.

Mrs Robinson decided to leave the next day. An excursion by steamer on the lake was planned; she would say she was tired of the water and wanted to see the churches in the town, choosing her moment, speaking in front of witnesses so that although Roderick would chide her, he would do it in the winsome manner he adopted in front of other people, as much as to say, look what I have to put up with, with this silly woman, but he would enjoy escorting Mrs Clifford. Mrs Robinson would go to the station, which was near the hotel, and catch a train to Geneva airport, then buy a ticket to Australia. That night she hardly slept for excitement, and in the morning she woke early, needing the bathroom.

She padded quietly out of the bedroom, a thin figure in her long cotton nightgown, and crossed the carpeted lobby to the bathroom. She did not see the soap on the shiny tiled floor, where Roderick had dropped it the night before, and she slipped, striking her head on the side of the bath. She gave no cry as she fell.

An hour later Roderick found her. Her face was pale and her limbs cold, but she was breathing. He stepped across her to reach the lavatory, relieved himself, washed his hands carefully, rinsed out his mouth and spat, then stepped over her again to return to the bedroom where he crossed to the window and gave himself up to ten minutes' hard thought. After this he picked her up – she was surprisingly heavy – and put her back in her bed, covering her up. She made no sound at all. He was thinking that she must have had a stroke or a heart attack: then, returning to the bathroom, he saw the soap and decided that she was probably concussed. He uncovered her again and opened the window while he bathed and shaved, then dressed, spraying himself with eau-de-Cologne which he had bought at the start of the holiday. Crisp and brisk, he went down to breakfast, nodding across the dining-room at the rest of the group. Mrs Clifford was sitting with Kay, the courier, and he asked if he might join them.

'My wife has a headache,' he told Kay. 'She doesn't want any breakfast, and she won't come on the excursion today. She's best left. I'll take her up some tea and toast.'

Giving a good performance as a devoted spouse, he poured out the tea, spread butter and marmalade on a slice of toast, and bore it upstairs. He would eat the toast himself and drink the tea instead of having a second cup downstairs. This would indicate that Lois had consumed the light meal before her death.

For the chances were that she would die, if left long enough without treatment. If she were to recover consciousness, she would be confused and would accept as the truth his version of events. He left her exposed to the chill air coming through the balcony window until the last moment before setting off, in his raincoat, and with a scarf wound round his neck, into the sharp October day.

The sky was clear and in the distance the mountains sparkled under a covering of snow. It boded well for the trip, and he would devote himself to entertaining Mrs Clifford; he fancied she enjoyed his tales of life in the Far East.

Before departing, he pulled the covers up over Mrs Robinson as far as her waist, leaving one arm out as if she had fallen asleep in that posture, and in the bathroom he rescued the errant soap, put it in the rack at the side of the bath, and wiped the slippery place on the floor. He hung on the bedroom door the red notice indicating that the occupants did not wish to be disturbed, walked down the passage and rang for the lift.

Mrs Robinson was dead when, in the late afternoon, the housekeeper entered after tapping and tapping on the door with no response, and after reception had telephoned the room several times to ask when it could be cleaned.

Roderick, returning with his travelling companions after an enjoyable outing, was greeted by the anxious face of the hotel manager and by two policemen. When the news was broken, he went into his rehearsed speech about how his wife had felt unwell. He was told there was a bruise on her head and that she could either have fallen or been struck down. He said that must have happened after he left; no doubt she went into the bathroom; perhaps she fell there; the floor was dangerously slippery, he added, frowning, the word *damages* hovering in the air, unspoken. She'd had tea and a piece of toast before he left, he said.

It was Mrs Clifford who said she thought it was odd that he had spread marmalade on his wife's toast, for she knew that Lois Robinson preferred honey or jam and, indeed, on the boat had said that she never ate marmalade; nor did she take sugar in her tea, yet her husband had put two spoonfuls in her cup. He, however, did take sugar, she had noticed; he liked marmalade, too, and had several times asked for it on the river boat when it was absent from the breakfast table.

'The autopsy will show if she ate the toast and drank the tea,' said the police officer.

He already knew that Mrs Robinson's holdall contained over £3,000 in travellers' cheques, an address in Sydney written on luggage labels, and a timetable of flights from various cities to Australia, as well as her passport. If she had drunk the tea, her lips would have marked the cup and her fingerprints would be on the handle. Tests would prove if this was so. Meanwhile, it was a suspicious death, as she had been dead for hours.

Roderick, demanding to see the British Consul, was taken off to the police station.

Mrs Clifford was glad she had been so observant. This characteristic had prevented her from making serious mistakes in the past.

GREEK
TRAGEDY

Patrick Grant sat beneath the vine on the terrace of Ariadne's taverna and, for the first time in nearly a week, felt at home. Below the whitewashed building above the small town lay the Ionian Sea, where the cruise ship *Andromeda* rode at anchor. Earlier, he had disembarked by launch, crossing the choppy water to the quay, a long stone jetty where the island ferries moored and the caiques tied up.

He had been to this island before, years ago, when he and Liz had at last risked a holiday together. They had rented a villa beyond the town, a small stone haven with three rooms and a bathroom whose plumbing was unreliable. Most evenings, they had wandered into the town to eat at one or another of the tavernas scattered along the waterfront or in the squares and alleys radiating from it, and Ariadne's had become their favourite. Here, it was always cool, and the fish dishes were rightly celebrated. Liz, drinking Demestica – neither of them liked retsina – would bloom and become animated, practising the little Greek she had learned.

During the day, she swam a lot, walking to a small cove near the villa while Patrick worked on his book. He would join her before lunch, usually cheese and salad at home, and in the afternoon he would work again while she, finding it too hot outside, would stitch at a tapestry she had bought to occupy herself while he was absorbed. Sometimes she did a little desultory sketching, but was dissatisfied with the results; she read a good deal, too. Patrick's book discussed the tragedy inherent in Shakespeare's comedies; it was aimed at a popular market and had been a minor success.

What if, he had later thought: what if he had abandoned the book for the two weeks of their holiday and given Liz, not

Shakespeare, his attention? As it was, six months after they returned to England, she had married a widowed doctor and had acquired three stepchildren, to be followed by two sons of her own.

Soon after this, Patrick had been offered a chair in Shakespearean studies at a Canadian university, and spent twelve years in British Columbia.

Now, time fell away and he almost expected to see Liz come towards him, smiling a little anxiously, as he belatedly realised she had done. She hadn't been wholly happy with him, though they had shared moments he would not forget. He, a distinguished scholar and skilled at observing other people, had never been able to manage his own personal life.

These were uncomfortable thoughts.

The terrace had been deserted when he arrived, pleased at having found the taverna still here, and so little altered. He was dawdling over his Greek salad, savouring the juicy olives and the feta cheese, when a noisy group of young people came trooping across the tiled floor to sit at tables on either side of him. Why couldn't they seat themselves further away, he thought grumpily, as their conversation loudly continued. One young man described to another the delights of a meal eaten in Acapulco, then a further gourmet experience in Rio. He recognised one of the men as the ship's photographer, the second as a dancer from the team of entertainers. The others, at the second table, were also members of the group of dancers, two men and two girls. They all began to talk across him. Why had they not sat together? Why this parade of their worldly gourmandising? Their generation spent months, even years, touring the world, touching down briefly here and there. Some did get to know other cultures, but this group, like the cruise passengers who spent only a day ashore here, a few hours there, imagined they had seen the world.

Patrick's mullet arrived and as he ate it, with the remainder of his salad and some coarse Greek bread, he noticed that the conjuror, accompanied by a thin girl whom Patrick recognised as the one sawn in half on the first night at sea, had

taken a table across the terrace under a trellis where
bougainvillea trailed over a pillar. They seemed happy
together, talking. The bright blue of a morning glory wound
itself up a wall behind them, reflecting the blue of the girl's
skimpy dress. Patrick's bad humour dissolved; let the young
people enjoy their boasting: the day was too perfect to be one
in which to harbour resentment and old sorrows.

I am content, he thought; at this moment, I am perfectly
content. Why have I spent so little of my life like this, in
mindless idleness? Of what use were all the hours he had
dedicated to papers on jealousy as a recurring Shakespearean
theme, ranging from *The Winter's Tale* to *Othello*?

Jealousy, he thought, looking across at the conjuror and
the girl: had they a relationship outside their professional
one? Probably. Did jealousy affect it? Perhaps they were
married; people did still marry, though regularising unions
seemed to be unfashionable today.

He inhaled deeply. The air was warm, and here they were
sheltered from the brisk sea breeze which had made the
launch crossing exciting, with spray breaking over the open
stern seating, causing the passengers to shriek. Maybe it had
not been such a bad idea, after all, to come on this cruise. In
recent years he had several times joined cultural tours in the
company of other scholars; now he was a lecturer himself,
deputising for the friend of a friend, who had telephoned him
ten days before the ship sailed with a desperate plea. The
regular lecturer, who gave short talks about the ports visited,
had been in a road accident while ashore in Rome. He had
been flown home with a broken leg, crushed ribs, and a
broken arm. *Andromeda* was without a lecturer and needed a
stopgap for the next cruise to allow the shipping line time to
find someone who would be able to see them through till he
had recovered. Patrick, who had been appointed Master of St
Mark's College, Oxford, would not take up his new position
until the following year; he had time to fill, and had been
persuaded to accept the three weeks' assignment.

It was not Patrick's sort of cruise. He was sure that among

the passengers there were many estimable and interesting persons, but so far he felt he had met none. He had been directed to a table in the restaurant where his companions were two widows, one blonde-rinsed, one grey-haired; a couple in their late sixties, Mr and Mrs Jones; and another younger couple, Mr and Mrs Boyd. The blonde widow came from Chichester, the other from Norfolk; they were school friends who, since the deaths of their husbands, had taken annual holidays together and this was their third cruise. The Joneses were of retirement age; Patrick did not know from what they would have retired. Mr Boyd was a dentist and his wife was an estate agent. The last member of the group was a woman of about thirty-six, Millicent Fortescue, travelling alone. She was dark and thin, quite tall, and had little to say unless drawn out by someone else at the table; Mr Boyd was good at this, no doubt due to a lifetime spent putting people at their ease in his surgery, thought Patrick, who felt nervous of Millicent lest she interpret mere civility as personal interest.

Millicent Fortescue was a teacher.

'Not at school?' Patrick had asked her. It was, after all, term-time.

She was between posts, Millicent had crisply replied, and would be taking up a new position after Christmas. This was an unusual time for a change, Patrick reflected; the end of the academic year was the appropriate moment for a move, though of course there were exceptions. He wondered, briefly, why Millicent's year had been interrupted. Perhaps she had been ill; a cruise had always been regarded as perfect convalescence.

Now, five nights into the cruise and at peace on this Greek island, he had determined to banish all thoughts of his table companions from his mind. The appearance of the conjuror and his assistant, and the other entertainers, had reminded him of the reasons for his presence here, and his nostalgic mood had been broken. Perhaps it was as well: looking back was not always wise.

He finished his meal and strolled away down the steep hill

towards the rows of tourist-trap shops. Some sold excellent leather work and jewellery: he had bought Liz a bracelet here. Now he had no one for whom to buy trinkets, he thought dolefully, and then remembered his sister and his niece, Miranda, now twenty and about to start her third year at Exeter university. Her usual garb was black: black leggings, black baggy sweaters, a small black velvet hat with an upturned brim – rather enchanting, he had thought, when he last saw her, but sombre. Gold earrings and bracelets did not fit her current image. He sighed. She would probably grow out of this phase but, set as she was on becoming a criminal lawyer, dark attire would always be her uniform.

He decided to buy her a bracelet anyway. That could be worn with any amount of *sub fusc*.

He enjoyed making his purchase, using the small amount of Greek he could command. Afterwards, with the package in his pocket, he walked on, hoping to buy an English paper if the stock had not already been cleared out by *Andromeda's* passengers; he should have thought about it earlier. At the end of the narrow street, he saw Millicent Fortescue, who turned right. The paper shop, if Patrick remembered correctly, lay that way, too, but he turned in the other direction and met Mr and Mrs Jones head on. They were arm-in-arm, Mrs Jones leaning on her husband; Patrick saw that she was slightly lame. Why hadn't he noticed this before? He used to be so observant.

The Joneses were wondering what to buy as presents for their grandchildren.

'Or should we wait till Yalta?' they asked him. 'What shall we be able to get there?'

Patrick applied his powerful intellect to the problem.

'Those wooden dolls?' he suggested. 'The ones that fit into one another. You must have seen them around.'

They had, but the grandchildren were boys.

'Wait and see, when we get there,' he advised. 'If there's nothing that seems right, there will still be Heraklion and Venice.'

'That's true,' they admitted. 'We're so lucky, Doctor Grant,' Mrs Jones continued. 'Our daughter and son-in-law have given us this trip as a ruby wedding present. Forty years, just imagine,' and as she spoke, the couple smiled at one another, a stout, bald man with a red face and a wrinkled woman with soft white hair in a cloud of curls. They still saw one another as at their first meeting, Patrick realised: a tall young man with blue eyes, and, no doubt, a slim and pretty girl.

He felt humbled, and in a weird, rather sour way, envious.

'Would you like some coffee? A drink, perhaps?' he heard himself suggesting, against his determined intention to remain aloof from the passengers and, indeed, everyone on board.

The Joneses accepted, plumping for tea with lemon, and were impressed by what seemed to them his confident knowledge of the language as he ordered, only to be answered in perfect English by the waitress who turned out to be an American student on an extended vacation.

'You've been here before, Doctor Grant,' said Mrs Jones, smiling at him.

'Several times,' he agreed.

'We've never been to Greece. It was our ambition,' said Mrs Jones. 'David is a parson. Our income doesn't stretch to these extravagances.'

'We've made a point of going to France,' said Mr Jones. 'We've learnt to know several areas well, particularly the Languedoc.'

'David's French is fluent,' said Mrs Jones.

Patrick should have discovered Mr Jones's calling before this; he might wish to say grace before meals. There could be a social dilemma. I'll ask the Captain, Patrick decided; or perhaps this question came within the Entertainment Officer's orbit or that of the Purser. He was sailing in uncharted hierarchic waters here.

While they sat there, Patrick managing, without a struggle, to appropriate the bill, Millicent walked past them, marching on without even a nod in their direction.

'Perhaps she did not notice us,' said Eleanor Jones. 'She's a strange woman. Very withdrawn.'

'Now, Eleanor,' admonished her husband.

'David thinks I'm a terrible gossip, but I like to know about people,' said Eleanor Jones. 'Don't you, Doctor Grant?'

'But you're not gossiping about Millicent Fortescue,' said Patrick. 'You've simply stated that you think she may be shy, and I would agree with that opinion.'

'She was dismissed from the school where she was head of the history department,' said Eleanor. 'She'd had an affair with the deputy head – he was married, of course.'

'Now you are gossiping, dear,' said David Jones.

'Was the deputy head dismissed too?' asked Patrick, intrigued.

'No, and you've put your finger on the nub of the matter,' said Eleanor. 'She was the scapegoat.'

'Now, dear, we mustn't judge,' reproved her husband.

'Why not?' asked Eleanor robustly. 'He was the adulterer.' She uttered the word clearly. 'And you're a minister. Who's to say what's right and wrong if you don't?'

'In principle, I agree,' Patrick encouraged her.

'It's again a case of the woman sinned,' said Eleanor.

'I didn't think people could be dismissed for that sort of thing these days,' said Patrick. 'After all, they were consenting adults, weren't they? Neither had seduced an under-age pupil.'

'They were unlucky enough to get caught out, er – together, as you might say, on school premises,' said Eleanor. 'In the head's study, to be precise. Miss Fortescue sued for wrongful dismissal and was awarded damages.'

'How do you know all this?' asked Patrick. 'Did she tell you?'

'No. But it was in all the papers – the tabloids, anyway. The Vanessa Fortescue case. I imagine she's using her second name on this trip, to protect her identity.'

'And the damages to pay for it,' said Patrick. 'But how did you recognise her?'

'I didn't. Our daughter did, on the quayside when we embarked. She knows someone who teaches at that school. Mind you, we're not going to let her secret out. She deserves some protection.'

But you've revealed it to me, thought Patrick, and if your daughter recognised her, others may have done the same.

'She was a very good teacher, I believe,' said Eleanor. 'I hope she won't find it too difficult to get another job.'

Patrick resolved, while remaining distant, to take more interest in Millicent, and to protect the Joneses from incurring drink bills beyond their budget. The custom at the table was for passengers to take turns buying wine; in spite of the low price obtaining on board, it could be embarrassing, and neither he, nor the other men at the table, had felt comfortable about letting the two widows pay their share, but the women had prevailed. Millicent had remained impassive through the resulting conversation; she would brook no opposition when her turn came, he felt sure, and would be capable of quoting the Equal Opportunities Act to support her: much good that had been in her own recent experience.

They returned to the ship by tender from the jetty. During the day the wind had grown stronger, and it was an adventurous journey as the launch bounded about over the waves; it was difficult for the seamen to hold it steady as the passengers disembarked.

'Have you noticed how small they are?' said a soft voice close to Patrick as he waited his turn to leap on to the small landing platform.

It was Betty, the blonde widow.

'How small who are?' he asked.

'The sailors. They're not big enough to make me feel secure,' said Betty, as a large lady ahead of them was manoeuvred from the boat and began ascending the steps to the opening in the side of the ship.

Patrick was already standing aside to let Betty precede him.

'I think you'll find they're quite wiry,' he said. 'But do go first, Mrs Hunter, and then I'll be behind you to catch you if you should slip. I'm not small.'

This was true. Betty Hunter thought him a fine-looking man in his way, tall and broadly built, with dark hair now greying at the temples. He was pleasant enough at dinner, but lacked the knack of uniting the table, making everyone happy. Too academic, she decided.

She was not being flirtatious, he thought, aware that she was perhaps less than ten years older than himself; this was one cruising hazard he had been warned about which he had not, so far, encountered.

The sailors, accustomed to helping much heavier, less nimble ladies than Betty Hunter, wafted her aloft without trouble and Patrick stood back to let a number of other passengers disembark from the launch before him. By the time he reached the deck of the ship, she had gone.

He enjoyed his sessions on the bridge, delivering, by means of the loudspeaker system to any who cared to listen, instructive descriptions of the ports at which they called and the landmarks they passed. He worked from the notes of the lecturer he was replacing, regretting that he had lacked time to prepare his own, but in these talks and those given as lectures in the ship's theatre, he embellished the text with his additions, and, having snatched up a pile of books before the ship sailed, read up on each area. He looked forward to Venice, where he could refer to Portia's pleading. It was a pity they were not going to Cyprus, he reflected, his mind turning again to jealousy and the fury of Othello. What was it that made people so obsessed? Gripped by such passion, they lost all rationality.

On the bridge, ordered calm prevailed but vigilance was never relaxed. Patrick learned to interpret the video screen which showed their progress, the marks depicting other ships. He was present when the various pilots arrived, each small launch in turn fussing up to the side of the ship like a piglet in search of a teat, watching from the normal passenger deck in Istanbul as the agile man clambered up a rocking rope ladder and was helped aboard.

Istanbul: the mystery of Asia: the mosques. He visited several, awed by their magnificence but irritated by the pressing crowds of touts and tourists. Their arrival had coincided with that of a number of other cruise ships and their promised berth had been given to an Italian liner, enraging the Captain, although he maintained outward calm. It upset the timing of the excursions since the passengers had to be ferried ashore. There was a jam of buses on the quay and again at every tourist sight. Patrick joined weary coveys of passengers from *Andromeda* trooping towards the underground cistern, an impressive spectacle built by the Romans more than 1400 years ago. Though a triumph of construction, it was a haunting, melancholy place, Patrick decided, avoiding drips from the ceiling and hurrying past pools on the stone slabs of the floor.

I don't understand the East, he thought, glad to return to the ship, which was remaining in port until midnight to allow passengers to sample the delights of night life ashore. During his years in Canada he had visited Hong Kong and Japan, and much of the United States, and had often returned to Europe, but wistfully. I am a European, he thought; that's where I'm comfortable.

Now he was about to settle in the Master's Lodgings at St Mark's for the last decade of his working life; that, he suspected and hoped, would be, for him, his most appropriate ambience. He had not yet turned his mind to the politicking and guile which he would need in his new position.

The final decade. He sighed, gazing back across the water at the spires and minarets of the city he was leaving. Shakespeare had set none of his plays here.

That evening Mr and Mrs Jones pressed him to join their table for the syndicate quiz held nightly in one of the lounges, and Patrick could not remember what flower had been represented on the reverse of the old threepenny bit, nor did he know in which year various football teams had won or lost notable encounters; in fact, he was astounded by his ignorance about what he considered trivia and at the mastery shown by some of his companions. All the same, he supplied the identity of the first Plantagenet king, and knew in which of Dickens' novels Mr Pecksniff appeared. A formidable team at another table established an easy lead; there were two retired headmasters among them, Patrick was told. It was small comfort; Patrick intensely disliked the exposure of gaps in his knowledge.

'Never mind, Doctor Grant,' said Mrs Jones cheerfully. 'Perhaps the questions will be more in our line another night.'

'Where is Millicent?' asked Mr Jones. 'I haven't seen her since dinner.'

Millicent had provided that night's wine; she had ordered it earlier in the day, thus foiling any protests by confronting the rest of the table with a *fait accompli*.

'She's gone to the film,' said Betty Hunter. 'What about a last drink? Doctor Grant?'

Patrick declined, saying he wanted to read up about Yalta. He was looking forward to the visit there; it should be very interesting to see what had happened to this town which was once a resort for high officials in the Politburo, as well as the home of Chekhov, but in fact he wanted to retreat to his cabin to read another of that writer's spare, compelling short stories.

He made his escape, and took a quick turn round the deck before going down to his cabin. There, at the stern of the ship, gazing at the receding churned pattern of its wake, stood Millicent Fortescue. She was at the rail, a thin, solitary figure, upright, tense, staring at the water which was fluorescent in the moonlight. Patrick hesitated, then approached.

'How was the film?' he asked, and she turned sharply, looking startled.

He saw that for an instant she did not know who he was, so rapt was she in her thoughts and her isolation. Then she answered.

'I didn't go,' she said. 'It was an excuse. I'm not too good at communal jollity.' She had regained her composure and added, 'Nor, I suspect, are you.'

'Not really,' he agreed. 'But I'm not a professional cruiser, like the man I'm replacing, and I suppose we can all learn. Aren't you cold?' She wore no wrap and her thin, pale arms were bare. 'It's chilly now. Shall we walk a little?' he suggested.

She found herself gently pacing beside him while he asked her whether she had been to any of their ports of call before. They circled the deck together, and then he escorted her to her cabin, which was on the same deck as his own.

Well, she hadn't leapt overboard tonight, at least, he reflected, unlocking his door. Next time, there might be no one to prevent her. Her stance at the rail when he approached had been so rigid, her mental separation from the present so profound, that he was sure it had been in her mind.

Yalta lay at the base of a ridge of mountains, looking rather like an Italian lakeside town. The air was fresh, almost icy, thought Patrick, going ashore with a group bound for the Livadia Palace. The Joneses and the Boyds were in the same bus, but none of their other table companions. Patrick had not seen Millicent Fortescue that morning; he successfully dismissed her and her problems from his mind, determined to enjoy his Ukrainian experience.

In the port area there were some young boys, about ten or twelve years old, he estimated, trying to sell crudely printed children's books, and army and navy uniform caps. They were nearly as persistent as the touts in Istanbul. He felt deep sadness; was this what freedom meant?

Their guide was a man of about thirty-five whose English was impeccable; he spoke frankly about inflation and the anxiety felt by everyone. At the Vorontsov Palace, his conscientious exposition won Patrick's admiration as the man described how the palace had been built with the most expensive granite, not local stone, to demonstrate the Count's great wealth. Pushkin, staying here, had fallen in love with the Countess: hence, Eugene Onedin. It was easy to imagine the family living in this building where Winston Churchill had stayed for the Yalta Conference, an old man who had endured a six-hour car trip from where his plane had landed.

Walking in the gardens of the Livadia Palace, scene of that historic meeting at which fateful decisions about the division of Europe were made, Patrick wryly surveyed the sleeping lion on the steps, drowsing while his brothers stayed alert; Churchill, feeling tired, had seen it as a warning. What a setting: no wonder the last Tsar and his family had loved it. Poor Anastasia, the survivor who had been denied recognition by her own grandmother; what suffering she had endured, ending her days in America as Anna Anderson, acknowledged by so few. Patrick was convinced that she had been the real Anastasia and now it was possible that genetic fingerprinting would, posthumously, prove the truth of her identity.

He was in a thoughtful mood, that afternoon, when he walked alone through the pestering small and larger pedlars pursuing the tourists through the streets. He had been disappointed at not entering Chekhov's house: too small, their guide had said as they drove past it, high on the hill among the trees. He emerged on to the promenade. In this town, privileged Russians spent vacations. He hoped that while he presided over St Mark's it would be possible to encourage visits both ways; he would do it, if he could keep his head above academic red tapes.

The Joneses were sitting on a bench gazing out to sea. They looked tired, and told him they had found the sight of children trying to make money from the tourists most depressing. They had bought a Russian sailor's cap for their youngest grandson, simply because the vendor reminded them of him.

Patrick, gloomy too, changed the subject by asking them if they had seen Millicent that day. They had not.

'She seemed rather low last night,' he offered. 'I met her up on deck.'

'She's still bitter,' stated Mrs Jones. 'And probably worried about her future.'

'But she'll get another job, won't she? A good one?' Patrick asked. 'Her story won't follow her round. Or even if it does, do such things matter these days?'

'In some circles,' said Mr Jones.

'We must hope the cruise will benefit her health, at least,' said Mrs Jones. 'She feels betrayed, of course.'

But who had betrayed whom? The husband did not come out of this in a good light, thought Patrick; he had behaved badly towards both his wife and Millicent.

On board again, he returned to the bridge to describe what could be seen ashore as they sailed away. Was anyone listening to him, he wondered, mentioning Chekhov; they were probably all below in the various bars.

Dinner that night was lively, though everyone had been disturbed by the lack of goods in the shops and by the street touts. Blonde Betty had bought a beautiful white shawl made of gossamer wool, so fine she thought it would pass through her wedding ring. She did not know what she would do with it, but she had wanted to buy something.

'Did you notice that the Black Sea really is black?' she asked. 'The water, I mean. Is that why it's called the Black Sea?'

None of them, not even Patrick, knew the answer to this, but he had noticed the inky colour of the water. Perhaps the sea was very deep, like Loch Ness, also inky, and perhaps it had a dark rock or shale base, he suggested. He began to look forward to seeing Homer's wine-dark sea again, not claret-coloured, certainly, but a deep purplish hue; was wine more purple then?

Late that night he listened to the world news on his radio and there was a brief item about a man and wife found dead in their car in Sevenoaks. The man, a schoolmaster, had not been at school the previous week, off sick, it seemed. A suicide pact was suspected. The item was repeated in the morning news sheet delivered to cabins early by the steward; Patrick glanced at it, more interested in the general news.

Their next port of call was Crete. Patrick gave a morning lecture about the island, repeating it in the evening. He had good audiences at both sessions in spite of the other attractions for a day spent at sea – clay pigeon shooting, deck games, bridge or bingo, according to taste. To his surprise, Patrick saw Millicent/Vanessa at the clay pigeon shooting station by the stern, not far from where he had seen her two nights before. He watched her shatter six clays with six shots, but he went off without speaking to her, bound for the indoor pool which was larger than the one on deck. He shared it with a stout elderly lady who ignored him while she swam up and down with a steady breast-stroke, a floral bathcap on her head.

Next morning, Heraklion sparkled in the early autumn sunshine. At this time of year, rain could begin suddenly and a cloud sitting on Mount Ida was a portent of unsettled weather, but today looked set fair. Patrick hastened ashore soon after breakfast and bought several English papers, covering the past few days. He put them in the zipped case he carried with him, then took a taxi to Knossos where he spent an hour before travelling back to town by bus. He had time to fill in before he met his old friend Dimitri Manolakis*, now retired from the police and running a security advisory service, so he sat at a table in the courtyard of the restaurant where they were to lunch together, ordered a beer, and began reading the newspapers. The world situation was what interested him, but he had been unable to get *The Times* except for the previous day, and the earlier papers were tabloids. In the first, on an inside page, he read an expanded account of the alleged suicide pact in Sevenoaks. There were pictures of the dead schoolmaster and his wife, and of their children, both at university. A paragraph mentioned that the schoolmaster's name had been romantically linked with that of a former member of the staff who had sued, successfully, for wrongful dismissal. She was named.

Reading this, Patrick's heart sank. Would Millicent/Vanessa see this? Had anyone telephoned her to tell her of her lover's death? Was that why she had been up on deck,

*See *Mortal Remains* and *Cast for Death*

contemplating the ocean in what he had seen as so fatal a manner? What a dreadful business, almost a Greek tragedy. Then he wondered if other passengers would read the report and make the connection. Few would realise Vanessa Fortescue and Millicent were the same person, he decided.

She must have heard the news. It added up. Poor woman.

He turned to the later papers and from them learned that the story was more complex than had at first appeared. It wasn't a carbon monoxide matter, using the car's exhaust, as he had assumed; a gun had been found in the car and the police were treating the deaths as suspicious; enquiries were afoot to discover who had last seen the couple alive and if anyone had been noticed near their house or garage recently. The car, containing the bodies, had been locked in the garage.

He shivered, full of foreboding, and read the few lines *The Times* had chosen to print on the subject. The killer could have made the calls which gave the excuse of illness, then left to establish an alibi so that by the time the bodies were found, he could have been hundreds of miles away, beyond suspicion. Or she: the killer could have been female.

Whoever it was would have left clues: if not fingerprints, other traces which forensic scientists would discover and identify.

He spent the afternoon with Manolakis, was shown his business premises and some of the latest security devices, and exchanged news. Manolakis, once so lean, had put on weight, and his grizzled eyebrows were luxuriant.

Patrick told him about the Sevenoaks killings.

'You can't be sure it was an outside murder,' said Manolakis.

'The forensic evidence will prove it, one way or the other,' Patrick said. 'Is it likely that the husband, having got away with it, would turn on his wife and himself?'

'The wife might have changed her mind about forgiving him,' said Manolakis. His English was now very good, much better than when they last met.

'I don't think so,' said Patrick. 'Millicent Fortescue is a first-class shot. She was picking off clay pigeons on the ship like a pro.'

'You think she did it?'

'Yes.'

'Why?'

'Because she was jealous,' said Patrick.

'Was a rifle used in Sevenoaks?'

'I don't know. The newspaper simply said a gun.'

'She couldn't have shot them in the garage. Someone would have heard.'

'Maybe she surprised them somewhere else – on some favourite walk she knew of, for instance. Or she could have hidden in the car.'

'And shot them at point-blank range? She'd have been covered in blood,' said Manolakis.

'Yes, but she could have got rid of incriminating clothes,' said Patrick. 'This was carefully planned. She could have trailed them, shot them when they were out walking, driven them home in their own car. She was a family friend. She'd have known about keys, and so on.'

'They'd have been heavy for her to move.'

'She'd have managed, if she had time in hand,' said Patrick. 'Jealousy is a very strong emotion.'

'You know that, don't you, my friend?' said Manolakis, stroking his grey moustache.

Patrick shivered, and almost felt a wave of hatred for the Greek who, unlike himself, had not wasted time with Liz all those years ago.

'You should find yourself a wife,' Manolakis advised. 'You shouldn't lock yourself up alone in that ancient college, however grand your position is as principal.'

'Master,' Patrick corrected. 'It's too late now, Dimitri. I'm too selfish to make room in my life for someone else.'

'Find a mistress, then,' said Manolakis.

'I might do that,' said Patrick, and laughed self-consciously. But it wouldn't do for the Master of Mark's to lead the sort of life which could invite scandal.

Andromeda was due to sail at six o'clock. Patrick returned on board some time before that and went to have a swim. He felt troubled. Should he warn Millicent, seek her out, show her the newspaper reports? If she was not the killer, she should be told about the deaths; if she was responsible for them, she should learn that the bodies had been found. He would think about it while he swam, letting the water ease his tensions.

He found Millicent in the pool, lying on the bottom, alone, and dead.

He got her out of the water, just in case she was still alive, but there was no life in her. He telephoned for help, then stood across the doorway of the fitness complex, a towel wrapped round him, to prevent others entering before someone in authority arrived.

They kept it very quiet. The ship's doctor and the Chief Engineer dealt with everything, locking the pool area. Patrick watched while photographs were taken. He described how he had found her, and had seen no one else about. The doctor, looking at the dead woman's eyes, said she might have taken sedatives before her swim, then lost consciousness and drowned.

In case she lost the will power, Patrick thought: or was she playing Russian roulette? For someone might have come along before any drug took effect.

'An accident, maybe,' said the Chief Engineer.

Patrick offered no opinion. Why had she not gone quietly to sleep in her cabin, to be found later by the steward?

She had left no note. It would have to be decided at the inquest, by which time her links with events in Sevenoaks would have been revealed.

It was not her way to be self-effacing. She need not have sued against her dismissal, even though her cause was just: the money she received was scarcely worth the publicity its award had attracted, but she had made a statement. She had made another, now.

And in Sevenoaks.

Warner Books now offers an exciting range of quality titles by both established and new authors. All of the books in this series are available from:

Little, Brown and Company (UK),
P.O. Box 11,
Falmouth,
Cornwall TR10 9EN.

Alternatively you may fax your order to the above address. Fax No. 01326 317444.

Payments can be made as follows: cheque, postal order (payable to Little, Brown and Company) or by credit cards, Visa/Access. Do not send cash or currency. UK customers and B.F.P.O.: please send a cheque or postal order (no currency) and allow £1.00 for postage and packing for the first book, plus 50p for the second book, plus 30p for each additional book up to a maximum charge of £3.00 (7 books plus).

Overseas customers including Ireland please allow £2.00 for postage and packing for the first book, plus £1.00 for the second book, plus 50p for each additional book.

NAME (Block Letters) ....

....

ADDRESS ....

....

....

☐ I enclose my remittance for ....

☐ I wish to pay by Access/Visa Card

Number ☐☐☐☐☐☐☐☐☐☐☐☐☐☐☐☐

Card Expiry Date ☐☐☐☐